Beware of Bad Boy

Book One of the

Beware of Bad Boy series

April Brookshire

www.aprilbrookshire.net

ISBN-13: 9781492935506

PROLOGUE

"It is amazing how complete is the delusion that beauty is goodness."
-Leo Tolstoy

Eight years ago . . .

Please don't say my name.

"The judges' results are in. . . ."

I looked at the girl next to me to see her shaking in excitement.

Please don't say my name.

"The winner of this year's Little Miss Pageant is. . . ."

My mom was in the front row with a weird smile on her face again.

Please don't say my name.

"Gianna Hilary Thorpe!"

Oh no.

I wiped my hand against my dress, scraping it against the sequins. The lady who said my name put the sash around me and the tiara on my head. It looked just like the last one I got.

My mom was taking pictures from the edge of the stage and I smiled just like she told me to. The flash made it hard to see anything else until she was done. Daddy was still sitting in the audience, looking bored. My mom always made him come to these things. I thanked the announcer lady and did what I was supposed to do when I won. Walking across the stage, I grinned big and waved at the people out there. Some of them didn't look happy because their daughters didn't win.

I didn't like them looking at me and I felt bad for the other girls the same age as me who didn't win. Some of them didn't like me and I think some of the moms didn't like my mom. But she got really mad if I said I didn't want to do pageants anymore. Last time I told her that she said if I didn't do them, we weren't going to Disneyland this summer. I really wanted to go.

When the pageant was over my daddy picked me up and carried me out to the hallway. "You did a good job, baby girl."

"Thanks, Daddy. Now I get to go to Disneyland."

He made a face and asked, "Is that what your mom said?"

"Yeah."

My mom was walking next to us and looked at my daddy 'cause he sounded mad. "It's just to motivate her."

Daddy still didn't look happy. "Let's just get her out of this dress and wash off the makeup. She's had a long day."

Mom rubbed her pregnant belly. It was getting so big and I couldn't wait for my little brother to be born. I was glad it wasn't going to be a girl. I'd feel bad if she had to do these stupid pageants too.

After I was cleaned up and wearing comfy clothes again, we went to eat at a restaurant. I ordered spaghetti and was glad I wasn't wearing the fancy dress anymore when some of the sauce got on my shirt. My mom was eating chicken and rice. She always ate that when we went to restaurants. My daddy was almost done with his huge steak.

"Mom?"

"Yes, honey?"

"Can I go to Cece's birthday slumber party?"

My mom frowned. "When is it?"

I told her and waited for her to tell me yes or no.

"Gianna, you have a pageant weekend."

I felt like I was going to cry. Best friends weren't supposed to miss each other's birthdays. I didn't want to be a bad friend.

My daddy swallowed the food in his mouth and glared at my mom. "I'm sure missing one pageant won't be the end of the world, Julie." My daddy always called my mom *Julie*. I remembered when I was little and he used to call her *babe*.

"I know!" my mom said brightly. "Why don't you invite Cece over for a slumber party the following weekend? I don't think we have anything going on then."

"Or she could skip the stupid pageant and go to the damn party like a normal little girl," my daddy argued.

I didn't want them to fight again, especially over me. "That's okay. What mom said is a good idea. I can invite Cece over." Then I decided to add, "And maybe some other girls, too?"

My mom looked relieved. "Sure, honey, it's a plan."

I leaned against the side of my daddy, sad I was going to miss the party but happy I wasn't a horrible friend. I'd get Cece the best present ever. Daddy wrapped his arm around me and I felt good I had him to stick up for me.

The next month, I missed Cece's party but gave her the most awesome present ever when she came to my house for a slumber party. I invited three of the other girls from ballet class and we had lots of fun.

When my little brother, Chance, was born, we were really happy and when I smiled for family pictures, it was a real smile.

Daddy finished medical school and we went to the same restaurant to celebrate with grandpa and grandma. They lived in Florida now, but said no way would they miss it because his school had cost them a lot of money.

Disneyland was so cool, my favorite place in the whole world. Chance cried a lot so I didn't think he liked it as much.

But everything changed soon after that trip to California. My daddy said he got a residency at a hospital in Texas and he had to move away. He said he loved me and my baby brother very much but he didn't want to be married to mom anymore. He would visit as often as possible, but Chance and I had to live with mom in Denver because he was going to be working all the time and couldn't take care of us.

My mom was really mad.

Chance didn't even know what was going on.

I wanted to go with Daddy to Texas so bad.

CHAPTER ONE

"Even when I see a beautiful woman, I think, 'Aw her life must be amazing.' Everyone does it. That's human nature to believe that beauty is everything."
-Marina and the Diamonds

GIANNA

"Gianna, you like Scott. He's been good to you and Chance. Why do you have such a problem with his son coming to live with us?" With her face is a mixture of motherly exasperation and bewilderment, my mom stood, hands on hips, waiting for an explanation.

Before replying, I peeked out the kitchen window to see my stepdad still out back with my little brother. "Mom, I do like Scott, he's a nice guy. I just don't understand why his son has to move in. Can't he just send him to military school or something? Isn't that what parents are supposed to do with delinquent sons? We've never even met the guy and we're supposed to occupy the same house as him. You may as well invite some stranger off the street into our home!"

Okay, I realized that was an exaggeration, but I couldn't help it. Scott was easy to accept because my mom loved him and he'd always been awesome to me and Chance. It didn't mean I had to like his son, especially one with a bad reputation for being a complete loser.

"Gianna Hilary Thorpe! That isn't the same thing at all. Scott's son is family whether you like it or not. And you forget I did meet him once, when Scott and I took him out for dinner downtown. So he isn't a stranger to me and soon he won't be a stranger to you either." She started stirring the gravy on the stove faster in agitation, but with skill managed to keep the liquid contained. It wasn't so easy for her to contain her frustration.

"Fine, mom," I conceded grudgingly, seeing that whining would get me nowhere. "But he's sharing a bathroom with Chance." Hopefully the loser would do something to get kicked out of the house or sent back to his mom.

"Of course, you need your privacy, honey. I'm sure he'll need his, too," my mom agreed with evident relief.

What he needed was a good kick to the ass that left an imprint of Scott's shoe. Grabbing my keys and duffel bag, I told my mom, "I'm out. The first football game is this Friday and we're working on new cheers."

"New cheers! Honey, I can't wait to see them!" My mom always went spastic over anything to do with my cheering. If being a cheerleader ended up being my greatest accomplishment in life, high kick me in the face *now*.

The lot nearest the gym at school was mostly empty since school didn't start until tomorrow. I got a text as parked and grabbed my phone from the cup holder. It was from Cece.

Cece: *Found perfect song for next routine*

Me: *Better get it approved with picky Jared*

Cece: *We'll come up with something first, then lay it on him*

Me: *I'll call you later to talk I'm just getting to cheer practice*

Cece: *Death to all cheerleaders!*

Me: *Then who would make the world a peppy place?*

Cece: *Gay hair stylists?*

Me: *Quit stereotyping!*

Cece: *It's true! I always leave the salon with a bounce in my step when Tony gets done with me!*

Me: *You always have a bounce to your step anyways, TTYL*

Hannah must've seen me pull up because she waited outside the gym doors for me.

Never a good sign. "Gianna, you need to talk to Kendra. She's being a major bitch!"

What did I ever do to give these girls the impression I was a therapist or mediator?

Hannah was still seething over Kendra stealing her boyfriend last March. If they stopped for five seconds and really looked at the guy they were fighting over they'd be friends again. Having a nice car and rich parents didn't make him any less sleazy.

"Why don't you just punch her in the face? It'll make you feel better," I suggested under my breath while walking around her and pulling the heavy door open. Better yet, punch *him* in the face.

The summer heat outside was a stark contrast to the blast of cool air that hit me. Maybe it would cool Hannah off, too. Most of the girls were already there, doing warm-ups. A couple of the girls were wearing shorts and t-shirts in the school colors, navy blue and gold, with lightning bolts on them. I wore grey Capri sweats and a black tank top layered over a white one. My sneakers squeaked on the shiny gym floor.

Along with some new cheers, we were working on a new halftime dance routine. With the girls' input, I doubted it'd be as cool as the one I'd come up with having Cece's help this weekend. The song everyone decided on was a pop song with corny, but fun, lyrics. At least I had more say in the dance steps than I did in the music.

"Okay, everyone!" Ashley, our head cheerleader, announced. "Let's get started!" We got in formation in the center of the basketball court as the music began.

*****

After practice I'd barely had time to come home and shower when *he* showed up. Although, since he was supposed to arrive this morning he was actually late. I checked the clock and figured about four hours to be precise.

"He's here! He's here! My new big brother!" My little seven-year-old little brother, Chance, was screaming at the top of his lungs, acting like Mickey Mouse was stopping by. At least someone was happy the delinquent was coming to live with us. Scratch that, Scott was pretty stoked also. My mom seemed okay with it, but I wondered how much of that had to do with wanting to please my stepdad.

I looked out the front window to see a red vintage Camaro parked at the curb. My stepdad turned off the lawnmower and went around the car to hug his son. He was far away, but dark hair and sunglasses was what I took in at first. I knew from the old photos on Scott's desk that his son didn't look much like him. Scott had sandy brown hair and green eyes, but his son got his looks from his mom. She was Greek or Italian or something. They moved to the back of the car now to unload the trunk.

I'd planned on sitting around in comfy clothes, catching up on my favorite HBO show. That idea didn't seem as relaxing anymore. Feeling unprepared to deal with the new situation, I passed by Chance on my way up the stairs. I pulled a shirt and pants off their hangers and quickly dressed. I put my shoes on in the kitchen, grabbing my keys and wallet off the counter. Just as the door to the garage was closing behind me, I heard the front door opening. Hopping into my Jeep, I pushed the button to open the garage and backed out of the driveway expecting my mom to run out to stop me at any moment.

She'd be so pissed when she figured out I'd left. I knew she wanted us to welcome Caleb as a family, but he didn't feel like family. I couldn't help my animosity and had a grudge against a boy I'd never met, with good reason.

He started it!

My parents divorced soon after Chance was born. Sometimes I thought my mom named him Chance because she viewed him as a second chance for their marriage. Well, that didn't work out so well. They fought before he was born, and they continued to fight after he was born. When he was just months old, my dad moved out and the following year the divorce was final. It still bummed me out, but I was glad my parents weren't unhappy anymore, especially my dad.

Four years ago my mom met Scott and they were married a year later. The wedding was beautiful and must've cost Scott a fortune. I was maid of honor and my little brother was ring bearer. Caleb was notably absent.

Even though we lived in a suburb north of Denver, I'd never met my stepbrother who lived with his mom downtown. Why? Because he was a selfish punk.

While I was happy my mom had a good marriage with Scott, my stepbrother didn't feel the same way. He refused to come to the wedding. He refused to visit his dad at our house in Broomfield. Scott drove downtown every other Sunday afternoon to visit his son, where I imagined my poor stepdad desperately tried to maintain a relationship with the ungrateful punk. My mom wasn't perfect, but I was protective enough of her to despise Caleb for rejecting her so thoroughly. How would he feel if Chance and I were the same way with his dad?

Figuring I was already going to be in trouble for taking off without permission, I may as well make it worth it. Heading towards the freeway, I decided to go visit Cece.

CHAPTER TWO

"The reason that the all-American boy prefers beauty to brains is that he can see better than he can think."
-Farrah Fawcett

CALEB

This was the boring life my dad chose over my mom? I couldn't believe I was going to be stuck here until I graduated high school. After complaining for years about my dad giving up on their marriage, my mom chucked me out the door to go live with him and his new family.

So maybe I got into trouble every now and then. So maybe I got expelled from another school last May. When did *boys will be boys* turn into *I can't take it anymore, you're going to live with your father*?

Three years ago my dad brought this blonde woman to meet me and told me she was going to be my new stepmother. I went home, told my mom and she freaked like her heart was breaking. The thing she was stuck on at the time was that my dad's new wife was so much younger than her. My future stepmother appeared nice enough, but I loved my mom and I couldn't stand her pain. I told my dad I refused to ever be a part of his *new* family. Even though she never said it outright, I know it made my mom feel a little better when I was resistant to having anything to do with my new stepmother and her kids.

Now, barely three years later, my mom couldn't seem to pawn me off to that new family fast enough. Being her only child only got me so far. She'd had enough of my antics and was ready to send me to dad to straighten me out. I thought the way our home life worked was just fine. My mom did her thing and I did mine. The problem for her was she didn't like the things I got up to.

When I pulled up to a giant two-story house which looked like it belonged on a sitcom, I couldn't help but compare it to the apartment I shared with my mom. Our apartment was in a trendy Denver neighborhood. This place was definitely a far cry from trendy. The neighbors probably expected quiet and everyone was in bed by ten at night.

My dad had been mowing the lawn when I pulled up and his wife was gardening in a flowerbed. My artist mother would have called it very Norman Rockwell. I hoped I wasn't expected to take part in any of it. I especially wasn't going to be pushing a damn lawnmower around the front yard.

As soon as I'd parked, my dad turned off the lawnmower and met me as I got out of the car. We grabbed some of my bags from the trunk and I was ushered through the white front door with a fancy gold knocker. My dad happily patted me on the back while Julie, my stepmom, yapped about how excited everyone was to have me there.

All of a sudden a skinny blonde kid came crashing into my legs. "Caleb is here! He's going to play PlayStation with me!" The welcoming party sure was confident. When tugging on my hand in the direction of what I guessed was the game console didn't work, he only pulled harder.

"Caleb, this is my son, Chance, and he's obviously excited about your coming to live with us. Chance, honey, Caleb just got here. He needs to get settled in first, so please stop yanking on his hand." It was weird how she spoke sternly with a smile on her face.

Maybe my dad went out and married my mom's opposite. When my mom used that tone you better believe there was a frown to accompany it. My mom was the moody artistic type, more likely to tie a scarf around her waist than her neck. This lady dressed different too, very preppy in her polo shirt. "Caleb, come sit over on the couch so we can all get to know each other."

I followed them into a living room, feeling awkward. Jesus Christ, could a person fit more floral printed furniture and paintings into one room? I spied what seemed to be some sort of shrine on the other side of the room. A long table against the wall was covered in pictures of a blonde girl at different ages. Different outfits, too. Some looked cheerleading related and some had her in ballet getups. The pictures were far from where I sat, but she looked sort of pretty. I didn't remember how old the daughter was, high school age at least, but she looked good enough to bang if she weren't my dad's stepdaughter. That definitely put her on the *Do Not Bang* list.

Julie and Scott followed my gaze and, believe it or not, Julie got even more excited. "Oh, Caleb, that's my daughter, Gianna. Chance, go get your sister. She should be here to welcome Caleb." Interesting that her name was Gianna, an Italian name when I doubted she had an ounce of Italian blood in her. My mom was Italian-American and she didn't even have an Italian name.

"I can't go get her mom 'cause she left right when Caleb got here. I told her he's here, then she ran upstairs, then she ran downstairs, went to the garage and left," Chance explained in a rush.

"Oh well . . . she must've been late to meet a friend, but you'll get a chance to meet her later, Caleb. I know, I'll show you to your room now." Julie's cheeks were pink as she excused her daughter's absence. Perhaps my new stepsister wasn't so happy about me being here.

Three hours later I was contemplating living in my car. I needed to escape. If I had to put up with any more of this family time crap I was gonna choke someone. That someone may just be my new stepmother. After I was shown my new room, painted *baby blue* with *sailboat* border on the wall, Julie insisted on getting to know me more. This consisted of two hours of Julie asking me questions, my dad staring at her like he loved her curiosity and Chance yanking on my sleeve to get my attention. Julie was hot and all for a lady in her thirties, but I didn't know what my dad saw in her beyond that. If her daughter was anything like her, I'd be walking around the house with a roll of duct tape for her mouth.

Finally a reprieve when my dad asked to speak with me privately in his study. A study for fucks sake! It was even decorated like the study cliché with manly plaids and dark woods. I sat across from him and picked up a Mallard duck statue with a question in my eyes.

He shrugged with a smirk on his face. "I let Julie do the decorating."

Setting the duck back down, I laughed. "You should hire a professional to redecorate."

"Nah, it doesn't bother me."

"The sailboats in my room have to go."

"Whatever makes you more at home, Caleb. I'm sure Julie

won't mind. We really want you to be comfortable living here."

"Thanks, dad."

He cleared his throat and sat forward. "I wanted to talk to you alone about why your mom wanted you here."

I gave him a skeptical look. "You mean, why she didn't want me there anymore?"

"Don't be a brat, Caleb. You know your mother loves you. She just thought the lifestyle down there wasn't benefitting you."

Actually, I liked my life a whole lot. My life was awesome in Denver. "Of course she loves me," I agreed. "She just thinks I'm a pain in the ass."

"You have been in the past," my dad said. "But let's leave the past where it belongs and why don't you look at this as a fresh start? I'm here if you need to talk or if you feel like you're slipping into bad habits again."

I wouldn't refer to them as bad habits. More like me being me and other people having a problem with it. Maybe if I promised to be a good little boy, my mom would let me come home? I so didn't want to be here, living in the suburbs, going to another new school and missing my friends. Too bad my mom knew me so well. She wouldn't believe for a minute I'd already changed my ways.

"Will do, dad," I stated halfheartedly. Life was about to get very boring.

Julie yelled that dinner was ready and we headed towards the dining room to have what she described as "our first family dinner." Oh joy. At least the food smelled damn good. My mom didn't cook much and when she did it was out of the box, so I'd finally found a plus about moving in. The spread on the table was mouthwatering and definitely home-cooked. If all family dinners were like this, I'd have to start working out more.

Right as we were digging in, a door slammed shut nearby. Julie smiled one of her exuberant smiles. "Gianna, honey, we're in the dining room!" Ten seconds later, in walks one of the most smokin' hot pieces I'd ever seen.

CHAPTER THREE

"She got her looks from her father.
He's a plastic surgeon."
-Groucho Marx

GIANNA

I was glad to escape the meet and greet with Scott's son. No way would I have been able to be sincere. It gave me time to think and decide on the best game plan for dealing with my new stepbrother. I would cautiously give him a chance since we'd be living in the same house for the foreseeable future. I pulled my Jeep into the garage and entered the house through the kitchen.

"Gianna, honey, we're in the dining room!" I heard my mom call out. I headed that way, feeling a mixture of anxiety and curiosity.

Walking into the dining room my eyes instantly fell on one of the hottest guys I'd ever seen. He had black hair almost long enough to fall into what I thought were hazel eyes. He stood up when I entered, making to move around the table. At a little over six feet, he seemed to tower over Chance who was still seated and shoving mashed potatoes into his mouth. As he passed by my mom I studied his getup: black tank top that showed off muscular arms, straight jeans hanging on lean hips and retro Vans.

My mom introduced us as he neared, "Caleb, this is my daughter, Gianna. You'll be starting at her school tomorrow. Isn't it so convenient you're in the same grade? Maybe you'll share some of the same classes, but either way she'll be able to show you around." I didn't second that offer.

Caleb met me where I still stood in the doorway. I didn't like the smirk on his handsome face. The light from the hallway behind me glinted on a piercing in his eyebrow. I was startled as he pulled me in for a hug. His muscles contracted as I gripped his biceps, not about to wrap my arms around him.

"Nice to meet you, sis," he said with a chuckle. I felt his warm breath on my ear as he added in a whisper only I heard, "Wanna sleep in my bed tonight?"

Feeling his hand reach down to pat my butt, I pushed him away and yelled, “Get off me, asshole!”

“Gianna, what’s gotten into you? Caleb was just trying to be friendly. Is that any way to greet him?” She looked appalled while Scott wore a disappointed expression. Chance stopped eating, his eyes riveted to the dinnertime drama.

“Yeah, well he was trying to get a little *too* friendly. Mom, do you-”

Caleb cut me off before I could finish, his face displaying false hurt and confusion. “I’m sorry, Julie. I’ve never had a sister before and didn’t know hugs weren’t allowed.” As I saw Scott’s eyes narrow I realized at least one person was suspicious. He may be able to fool my mom, but his dad obviously knew better. Not that Scott would call him out on it and risk upsetting his wife.

“It’s okay, Caleb, hugs are allowed. We’re a very affectionate family,” my mom encouraged. *We were*? “That was very sweet of you,” she said before throwing me a hard look. “Now let’s just sit down to enjoy our first dinner as a family and we’ll talk about this later, Gianna.”

I couldn’t believe my mom was falling for his crap! No wait, I totally could when I thought of how my mom always liked to sweep problems under the rug, pretending they didn’t exist. Like when our family was splitting up and she insisted her and my dad would reconcile. Or the past three years when Scott’s absentee son was only a picture on his desk when he should’ve been a frequent visitor.

After dinner, which I finished last with being late, I ran up to my room, ignoring the fact my mom wanted to talk to me. I turned on some music, a new electronic group Cece wanted me to check out, and flopped down on my bed. I looked at my phone to see eighteen new text messages. I ignored the ones from people at school and found one from Cece.

Cece: *How’s the new brother?*

I immediately texted her back.

Me: *Stepbrother! And I’ll probably start a fire outside his bedroom door tonight*

Cece: *That bad?*

Me: *Worse*

If life got any worse, I’d be moving to Houston to live with my dad. Scratch that, I could never leave Cece and the boys. Guess I was stuck with-

A loud banging on my wall interrupted my thoughts.

"Turn that shit down!" Caleb shouted through the wall separating us.

Glancing at my door to check it was locked, I turned the volume up on a crappy song that made me wonder what Cece was thinking when she called this band *genius*.

It was funny how people were always telling me how lucky I was. Lucky to be so beautiful. Lucky to do well in school. Lucky to be dating Josh. Right now, when it came to stepbrothers, I was feeling decidedly unlucky.

CALEB

Damn, how lucky could one guy be? I'd already worked my way through all the hot chicks at my old schools. Now I'd get to live in the same house as an even hotter chick. Maybe living in the 'burbs wouldn't be so bad after all. One thing was for sure, playtime with my *sister* was going to be fun. Even if she was hands off, I'd still be able to check out that ass whenever I wanted.

Too bad she had shit taste in music. The ruckus coming through our adjoining wall made me turn up my own music to drown it out.

Going through my phone, I checked my messages. One from a one night stand the other weekend asking why I hadn't called her back yet. She'd made weird sounds when she was coming. Another from Dante wanting to know if my new stepmom was hot. A text from Hailey checking if I wanted to go out tonight.

I answered Dante and Hailey, telling no to both. Although, my stepmom could be hot if she didn't have the suburbia stick up her ass. If I were home at my mom's I would've taken Hailey up on her offer, but no way was I going to make it all the way back home driving drunk. Plus, my dad would be pissed if I ruined my new start so soon.

Feeling tired, I kicked off my jeans and pulled off my tank. I'd unpack my stuff tomorrow. At least the bed was comfortable, with all these pillows and the fluffy comforter.

*****

I woke up with the sun shining on my face and my first thought was to buy some blackout curtains. I'd need them to sleep in on the weekends I spent here. I planned on crashing at my mom's as much as possible otherwise I'd be bored as hell stuck here.

Three knocks on my bedroom door accompanied Chance yelling through it, "Caleb, Scott says to wake up!"

"Yeah!" I grunted, dragging myself out of bed. Unfortunately, I couldn't skip the first day of school. It really pissed teachers off. It was creepy to open my door and find Chance standing out there. "What's up, little dude?"

"Are we playing video games after school?" he asked intently.

"Um, sure," I replied, then added as he was running off, "As long as your mom says it's okay!" Or whatever.

The bathroom Julie had indicated I'd be sharing with Chance was free. It was decorated with yellow rubber ducks, the shower curtain, the towels, even the freaking soap dispenser. No way was I ever letting my friends up here. The teasing would never end. Soaping up in the shower, I wanted to laugh my ass off. Maybe I'd redecorate this room also. I'd see how the kid felt about skulls, Julie would love that.

Leaving the bathroom with a towel wrapped around my waist, I passed by a pissy-looking Gianna who made an obvious effort not to look at my bare chest. "Want to put some clothes on?" she asked sarcastically.

"Want to help me get dressed?" I countered and laughed obnoxiously when I heard her curse softly. Looking at the alarm clock I failed to set last night, I saw I was running late. I was dressed in two minutes flat and took an old backpack with me downstairs.

"Caleb, honey, here's your lunch money." Julie handed me some one dollar bills. Was she for real? She passed out lunch money every day? My mom transferred money into my bank account every few weeks. But, hey, I was never one to turn down free money, so I pocketed the cash thinking I'd enjoy the extra spending money.

"Thanks, Julie, you're the best stepmom ever," I told her, seeing the compliment had the desired effect from her pleased smile. Oh yeah, I knew how to work the charm so she'd be more willing to give me money in the future.

Julie handed me a plate of pancakes and glass of milk. It worked for me. I sat down at the kitchen table across from Gianna and dug in. There was a blue backpack on the chair next to her. She was ignoring me, concentrating on her food.

"Oh darn," I said sorrowfully.

"What's wrong, Caleb?" Julie questioned immediately.

Slapping my forehead in a dumbass gesture, I explained, "I forgot my school supplies at my mom's." Total lie, I just didn't bother getting any even though my mom bugged me all last week.

Gianna's eyes narrowed on me at her mom's next words. "I'm sure Gianna can lend you some."

There was a pronounced silence as Gianna stared me down. Finally, and with obvious reluctance, she said, "Sure." I kept eating my pancakes, washing them down with milk. With agitated movements, Gianna got a notebook and some writing utensils out of her bag, shoving them across the table at me.

Picking up the pink notebook she gave me and a pack of pens, I slipped them into my backpack. "That's sweet of you, really." I'd seen the less girly colored notebooks in her bag so I grasped she'd done it on purpose.

She looked proud of herself and I was sure it was the pink notebook putting that smirk on her face. "No problem, Caleb." Her insincere smile had me wondering if being gorgeous made her a bitch. She wouldn't be the first beautiful female with a crappy personality.

Drinking the last of her orange juice, Gianna zipped her bag up and headed for the garage door. Julie stopped her by suggesting, "Honey, Caleb should ride with you today since he doesn't know the way to school. That way you guys are together so you can show him around."

With my back to Julie, I gave Gianna a smug grin and relished her scowl. "Fine, hurry up," Gianna called out before the garage door slammed behind her. I took both my dishes and Gianna's to the sink, earning an approving look from Julie.

Gianna sat in the driver's side of a white Jeep Liberty. Taking my time, I hopped into the front passenger seat. She started the car as the garage door came up and DMX blasted from the stereo.

"You like DMX?" I asked disbelievingly. She didn't look the type to enjoy rap music. More like a Katy Perry fan.

"Yes, and I'd much rather listen to him than you right now, so if you don't mind. . . ."

What a raging bitch. Fine by me, I thought to myself, I'd just check her out in silence. Damn, her body was rockin'. She wore a denim skirt that showed me lots of those luscious legs, a tight-fitting white t-shirt and white Adidas. As I listened to DMX's aggressive lyrics, I wondered if angry cheerleaders on the rag were now listening to rap music.

Five minutes later, we pulled into the school parking lot. It was newish looking, unlike the schools I'd attended downtown. The massive two story building was a light brick. As she parked her Jeep, Gianna's hand suddenly gripped the steering wheel tightly. What was up with that?

Climbing out of the vehicle, we were literally swarmed. Several people converged, all trying to get Gianna's attention, both male and female. Guess the girl was popular. The look on her face was interesting. She didn't seem to enjoy the attention. The curve of her smile hinted at a grimace. The way she held her body indicated discomfort.

I got a couple curious glances from her fan club. One girl who walked on the other side of Gianna nudged her to ask, "Who's he? He's cute."

Gianna looked at me as if she'd forgotten I was even there and said indifferently, "This is my stepbrother." Just her stepbrother, not even my name. Rude.

Since Gianna apparently wasn't going to bother with any introductions that was their cue to offer it themselves. I met a Shawn and Erin first. Talk about popular by association. While I was being bombarded, the girl who'd asked about me was now hanging on my arm and trying to get my attention. I saw Gianna hide a smile and walk away from the group.

"Gianna never told us she had such a nice stepbrother. My name's Hannah." I looked the girl up and down and decided she was definitely worth my time. Since Gianna didn't seem bothered with me finding my way around a new school, I'd allow Hannah the honor.

"Show me to the front office?" Gracing her with my sexiest smile, I let her grab my hand and lead me towards the front entrance. On our way there, I saw Gianna walk up to a blonde guy smiling at her. He immediately pulled her into a hug and kissed her. For some reason this really bothered me. Maybe it was a protective brother thing. Bitch or not, she was my stepsister now. I shook the feeling off, taking on a *who cares* attitude about it. It didn't matter to me who kissed those lips.

My classes sucked just as much as they did at my last school. My English teacher last year was fresh from college and not bad to look at. The one I had this year had hips almost as wide as the doorway to her classroom. I had a couple classes with Gianna, not sure if it was a good or bad thing. She didn't seem like the type to let me photocopy her notes.

She didn't show me around even after the classes we had together. The idea of ratting her out to Julie crossed my mind. Hannah was more than eager to help me out and I wondered what else she was eager for. At lunch time, I found out the guy Gianna kissed was her boyfriend Josh and that they'd been going out for almost a year. I sat at the same table as Gianna and this Josh guy, but at the opposite end. It seemed as though I'd been inducted into the popular crowd. As if I gave a shit. I'd piss off more than one of these girls before long. Gianna ignored me, but my ego was nurtured by several of the other girls.

Gianna was a favorite topic amongst our classmates once they found out who I was. I learned more about her during the forty-five minutes of lunch than I did the day before being in the same house as her. No wonder she was such a prissy bitch. All of her peers practically worshipped her. In this shallow society of high school, she outshone the other females, and there were a lot of pretty girls here. This was why half my friends were older.

Her boyfriend was no different than the rest. He stared at her as if entranced and seemed to only take his eyes away from her to look at his food. Once though, he caught my eyes and gave me a dirty look. Oh, so it was like that? Josh, in his Abercrombie shirt, perhaps didn't like that his girlfriend had a stepbrother living in the room next door. Tough shit.

Actually quite a few guys stared at her like Josh did. Gianna's behavior puzzled me, however. She mostly sat there picking at her food and looking up every once in a while to answer a question. Now that I thought about it, I was doing the same thing as these dumbasses, staring. Fuck that! I was going to stop examining Gianna and start planning when I'd be getting Hannah in my backseat.

After lunch, I had one other class with Gianna. Did the girl ever smile? When the last class of the day was out, I met Gianna at her Jeep and she drove me home in silence before going back to the school for cheerleading practice. After she took off, I hopped into my car and drove down to Denver to visit friends and hopefully find some fun.

GIANNA

With the first week of school almost over, I was dying for Saturday to come. It was the same this year at school as every other year. People still wanted to be my friend no matter how unfriendly I was. I quit pretending years ago it was my personality that drew them. It wasn't all that flattering to be liked for the way you looked. Even when I tried to discourage them they seemed to take it in stride. I think they figured a girl with my looks was supposed to be stuck up and bitchy, so I was merely acting the part.

Sometimes I looked at some of the other girls at school and wondered what it would be like to be average-looking. Have friends at school that liked you for who you were, not what you looked like. A normal school life appealed to me. The only people I knew who liked me for who I was were what I liked to call my weekend friends. I escaped Broomfield, my mom, school and even Josh every Saturday and tasted freedom.

Did Josh like me for myself? Sometimes I wondered with him. He started saying he loved me early on in our relationship, but maybe it was the way I looked that he loved so much. Did I love him back? I wasn't sure. If it was love, wasn't I supposed to get butterflies in my stomach when I saw him? Maybe I should break up with him, but I didn't want to hurt his feelings. Dating him kept most of the other guys away, which I liked. Lately, I'd even begun telling him how frustrated I felt about life at school. He seemed to understand.

Today was Friday and I had to cheer tonight at the first football game of the season. Josh was starting quarterback this year and he wanted me to go to a party afterwards with him. We'd been going out for a while and he'd been pressuring me lately to finally have sex with him. I knew I definitely didn't want that. Still waiting for those butterflies. If he tried pressuring me too much, I'd have no choice but to break up with him.

Right now I was doing the usual lunchtime routine. Sitting with the popular crowd, picking at my food and wishing I were anywhere but here. At the other end of the table was Caleb surrounded by a bunch of girls and a few guys he seemed to have made friends with. At least it was a little quieter now at my end of the table.

Hannah was sitting next to him as she'd been all week. God, she was such a two-faced bitch. She always acted like we were best friends but, I swear, sometimes the looks she gave me were a mixture of envious and hateful. She didn't hide it as well as she thought. She was under the impression she was Caleb's girlfriend. Didn't she realize that to a guy like Caleb she was just the flavor of the week? I'd heard him on the phone last night flirting with some girl named Monica. It was disgusting listening to him purr on the phone to some stupid girl. Once it started sounding like they were about to have phone sex, I turned on my TV full blast.

CALEB

All high school parties were the same, chicks and dicks getting drunk and hooking up. The girls thinking screwing the boys would get them love and the boys thinking of how much they'd just love to screw the girls. I was gentlemanly enough to steer clear of the innocent looking ones, the ones whose tears and drama weren't worth it.

"Caleb, you're not even paying attention to me!" Jesus fucking

Christ, this chick was annoying. Whether I hooked up with her tonight or not, it was time to give her the boot.

I spotted Gianna across the room dancing with some random guy to a popular ragga song. I was shocked to see the girl could actually look happy. And *damn* could she dance sexy. I was getting turned on just watching her.

Before the song finished, I saw Josh walk over to the guy and push him to the ground. Gianna yelled over the music, "What the hell?" at Josh and stormed off. Josh followed at her heels, looking not the least sorry. I felt sort of pissed myself, but because Josh ruined her moment of happiness. Not that I was jealous of the guy, of course. The girl was the most bitchy, unhappy person I knew. Tonight was the first time I'd seen a genuine smile on her face. Not that I cared about her happiness. We didn't even like each other.

"Caleb, I asked you a question and I want an answer!" Hannah whined.

"What was the question?" I asked, turning my head back towards her. She was pretty, not like Gianna, but doable. It was just her personality which was hard to take.

"Are you going to ask me to be your girlfriend or not?" she impatiently demanded to know. It appeared I'd be giving her the boot before getting laid. When you heard the G-word, it was time to get the fuck out of dodge.

Two hours later and bored outta my mind, I was leaning against the side of my dad's house smoking a joint when a lifted truck pulled up a couple houses down. I couldn't really see through the windows too clearly, but all of a sudden I heard a feminine voice yell, "Get the fuck off me, Josh! I said *no*!"

I realized it was Gianna and ran towards the truck. Opening the driver's side, I pulled Josh out by the shirt and threw him to the ground. Before he could react, I kicked him in the stomach, glad I was wearing boots. I glanced up into the truck to see Gianna's shocked and crying face. Turning my attention back to Josh, I continued to kick the crap out of him. I was a firm believer in the saying *kick 'em when they're down*. Who said you had to fight fair?

I heard a car door slam and looked up to see Gianna running towards the house, opening the side fence to the backyard. Good to know she trusted I had this covered. Either that or she was embarrassed in her choice of douchebag boyfriends.

"I hope you learned this lesson, because if you ever lay another hand on her without her permission, I'll break your fuckin' face," I threatened Josh. His response was to groan pathetically.

Taking Gianna's route into the backyard, I could hear her crying and talking on the phone. I stopped just around the corner to eavesdrop. A person heard the best information that way.

"I can't take it anymore, Jared. I hate everything and everyone here. I'm so through with Josh and every guy like him. I would tell my mom I just want to go live with my dad in Houston, but I'd miss you guys too much." A few seconds later she said, "No, Jared, I don't need you to come kick his ass. My stepbrother already took care of it." She laughed and there was silence. "Yeah, I don't think he'll try it again." Another pause. "Yeah, tell Cece I'm sorry for getting her worried, I just needed to let off some steam. See you guys tomorrow. Love ya. Bye."

She sighed loudly as I walked around the corner. She jumped back before recognizing me. "Oh, I thought you were Josh."

"You shouldn't have to worry about him anymore," I told her, scanning her face for I didn't know what.

"I'm not so sure about that, but thank you anyways. I better go to bed. I have get up early tomorrow to go downtown," she informed me and started to leave.

"What for?" I asked her, not sure why I bothered.

"Oh, um, I study ballet every Saturday morning at Ballet Denver downtown. My friend Cece also goes there. I usually spend the night at her house every Saturday, so you won't see me again until Sunday." I didn't have anything to say to that, so she continued, "Thanks again, Caleb."

Oddly, I liked hearing my name coming out of her mouth. Shaking off the feeling, I teased her, "Good night, sis,"

Instead of getting mad like before, she laughed and walked into the house.

I stood out there and finished my joint.

CHAPTER FOUR

"In every man's heart there is a secret nerve that answers to the vibrations of beauty."
-Christopher Morley

CALEB

"Caleb! Caleb! Come play with me!" Ugh! What time was it? The break of dawn? Why was this midget bugging me so early on a Saturday morning? I'd be having a talk with my little stepbrother about there being a time for play and a time for sleep.

I lifted my head from the pillow and growled, "Go bug your sister, runt. It's too early to open my eyes."

"I can't 'cause she already left. And it's not early, it's late. I already ate breakfast *and* lunch." Chance took it upon himself to start dragging my blanket away.

I lifted my head to see my alarm clock, it was past twelve. That wasn't too early for a Saturday, so I decided to get up. I was supposed to hang out with my friend, Dante, today. He'd be pissed if I flaked out on him.

Dante was like a brother to me. We'd been best friends since the third grade when we'd both liked the same girl and used to get into fights over her. It drove the teacher and our parents crazy. Halfway through the school year, the girl moved away and we called a truce. We'd been best friends ever since. I often ate at their house because, unlike my Italian mother who was *supposed* to like cooking, Dante's mom was a genius in the kitchen.

I took a shower, dressed in something I could also go out in tonight and went downstairs. Going into the kitchen first, I grabbed a Gatorade and one of Chance's Lunchables from the fridge. My dad was on the couch watching ESPN. Julie was over by the shrine to Gianna, dusting the pictures and trophies, making them shine.

Catching my dad's attention, I told him, "Hey, dad, I'm driving down to Denver to hang out with Dante. I might be home tonight, or I might spend the night at mom's."

"Oh, Dante, haven't seen him in awhile. Tell him I said hello and remember it's a fresh start, son," my dad replied.

"Yeah, yeah, I'll be a good little boy. Scout's honor." That was funny, since they kicked me out of the boy scouts. So not my fault. My parents were pissed, but more embarrassed than anything else.

Speeding out of the neighborhood, I saw an old man throw me a mean look. There went the neighborhood with Caleb Morrison moving in. I put on The Strokes, tapping my wheel to the beat. Fifteen minutes later, I was out of suburbia and on I-25 heading south towards downtown. I had The White Stripes playing on my stereo now, and Jack White was singing about being friends.

I could see the skyscrapers down in the valley from this part of the freeway. As always, I thought to myself, *there's my city*. I couldn't imagine having to live up north in the suburbs for the next two years of high school. But if I did, the moment I got my diploma I was moving back to the city.

As the freeway started curving around Coors Field, I thought about last night. I'd really like to kick Josh's ass all over again. I didn't know what to make of Gianna anymore. The girl confused the shit out of me. She dressed all sporty-preppy, but listened to hip hop. She was a popular cheerleader, but seemed anti-social at school. She had a boyfriend, but didn't really seem to want much to do with him. And who the hell was Jared? I hadn't met any Jared at school. Why would she call him in a crisis? Whatever, the girl wasn't my problem. Let her mama worry about her.

When I pulled in front of Dante's house, he was sitting out front on the porch steps. He saw me, opened the screen door and yelled, "Mom, Caleb's here! I'm taking off!"

Climbing into my car Dante asked, "What's up? Aw, man, turn this shit off." The "shit" he was referring to was The Pixies. Definitely not shit. He hooked up his music and put on Drake. Dante didn't like any of the music he liked to call "white boy music." He knew I liked all music as long as it was good, so I wouldn't mind anything he put on.

Answering his question, I said, "I don't know what's up. I don't live down here anymore, remember? So, what do *you* have in mind for today?"

"You remember those chicks we met playing basketball at the park on Monday? We could call them up and see if they want to hang out tonight."

"Sounds good. There was this chick at my new school I was

planning to hook up with, but she was so clingy I had to ditch her ass last night."

"Cool, I'll call them and see what's up." Dante pulled out his cell and whined, "Damn, I just got a text from my cuz. Forgot I promised him I'd come check out his crew tonight."

"Taye? That's okay, we can just take the girls with us."

*****

We had to park a few blocks away from the club and walk. We'd picked up Nina and Skylar, the girls we'd met on Monday, at Nina's house and I was pumped to be out in the city on a Saturday night. These ladies were hot and I could tell they'd got all done up for us. The effort was much appreciated. It seemed as though we'd already paired off. Dante was walking up ahead with Nina while I walked with my arm around Skylar. The skirt Skylar wore was so short her ass was almost hanging out and I looked forward to pulling it up later tonight and sinking in.

Finally we reached the club where Dante's cousin was performing with his crew tonight. I hadn't seen his cousin, Taye, for months, but he was pretty cool so I didn't mind coming along. Besides, he'd been bragging the last couple times I'd seen him about how awesome his crew had become. I was curious to find out if he'd been telling the truth.

We got our drink and dance on with the girls. Thankfully, they both had fake IDs, otherwise their asses would've been waiting in the car. After being there for an hour, the lights turned off and spotlights came on in the far corner of the club where there was a raised area of the floor. The crowd cheered and turned their attention that way, expecting to be entertained. Standing under the spotlights was a group of about eight people dressed in gray hoodies. With the hoods up, they also wore black basketball pants and white sneakers. Their heads were down as the music started. A remix of "Planet Rock" by Afrika Bambaataa & Soulsonic Force filled the club at almost deafening levels. Three of them lifted their heads and started breaking. I had to admit it was pretty tight and I recognized Taye as one of the breakers. A Hispanic guy began popping while Taye played off his moves with ones of his own.

After a few minutes, the music changed to Aaliyah's "Try Again" and the six guys ripped off their hoodies while two girls ripped off both their hoodies and basketball pants. The guys were now wearing their basketball pants and white tank tops. The guys split up in groups of three and each group surrounded one of the girls. Each of the girls wore pink tank tops with skintight black shorts, a definite improvement.

The guys took turns popping and breaking around the girls, pretending they were competing for the girls' attention. Before one could finish dancing, another one was pushing him out of the way and standing in front of the girl he was trying to get the attention of. While all this is going on, the girls would rotate between standing there with one hand on their hip while ignoring the guys and popping back at the guy in front of them at the moment. A couple times, the girls would push a guy away then continue dancing. The guy who got pushed away from her would fall back into a dance move.

I found this performance fascinating. Definitely the best I'd ever seen. The reason it interested me was easy, because one of those girls up there was my new stepsister.

CHAPTER FIVE

"Imperfection is beauty, madness is genius and it's better to be absolutely ridiculous than absolutely boring."
-Marilyn Monroe

CALEB

What in the hell? I probably looked like a fool, standing at the back of the club with my mouth hanging open. Dante nudged me and my head swung his way. He gave me a what-the-fuck look. I shook my head at him, not wanting to shout an explanation over the music.

Gianna and her crew finished their performance, the DJ flowed into a new track and the crowd transitioned into dancing again. Other places I'd been to hired dancing or singing acts to mix up the club experience. It livened up the crowd when a surprise performance occurred since they always seemed spontaneous. It barely registered with me when Skylar and Nina took off to use the bathroom. I couldn't see Gianna anymore and was scanning the crowd when Dante yelled over the music, "Hey, man, I'm gonna go talk to Taye!"

"I'll come with you!" I yelled back, figuring Gianna would be nearby.

We worked our way through the masses and found Taye chatting up a petite brunette. When Dante was done greeting his cousin, I pounced on questioning him. "Hey, Taye, who's the hot blonde in your crew?"

His expression filled with disapproval. "Don't even think about it, Caleb. I know you, man. We don't put up with anyone fucking around with Gigi *or* Cece." Huh, Cece must be the Hispanic chick that danced with them.

"Gigi?" Now this would be good. "It's not like that, Taye. It's just I'm pretty sure I know her. Where'd she go?"

Taye gave me a skeptical look and pointed over to the dance floor where Gianna was dancing with one of the Hispanic guys from the crew. "She's over there with Jared."

My eyes darted over the pair, taking in her smiling up at the guy. So this was *Jared.* The guy she called when something went wrong. I'd rarely seen her smile and right now she was smiling as if she were high on life. *At Jared.* I didn't know why, but the uncomfortable feeling of jealousy coursed through me.

"Yeah, that's her, Gianna," I stated when Taye continued to stare at me with wary disapproval.

Finally, and almost reluctantly, Taye said, "Hey, you guys should come to the after party at Jared and Cece's house."

"Sure, why not?" I agreed nonchalantly. It would be interesting to see how *Gigi* handled me invading her group of friends. I'd known Taye for years but he and Dante didn't hang out much so I'd never met all of Taye's friends.

A while later Taye rode with us to the after party to show us the way. Nina sat between Dante and Taye in the backseat. Skylar sat up front with me since she was sort of my date for the night. We arrived to the house the party was at and unloaded from the car, with Skylar easing up next to me as we strolled up the walkway.

Urging her in front of me and ignoring the confused look on her pretty face, I let her and the others go in ahead of me and stood back when we entered the living room. There were people dancing in the center of the living room, showing off mostly. Gianna and the other girl from the crew were laughing and doing silly dance moves that mimicked the guys' serious ones.

Taye called, "Watch out!" and slid into the middle of the group doing a head slide on the hardwood floor. He flipped forward onto his feet to grab the Hispanic girl, Cece, and lift her up in the air.

The girl laughed and whined, "Taaaaaye!" as a giggling Gianna tried to pull her down. While the girls were distracted, Jared snuck up behind Gianna and poured a bottle of water over her head.

Gianna spun around in shock and Jared dashed away. Before Jared could escape through a doorway, Gianna jumped onto his back and they tumbled forward to the floor. Gianna straddled him while his face was to the floor. Triumphant, she declared, "That's what you get, punk!"

I would've never imagined Gianna had this playful side to her personality. Actually, I assumed she was sadly lacking in the personality department. Why did she act so moody at home and school, then here she acted the complete opposite? It was unexpected, for sure.

She hopped up off Jared when he started to get on all fours with the clear intention of getting the best of her. Her gleeful smile faded and her blue eyes shot wide when she locked in on me.

I smirked and said devilishly, “Hello, Gianna.”

GIANNA

Oh. My. God. What was Caleb doing here?

With this thought foremost in my mind, I asked him, “What the fuck are you doing here, Caleb?” At the hostility in my tone, everyone’s eyes focused on us.

Jared confronted Caleb with his arms arrogantly crossed over his chest. “I don’t know you, what are you doing in my house?”

To my surprise, Taye stepped forward. “It’s cool, Jared. He’s a friend of mine.” How did my friend Taye know my infuriating stepbrother? Taye turned to me. “It’s cool that he came, right? I’ve known Caleb forever ‘cause he’s my cousin’s best friend.” What was I to say to that?

“*And* I’m Gianna’s stepbrother,” Caleb piped in slyly. I guess there went pretending we were nothing to each other.

Jared was confused for a second before his face broke into a welcoming grin. He gave Caleb one of those awkward half hug, pat on the back things guys did. “Dude, nice to meet you. I’m sorry if I was an ass, but you understand. Us guys are always having to watch out for our girl, Gigi. Hey, so you must be the guy who beat down that Josh motherfucker. No one fucks with our Gigi. We’ve been telling her to dump his ass for months. Thanks for jumping in and taking care of it for us.”

“Us?” Caleb raised his eyebrows, all GQ handsome dressed in black pants with a grey t-shirt and black vest. His hair looked like the girl standing next to him, obviously his date, ran her hands through it in a moment of passion. As usual, his mere presence annoyed me. The girl was clinging onto his arm with a starry look in her eyes. Her short purple dress made her look cheap, which was probably Caleb’s usual type.

“Yeah, the crew.” Jared was still conversing with the guy I hoped was a figment of my imagination. “We worry with her up north and us down here. She doesn't have anyone to watch out for her there." *Please, Jared, just shut up now*. He made me sound helpless.

Caleb smiled charmingly and I noticed his subtle move to detach himself from the clinging girl. "No problem, anything for *Gigi*." The tilt of his lips turned sarcastic when he aimed his grin my way. I so wasn't okay with him calling me by my nickname. He'd no doubt turn it into a taunt.

Just great, now Caleb was best buddies with Jared? Someone could just kill me now. I rolled my eyes at them and stomped off to the kitchen to get a drink. Cece came up behind me as I pulled a wine cooler out of the fridge. "Gigi, your stepbrother seems pretty cool, not at all like you described him. Why didn't you tell me how hot he is?"

"Huh, I didn't notice," I remarked dryly. "But I guess he's hot, if you like the type." Her disbelieving expression called me out on being a big fat liar. A girl would have to be blind not to take note of what genetic perfection Caleb was.

"So, you think I'm hot?" I spun around and there was Caleb leaning in the doorway, his face smug.

Running a hand over my wet hair, I said coolly, "That's not exactly what I said."

"No, but that's what you meant." he countered. I opened my mouth to say something else but he interrupted, "Aren't you going to introduce me to your friend, *Gigi*?" He had an assessing glint in his gaze as he scanned Cece's petite figure.

"Don't call me Gigi. This is my best friend, Cece. Cece, this is my stepbrother, Caleb." I gestured back and forth indifferently.

"Caleb! Gigi's stepbrother!" Cece exclaimed excitedly, pulling a startled Caleb down into a hug. She added, "Welcome to the family!" Clearly caught off balance, his response was amusing.

"The family?" he repeated quizzically.

"Yeah, the gang. We're each other's second family. Well, actually, Jared really is my family because he's my older brother. But then, you're Gigi's brother, also." Sometimes Cece was too friendly for her own good. Sometimes even for *my* own good.

"Stepbrother," Caleb corrected her, emphasizing the *step* part.

Cece waved her hands in the air and said, "Whatever." As the notes of a new song filtered in from the living room, her face lit up and she danced off. “That’s my song!” *Cece, gotta love her.*

Caleb watched her leave in puzzlement. His focus turned back to me and I felt weird with him towering over me. He was much too close. “I think we need to have a little talk,” he suggested sternly. Before I could say anything, he grabbed my arm and pulled me out the back door.

Once outside, I shouted, “Let me go, Caleb!” I got ready to struggle, but he immediately released me. Feeling a bit deflated, I rounded on him defiantly. “What do you want?”

Something strange passed over his features, almost like confusion, before it turned into amusement. Disregarding my cutting tone, he crossed his arms over his chest and taunted, “Does your mother know what you’re up to every Saturday? Because I was under the impression she thought you went to ballet during the day and had a slumber party with Cece at night. I don’t think she’d be very happy to find out instead of sleepovers, you’re going to downtown clubs and parties.”

“No, she doesn’t know and you better not tell her!” If he tattled on me, it’d be all out war.

“And why should I keep my mouth shut? I think Julie has a right to know what her daughter is up to.” His mock concern only enraged me more.

Feeling threatened and more than a little panicked, I blurted out, “Because this is all I have! These are my only real friends! The only people who give a shit about me and who I can be myself with! Without this, I will go freaking insane!” To my embarrassment, my voice pleaded. “My mom wouldn’t understand and she definitely wouldn’t approve.” I tried to sound menacing as I finished with, “I won’t let anyone take this away from me.”

To my surprise, the look on his face transformed momentarily, softening. Then just as fast his smug expression was back and he shrugged. “I guess I could be persuaded to keep my mouth shut.”

“Persuaded?” I asked warily.

“Yes, persuaded,” he drawled in a voice I found disturbingly sexy. “Here’s the deal, *Gigi*. I keep your Saturday secrets and you do what I say the rest of the week.”

“You asshole, I’m not having sex with you!” I practically

screamed at him.

He burst out laughing. "Who said anything about sex?" Looking disdainful now, he explained, "Baby, I've never had to force or blackmail a girl to have sex with me. I'm not exactly hard up when it comes to getting laid."

"Pig," I muttered. The unwelcome image of him in a towel popped into my head and I scowled.

"You got that right," he agreed unrepentantly. He seemed thoughtful as he continued, "But since you suggested it."

Before I had time to process what he'd just said, he pulled me into his arms and his lips came crashing down on mine. At first I just stood there, not moving. I was about to push him away when he started nibbling on my lower lip and sucking it. It felt so good I couldn't help myself. With a groan, I put my hands in his hair and met his enthusiasm.

After a dazed minute, he pulled back. "Like I said, never had to force or blackmail a girl."

I was pissed off by his trick and belatedly pushed him away. "You jerk! I would die before I ever had sex with you! And that kiss *sucked*!" I slapped him on the chest as a final insult and walked back inside. His mocking laughter followed me into the house.

CALEB

I thought I was lucky before. Now, I not only got to live in the same house as the hottest chick ever, but she had to do whatever I said. My own personal pretty little slave. Life was good and so was that kiss. It promised to be one of the more enjoyable kisses I'd experienced. This new game would at least alleviate the boredom of suburbia.

CHAPTER SIX

"Beauty awakens the soul to act."
-Dante Alighieri

CALEB

I spent the next hour of the party observing Gianna in what I now liked to call her *natural habitat*. I relished the power I possessed over her. I just needed to figure out what precisely to do with it.

I noticed how Jared took every opportunity possible to touch Gianna in some way, or he'd find ways for her to touch him. An arm slung over her shoulder in a friendly manner seemed not to faze her. Maybe he meant it only as a friend, but either way, it bothered me. I was starting to think of Gianna as belonging in some way to me. Not in a relationship sort of way, of course, because I didn't do relationships. I just felt protective of her. It was completely natural, given our relationship as stepsiblings. It was also clear that the girl was mixed up and needed to get her life together. This double life business, where she was one way during the week at school and something else altogether on the weekends couldn't be healthy.

It amazed me that at home she clearly did what her mom and everyone expected of her. It was almost as if she wasn't a real person at home, but some alternative universe version of Gianna. Here, with people she was comfortable being around, I watched her and she seemed to be a more likable person. It was like Gianna and Gigi were two different people. Which one was the real Gianna? I was guessing Gigi. Why was Gianna the way she was at home? Why didn't Gigi exist at home and school? I'd definitely be finding out.

Dante was still hitting it off with Nina, but I'd lost interest in Skylar even though she'd suggested we go out to my car to be alone. The air of desperation in her eagerness was a turn off tonight. Normally, I'd be all over that.

I weaved through the crowd of people until I spotted Taye. Needing to get rid of her, I asked him to do me the favor of taking Skylar off my hands. He was more than happy to oblige and within seconds was sitting on the couch next to her.

I located Cece and asked her if I could talk to her privately. She nodded with a serious look on her face and I followed her to what must've been her bedroom, unless it was Jared with the purple walls and bedspread.

"What's up?" she asked, plopping down on the bed. I pushed from my mind the memories of other girls' bedrooms I'd been in. Gianna would have my balls if I put the moves on her cute little friend.

Figuring out the best way to play this out, I started by saying, "I'm worried about Gianna."

She immediately became alert and I didn't even have to say anything else, because *damn* did the girl like to talk. Her wild hand gestures combined with long curly black hair whipping around made it all the more animated.

"I know *exactly* what you mean, Caleb. We all worry about her, especially me and Jared. She's like a sister to us. I first met her when we started ballet together when we were little. She was always really quiet and the other girls thought she was stuck up because even then she looked like a mini supermodel. You should've seen her mom, though, she was so overbearing. Wanted everything to be perfect, especially Gianna, and always talking about how beautiful Gianna was. No wonder the girl was shy, with a mother like that. When we got to middle school, her mom started letting her spend the night on some Saturday nights. That's when Jared was really getting into breaking. We used to watch him and his friends and eventually we learned the moves and became part of the crew a few years ago. Now, Gianna is with us almost every Saturday night!" She ended the last sentence with a pleased smile.

I opened my mouth to comment on a couple things she said, but she wasn't done yet. "When Gianna started hanging out with the crew, she really came out of her shell. I feel so bad for her, though, being so gorgeous. You know she hates it, don't you? She knows that most girls only want to be around her because she attracts guys' attention. And, of course, *you* know why guys want to be around her." She tilted her head to the side and studied me. "No offense, but I'm getting a definite player vibe coming off you."

"None taken," I replied wryly.

She shrugged one small shoulder and continued, "Anyways, in eighth grade, she heard all the other popular girls at school, who pretended to be her friend, talking shit about her in the bathroom. After that, she tried making friends with some unpopular kids, but they acted weirded out and nervous around her, like they had to impress her. I really hope she stays broken up with Josh, though."

"Me, too," I got in quickly, thinking of last night.

"He's so obsessive about her. She told me once that she wishes she could come live with us, but she knows her mom would never allow it. I tell her to say fuck off to everyone, but she won't. She's always worried about pleasing everyone else around her, especially her mom, and in the process she makes herself miserable. Her mom has been conditioning her to be a certain way since she was little. It just makes everything jumbled in her head, her wants and her mom's expectations. So, what exactly are *you* worried about?"

Like I said, this girl liked to talk. Summing it up to her satisfaction, I told her, "Basically the same thing."

She popped up to give me a hug. "I'm so glad there's someone up in Broomfield looking out for Gigi." This made me feel guilty, for about two seconds.

"Don't worry," I assured her. "I'm going to make sure things are different for Gianna at home and school from now on." I was feeling mixed up myself. I hadn't decided my intentions in this new game between me and Gianna. I'd think about the stuff Cece told me and figure it out later. "By the way," I began, "the nickname, Gigi?"

Cece looked proud as she explained, "Cece and Gigi, they rhyme."

This girl was adorable. I could see why Gianna cared about her. However, if she were my sister, I'd probably put a muzzle on her when the yapping became too much.

GIANNA

I hadn't seen Caleb for awhile and was annoyed his absence even registered in my mind. Maybe he went home. A girl could dream. My life sucked enough already. What'd I do to make the universe punish me with an evil, devious stepbrother like him?

While I was sulking and feeling sorry for myself, I saw Caleb and Cece come out of her room down the hallway. What the hell? He was such a manwhore. He brought some girl named Skylar to the party and now he was hooking up with Cece. And what was wrong with Cece? This wasn't like her at all. Your best friend wasn't supposed to hook up with your stepbrother. Maybe they'd just made out. That was more like Cece. I wouldn't even care what Caleb got up to, but this was my best friend. They were totally off limits to each other.

Caleb walked up to me and I did my best to ignore him, but he put his arm around my shoulder and asked, "Miss me?"

"Fuck no," I told him acidly.

"Gigi, watch your mouth! Am I going to have to tell mom?" he teased me, faking astonishment.

I said through clenched teeth, "She is *not* your mom and it's Gianna to you"

"You know, Gigi," he started as if I hadn't spoken. "I was thinking you need to have more fun, and I think I'm just the person to help you out."

"Unlikely," I replied sarcastically. "I'm not into banging random sluts."

He was quiet long enough for me to turn my head to look at him. "Just a moment," he whispered. "Okay, image burned into my brain. Gonna have to save that one for later."

"So gross," I muttered, shuddering in distaste dramatically.

He ignored me and continued, "Tomorrow, when I'm in charge, we're going to work on this new goal of ours."

"I didn't realize you knew what the word *goal* meant. Unless you count that your only goal in life is to not have any real goals at all."

"You know, that may be true in the past, but now I have two goals. Making sure you have more fun is one of them." He glanced at his wrist where a nonexistent watch rested and said, "Hey, it's past midnight! Technically, it's Sunday now and you're supposed to do whatever I say."

Before he could say anything else, Jared came up to us and asked to talk to me alone. Seizing on the opportunity to ditch

Caleb, I quickly walked with Jared to the front door. When I glanced over my shoulder at Caleb, I saw a disgruntled expression on his face. Good, it wouldn't be fair if I were the only one annoyed.

Jared and I sat on the front porch. The late summer night breeze was nice. "Thanks for interrupting us. He gets on my nerves."

"Really?" Jared seemed surprised. "I thought he was pretty cool."

I nudged him playfully. "That's because he beat up Josh."

"I'm glad you broke up with Josh." I watched as the breeze picked up a chunk of Jared's dark hair. Then I noticed he seemed tense.

"Well, I don't know if we've technically broken up. I mean, the words haven't been said. I've been ignoring his calls and texts all day, but I haven't told him it's over yet. I do plan to officially end things with him. I'm just not looking forward to dealing with his protests."

Jared was thoughtful for a moment before saying, "Good enough for me." His lips were on mine a moment later. This was the second time in one night a guy surprised me like this. I hoped it wasn't a new trend.

CHAPTER SEVEN

"Whenever, at a party, I have been in the mood to study fools,
I have always looked for a great beauty
they always gather round her like flies around a fruit stall."
-Jean Paul

GIANNA

I couldn't believe Jared was kissing me! What was even stranger was that I wanted to kiss him back. This felt good, but I couldn't help comparing it to Caleb's kiss. Was Jared's kiss different in a good or a bad way? Kissing Caleb was like a fire igniting, probably because he made me so mad. Kissing Jared was like a slow burn. Why the hell was I thinking of Caleb while I was kissing Jared. I hated Caleb!

Jared pulled back from the kiss and put his forehead against mine. "I've been waiting to do that for a long time. Like I said, I'm glad you broke up with Josh."

"Excuse me," said a stiff voice behind us. We both turned our heads to see Caleb standing there. "Gianna, I need to talk to you before I leave . . . about family stuff."

Yeah right, family stuff. He just wanted to harass me again.

Jared squeezed my hand and stood up. "Sure, no problem."

Once the screen door slammed behind Jared, Caleb still hovered above me in the darkness. I couldn't see his face clearly but he was motionless. "*What*?" I asked him in exasperation.

"How long has this been going on between you and Jared?"

"It hasn't. I didn't know Jared had those kinds of feelings for me until about five minutes ago," I explained, then added, "Not that it's any of your business."

"He isn't right for you," Caleb pronounced as if he were some sort of authority on the matter.

"How would you know? You just met him tonight and you just met me a week ago. Besides, I saw you come out of the room with Cece." When he made an aggravated sound, I couldn't help teasing, "I think it'd be adorable, a sister and brother dating another sister and brother."

"Stepsister," he corrected me. "And nothing happened with me and Cece. We were just talking."

"Whatever, I just hope Cece didn't taste Skylar in your mouth."

Caleb chuckled and sat down next to me. "Like you should talk."

I had no comeback for that, so I changed the subject, "What did you want to talk about that's so important you had to interrupt me and Jared?"

"I want to talk to you about the fact it's almost two o'clock Sunday morning. Your ass is mine. Grab your bag, let's go!" he ordered like a drill sergeant.

"No," I refused.

He gave me an *oh yeah* look and pulled out his phone. "As a good stepson, I feel it's my duty to inform Julie that I found you at a wild party downtown."

He messed with his phone and I caved. "Fine!"

Stomping inside to get my overnight bag, I grabbed it from Cece's room only to have Jared stop me in the living room when he noticed it in my hand. "Where are you going, Gigi?"

"Um, family emergency. I'll call you guys later. Tell Cece I'll call her tomorrow."

"Okay, we'll talk about . . . things, later," he said pointedly. Reminded of the kiss, I felt awkward around Jared. How would it change things between us?

"Not likely," Caleb muttered from where he stood by the front door.

Caleb held the door open and followed me outside. As soon as we were out of earshot on the sidewalk, I spun around and demanded, "So, what now?"

"Now, you get in your Jeep and follow me in my car." He was already walking down the street towards where his Camaro was parked under a streetlamp.

"Follow you home?" I called out after him.

"Nope," was his infuriating reply before he got into his car.

I hated him!

We drove only fifteen minutes when he pulled into a parking garage. I followed him to where he parked and he hopped out to indicate I was to park in the spot next to him. Rolling down my window, I let him see how unhappy I was with him. "Where are we?"

"We're near my mom's apartment," he answered, making me feel better.

"Why are we going there?" I asked, wondering if his mom would be pissed for us showing up so late. Scott's ex-wife had always been some shadowy figure that I assumed disliked my family just like her son.

"Sleepover." He winked, opening my door and taking my hand. "Come on, it's only a block down." Urban living was weird to have to park your car so far from your front door must be a pain.

I squeezed his hand as hard as I could as we exited the parking garage. He threw me an incredulous smile. "Are you trying to hurt my hand?"

"Yup, did it work?" I returned his grin with a hopeful one.

He started laughing at me. "Sorry, princess, you just aren't strong enough."

We reached a building with glass doors where he punched in a code. "Won't your mom mind?"

"Nope, she's at her friend's art show in Phoenix." We went up the elevator to the seventh floor where Caleb led me to an apartment door to the right.

Upon entering, I stopped in the entryway as he locked up. "What does your mom do for a living?"

"Interior design, plus she sells her paintings on the side."

I could totally see her being an artist and interior designer from the looks of the place. While being homey, at the same time the place screamed style. Not a pretentious, elegant type of style. The kind of style that was cool without trying. It figured, with her being Caleb's mom, he must've got it from somewhere. Not that I'd ever utter that compliment. The apartment was larger than I thought it'd be. The paintings hanging on the walls were interesting and I wondered which ones, if any, were his mom's.

I pulled my eyes away from a painting of the Denver Skyline at sunset. Caleb stood in the middle of the sitting area, hands in pockets, watching me. "Caleb, what do you want from me? Are you doing this just to annoy me?"

"Maybe I don't want anything from you. Maybe I want to do something for you," he stated matter-of-factly.

"I don't believe you. You're too selfish of a person. You do whatever you want, no matter the consequences."

"And you don't do enough of what you want," he responded. "I've watched you this past week. You do what everyone else expects of you even if it makes you miserable."

"That's none of your business."

He ignored my totally true statement. "Why are you a cheerleader?"

"Because my mom wants me to," I answered honestly, not in the least embarrassed. It was normal to try to please your parents. If Caleb did the same thing he'd be in less trouble all the time.

"Why do you hang out with the girls you do at school?" he asked, looking intently at my face.

"Because they're popular like me," I said condescendingly, trying to make him feel like an idiot for asking me these questions.

He wasn't deterred and continued his amateur psychoanalysis. "Why were you with Josh?"

I shrugged as if it were no big deal. "I'm a cheerleader, he's on the football team and kept other guys from bugging me. My mom really likes him and he says he loves me."

"Do you love him?"

"Does it matter?" I gave him a dirty look. "And, *again*, is it any of your business?"

He nodded thoughtfully as if he'd just come to some conclusion. "What do you really want in life?"

"Jeez, Caleb, pretty soon you'll be switching from using psychology to philosophy on me."

"Just answer."

"I'm not really sure, I try not to think about things I can't have."

"Well, think about it. I'm taking you under my wing. You'll do as I say and be much happier for it." How magnanimous of him.

I rolled my eyes at his conceit. "Happy like you? Are you happy being a delinquent and a player?"

"Extremely," he shared with a smartass grin.

"If I have to do this, change my life for the supposed better, then I say you do to," I turned the tables on him.

"Hey, princess, I'm the one blackmailing you. If you had any dirt on me, I wouldn't care who you told. Besides, what could I possibly need to change?" He sat down on the couch behind him, relaxed and unconcerned.

"Uh, I don't know," I challenged sarcastically, "how about the fact that this is your third high school and you're a selfish punk who disappoints your parents regularly?"

"Well, there you go. I'm already changing my ways. I'm doing the selfless thing of seeing to your happiness. I already feel better about myself. Maybe you and your being responsible will rub off on me." He was so full of it. "Actually, I like the idea of any part of you rubbing on me."

"Pig," I mumbled loudly enough for him to hear.

"So, have you broken up with Josh yet?" he asked abruptly.

"No, not yet." And I wasn't looking forward to it.

"Well, there's our first order of business. Call Josh right now and dump his date-raping ass."

This was something I knew I'd to do anyways, so I didn't mind doing what Caleb was deluded enough to think were orders. Trying to come off as blasé about the whole thing, I grabbed my phone and dialed Josh.

He picked up after two rings and immediately started apologizing, "Hey babe, I'm so sorry about last night. I shouldn't have drunk so much at the party. You know I love you more than life and would never hurt you. I need to see you. Can I come pick you up?"

I stared at Caleb as I said, "Josh, I'm breaking up with you. It's over."

Josh began protesting the breakup like I'd expected, telling me we were meant to be together. He didn't let me get a word in edgewise. Caleb made motions for me to hang up, but I felt so bad because Josh was crying about how much he loved me.

While I waited patiently for Josh to finish talking, Caleb barked loudly so Josh could hear, "Gianna, baby, come back to bed, I need to feel your body against mine again."

Holy crap! Josh's waterworks turned off fast. "Gianna, who *the fuck* was that? Are you fucking someone else? You haven't even fu-" I quickly hung up before he could finish his rant.

I should've been pissed and tried my hardest to keep from

laughing, hitting Caleb in the shoulder. "What the hell, Caleb? Do you want him to go all psycho on me?"

Catching me off guard he pulled me down onto his lap. "Don't worry. I'll protect you, princess." I struggled to get out of his arms, but he held me in place for his kiss.

Dammit, I didn't want to kiss him, but my lips had a mind of their own. I weaved my fingers through the black hair at the back of his head and pulled it lightly. His kisses moved from my mouth to my neck. "I hate you," I reminded him and myself, but it sounded husky and weak to my ears.

His grin against my neck irritated me. "I know, princess. Hate me some more, I'm enjoying it." I pulled his head up by his hair and kissed him aggressively.

Caleb drew back with a hesitant expression on his face. Making a decision, he picked me up and carried me down the hall to a bedroom. "Caleb?"

He laid me on the bed and followed me down, bracing himself on elbows. We resumed kissing and I knew I should push him off me, but it felt so good. He did say I needed to start doing things I wanted to do. At the moment, this was what I wanted to do. It didn't matter that I hated Caleb. The stupid, sexy delinquent was turning me on against my own will. Still meeting his lips with my own, I inched my hands under the back of his shirt. He had one hand on my hip and the other behind my neck, rubbing lightly.

"You're so beautiful," he groaned.

That snapped me right out of my lust haze. He was simply another person wanting something from me because I was beautiful. Coming to my senses, I pushed him off me. "Ugh, get off me!" I didn't care how expertly he kissed anymore.

"What?" Caleb chuckled, studying my scowl. "I don't hear that often."

"That too! Thanks for reminding me what a manwhore you are!" Using my legs, I thrusted him away from me.

He kneeled on the edge of the bed with one leg on the floor behind him. "You're so mean to me. What'd I ever do to you?" His playing at being hurt was almost cute, but I had to stay strong and remember that everything he did had been used on a legion of girls before me.

"You're arrogant and obnoxious and I hate you!"

His look said, *oh really?* "Do you make out with all the guys you hate?"

I covered my eyes with one hand, regretting not running away the second I spotted him tonight. "No, just you." While my eyes were covered he took advantage and his lips came back to mine. My traitor lips greeted him like an old friend.

Unexpectedly, his kisses gentled before stopping altogether. I glimpsed his disgruntled face before he turned away. "Rest up. We have a big day ahead of us tomorrow."

I stayed quiet while he left the room and returned shortly after with my bag. Disturbed, I decided not to think anymore about how I could like kissing someone so much that I couldn't stand.

CALEB

What the ever-loving hell was I thinking? I couldn't seduce Gianna. She wasn't just some random girl that I picked up at a party. I couldn't have sex with her and ditch her like I did other chicks. I needed to avoid kissing her again. I had a feeling it wouldn't be so easy. She was so freaking hot and beautiful. But I had to remember she was off limits. If I hurt her the fallout would be epic. It'd piss my dad off more than anything else I'd done.

When I saw her kissing Jared, something inside me awakened for the first time. It was ugly and jealous. I didn't want her kissing anyone else, but I couldn't be with her myself. She deserved someone who would be willing to commit. I could never do that, refused to fall into that trap. I lived through my parents' tumultuous relationship before they finally divorced. Relationships weren't worth the headache they caused and they always fizzled out, leaving the people involved with nothing but regrets.

CHAPTER EIGHT

"Taking joy in living is a woman's best cosmetic."
-Rosalind Russell

CALEB

I woke up on the couch and remembered Gianna sleeping in my bed. Walking down the hallway, I half expected her to be gone. A peek through the cracked door showed me her sleeping form. She looked good in my bed, wearing pajama shorts and a tank top, with a sheet tangled in her legs. Even with her hair all messed up she was still the most beautiful girl I'd ever met.

Pushing the door open, I ran in and jumped onto the bed. Simulating an earthquake, I yelled, "Wake up, princess! I'm bored and need your grouchiness to entertain me." Her eyes snapped open in alarm, but when she saw me she scrambled upright to take a swing at me.

"You scared me, Caleb!" She fought a grin while trying to appear mad.

I dodged out of the way, laughing at her. "I'm hungry, make me some breakfast."

"Why don't you make *me* some breakfast? I'm the guest here," she grumbled, laying her head back on the pillow and pulling the sheet over her.

"Fine, lazy, but get up and get ready. We've got things to do today. Do I always have to be the responsible one around here?" I joked, earning a glare.

"I need to go home. My mom will be expecting me," she argued.

"Don't worry. I'll take care of Julie. She loves me."

"She's the only one," she muttered under the sheet.

"That's not nice. I'm going to have to tell mom you're being mean to me," I threatened.

Gianna threw the sheet off her head to shout, "She's not your mom!"

Thank god for that, I thought to myself. Otherwise I'd have been making out with my sister last night. About last night, what would she do if I kissed her now? Better not. I couldn't mess around with her like that. I turned away, shutting temptation out.

"I'll go make breakfast. I hope you're not counting calories 'cause we're eating pancakes." While in the kitchen, I was determined not to think about Gianna naked in my shower.

Thirty minutes later, I'd already eaten when Gianna came out of the bathroom dressed casually with her dark blonde hair still wet. "Go ahead and eat while I take a shower. I left a pen and paper on the table. Your homework for today is to write down all the things you'd do if there were no consequences."

"Why should I do that?" she asked belligerently.

"Because I said so and I'm the boss." It was that simple. Whether or not I'd actually rat her out to Julie, I didn't know. If she didn't do what I said, I'd decide then.

"Whatever, go take your shower. You stink."

After my shower, I found Gianna sitting on the couch with an amused, self-satisfied look on her face. I sauntered over to the dining room table to read her list.

1. Punch Caleb in the face.

2. Steal Caleb's car and go for a joy ride, which may involve crashing into a brick wall.

3. Find a way to get Caleb expelled from my school, so he'll have to live somewhere else.

I glanced up at Gianna to take in the smug grin on her face. "What?" she asked innocently. I rolled my eyes at her and kept reading.

4. Go tagging (that means spray painting your name in public places, white boy!)

5. Get a tattoo

6. Street dance downtown at the 16th Street Mall

7. Quit cheerleading

8. Go on a road trip to Vegas

9. Punch Caleb again

10. Ditch school

11. Make new (real) friends at school

12. Go out clubbing and get drunk off my ass

13. And other things that are none of your god damn business!

My eyes moved to Gianna again but she didn't meet my eyes. "You better not make fun of me. You wanted the list, so there it is." The list wasn't particularly creative or adventurous in my book, but it was a start.

"I wasn't going to make fun of you. But before we're done, I'll find out what number thirteen means. I think I should be able to help you out with most of that. Of course, we won't be doing anything to harm me or my car." That was for sure.

"What do you mean that you'll be able to help me out? I can't do those things. My mom would kill me, especially if I quit cheerleading. I think she'd rather me get a tattoo than quit cheerleading." Her sour expression reminded me of Chance when my dad told him to do his homework the other day. Watching my dad parent another boy was odd for me. But I had to say, at that age I'd put up a much better fight than Chance.

"Well, you don't have a choice, remember? You do what I say, or I tell your mom your secrets."

"You have to be the most horrible stepbrother ever," she said, as if it would hurt my feelings. I took that as a compliment. Not being devious would be boring.

"Yep, time to go. I called your mom and already let her know you'll be helping me at the downtown library with a school report. I told her we want me to get a good grade, so we'd be home late. We'll take my car, because it's cooler than yours." With that, a reluctant Gianna and I left the apartment and trekked to where my car was parked.

"Your car is not cooler than mine," she commented while I backed out of my spot. "By the way, where are we going?"

"We're going to buy some spray paint." Traffic was light late Sunday morning, so I maneuvered through the streets with ease.

She gaped at me. "We can't really go tagging! It's the middle of the day! Do you want to get arrested?"

"No, I definitely don't want to get arrested again, so we'll just have to be very careful."

"*Again?* Oh my god! You've actually been arrested? What the heck for?" I could tell she was both shocked and dying of curiosity. Hello? Juvenile delinquent here. Getting arrested was like a rite of passage. It was the second and third time around that wasn't fun anymore.

I smiled mysteriously at her just to rile her up. "Wouldn't you like to know?"

The nearest hardware store wasn't really near at all, so it took some time to get there. When we found the spray paints, she picked out hot pink and aqua blue. I grabbed your basic black and white. There was beauty in simplicity, as my mom always said. Dante and I used to do this in middle school. Even though this was baby stuff, it brought back good memories.

I hadn't been to our favorite tagging spot for years. It was an industrial area full of warehouses and big ugly brick buildings. Since it was Sunday, there wouldn't be many people around. We parked in a mostly empty lot and got out of the car to search for the right spot.

Gianna was as nervous as a guy getting laid for the first time. I shook my head at her and grasped her from behind to whisper in her ear, "The police are after you, Gianna. They have a stakeout going on, just waiting for you to show up here with a can of spray paint."

She squirmed out of my arms. "Shut up, Caleb! Not all of us are okay with having a rap sheet. So, where are we doing this?" Along with her nervousness, I could also sense her excitement, like a guy having his first threesome.

"How about around the back of that building?" I motioned to a warehouse which didn't have any cars parked out front.

We made our way around back and I shook her cans of paint, then mine. She had a look of concentration on her face while just staring at the wall. "Well, what are you waiting for?" I asked her.

"I can't decide what to write."

"If you want, I'll pose nude for you and you can paint me," I teased her.

"And what if some poor old lady or little kid sees it? I think I'll just write my name." She began painting so I did too. Twenty minutes later, I heard her announce, "Done."

Backing up, I examined her work. She'd written *Gigi* in aqua blue with hot pink around it and underneath she'd wrote, *DCK Breakin' Crew*. It was dripping in spots, but not bad.

"What does DCK stand for?"

"That's the name of our crew, Denver Cool Kids Breakin' Crew. Jared came up with it." Her cheeks were pink and it was obvious she had some idea of what would come out of my mouth next.

"Figures that douche would come up with something so lame. Sounds like something that'd be on a Disney show."

"Well, we could change it, but we've had it since middle school. It's what we're already known as," she said defensively. Jared was still a douche, even if he came up with the name when they were little kids.

She stood back to look at what I'd painted to the right of her artwork. "You are such a pervert."

"Doesn't make it any less true, princess," I studied my handiwork. I liked it. I'd drawn an arrow pointing towards her name and words saying, *She's Hot For Me*. I'd also signed my name in cursive at the bottom.

Gianna tried to kick me in the shins, but I dodged her puny efforts. She was about to try again when a back door of the warehouse opened, about thirty feet from where we stood, and a middle-aged guy came out with a trash bag in each hand.

He took one look at us then at the spray cans in our hands and yelled, "I'm calling the cops, you punks!" He dropped the trash and hurried in our direction, pulling a cell phone out of his pocket.

"Run!" I told Gianna, already planning to come back later and snap a picture of our artwork. Poor girl was frozen in shock, so I yanked her by the arm to get her moving. I had to take the time to grab all of the cans of paint because the police did have my fingerprints on file. Of course, they'd have to go to the trouble of dusting for prints on paint cans. You'd think they'd have more important things to, like solve felonies.

We ran all the way to my car and scrambled inside. Cautiously, I turned to Gianna, expecting to see her scared and in tears. Instead, a big grin stretched across her face and she appeared exhilarated.

"Did you have fun?"

Still wearing the grin, the words burst out, "Yes, I think almost getting caught made it more exciting! What are we going to do next?"

I couldn't help myself. She was so cute in all of her juvenile delinquent joy. I carefully captured her face and then her lips with my own. She was momentarily stunned, but kissed me back. A new warmth inside of me expanded. I drew back, relishing the sudden shyness in her eyes.

"Now we go eat lunch then visit a friend of mine."

CHAPTER NINE

"A bachelor never quite gets over the idea that he is a thing of beauty and a boy forever."
-Helen Rowland

GIANNA

Caleb parked in another parking garage downtown and we walked several blocks to the Rocky Mountain Diner. "You know, I've never been here."

"They have the best food here. I'll order for you," he offered, guiding me to a booth with his hand on my lower back.

We sat down and a forty-something waitress approached with menus. "Where've you been, honey?"

"Jean, I have bad news, devastating really, I had to move up north to Broomfield with my dad. I'll probably only be able to make it in here once a week." He looked so pathetic and sad that the waitress ate it up.

She patted his cheek soothingly. "Poor baby, who's going to feed you?"

"Don't worry, Jean, I have a new stepmom and she's got mad Betty Crocker skills. Actually, this is my stepsister, Gianna." He motioned towards me, bringing Jean's attention to me.

"Oh, what a pretty girl. You'll have to watch out for her, Caleb."

"I'm trying my best, Jean, but she's kind of wild." *Smartass.*

"You're such a good boy, Caleb. What will you have today, the usual?" Jean had a pen and notepad ready to take our order.

"Yes, we'll both have that. Thank you, Jean."

Jean left to give the kitchen our order and I hissed at Caleb, "You are so full of it."

"Yeah, I know," Caleb said proudly, leaning back in his seat. He pulled the list out of his pocket and I saw him cross off numbers one through four and number nine. "So, princess, what does number thirteen entail?"

"Wouldn't you like to know?" I imitated what he'd told me this morning.

He was unconcerned. "I'll get it out of you eventually. So, how much fun are you having under my guidance?"

We were sitting there laughing about almost getting caught earlier when some random girl plopped herself sideways onto Caleb's lap. Her arms snaked around his neck at the same time. "Caleb, where've you been? I've missed you." She was doing that annoying baby-talk thing girls did when trying to sound cute.

Her nasty-ass lips were on his before he could respond. I felt like yanking her off of him by her cheap extensions. Caleb pushed her off him, saying, "I moved, Cathy."

"It's Casey," she corrected heatedly.

"Yeah, whatever, anyways I'll call you," he said in that tone that meant *I won't really call you, I just want to get rid of you.*

His meaning was obvious to me and probably anyone within earshot, but Casey must've been delusional. "You will?" she practically squealed. "You promise?" It was the disgusting baby-talk voice again.

Caleb was clearly annoyed, wanting her to be gone. "Promise."

Casey went back to her table, but not before throwing me a venomous glare. I restrained myself from tripping her, just barely. It wouldn't do to have Caleb think I was jealous. Which would be totally untrue and ridiculous. Getting jealous over a guy like Caleb would be like getting jealous over a swing at a public park. It was free for anyone to have a ride.

He must've sensed my inner turmoil from the look on my face, because he drawled, "Jealous?"

"How'd you know?" I asked in fake astonishment. "I so wanted her to sit on my lap and put her STD mouth on me!"

"I *thought* I was getting a lesbian vibe from you!" he joked, still seeming annoyed underneath the levity.

"So, are you going to call her?" If he said yes, my respect for him would suffer even more. Besides, I stupidly wanted him to say no. I was pretty positive he'd slept with that girl at some point and it bothered me despite my not wanting it to.

"I don't even have her number."

Good boy, I respected him more for his decision.

"Plus, I don't usually offer seconds."

And the dial on the respect meter just went back down.

I could hear that Casey bitch talking shit about me with some other girls in a booth somewhere behind me.

She looks like she got plastic surgery on her face, said one voice.

I bet she used to be a dog, said another.

He'll totally dump her and call you, Casey, 'cause you're way hotter, said a third.

Fed up, I scratched the back of my head with my middle finger and heard a round of gasps. I smile serenely at Caleb, who was clueless to the verbal and nonverbal catfight he'd instigated.

Our food came a little later and he'd ordered us both huge hamburgers with steak fries. "I can't eat all of this," I told him. "I'd need two stomachs."

"Don't worry, I'll eat whatever you don't finish," he assured then bit into his burger.

"That's probably why you ordered us the same thing, huh?" His smile was answer enough.

I ate as much as I could and let him finish my food as promised. "Whenever we go out to eat, my mom makes me order a salad or chicken and rice. I haven't had a good fattening restaurant burger in forever." At home she made tasty food to make Scott happy, so I got to eat that, but she sometimes gave me a disapproving look if she thought I was eating too much.

"That is just wrong. You're far from fat," he remarked, eyeing my stomach area. I had the sudden urge to cover it with my hands.

Fighting a blush, I told him, "Yeah, but she's paranoid that I'll gain weight. Sometimes I wonder what'd happen if I did. She'd probably have a nervous breakdown or something."

"Please don't get fat. I like looking at your hot body too much," he teased.

"Pig." He had nothing to say to that, since it was true.

Caleb paid for our meal and we left the restaurant, walking in the opposite direction from where his car was parked. "Where are we going?"

"You'll see, princess," he replied with a wink.

We crossed quite a few blocks before stopping in front of a tattoo shop called Donna's Designs. "Are you serious? I can't get a tattoo. My mom would drag my ass to the nearest place to get it removed."

"Then you just have to get it somewhere she won't see it. I think I know the perfect place." He smacked me on the butt to make his meaning clear.

"Like I said, you're a pervert." I slapped him on the arm in retaliation.

"Anyways, you don't have to get it today. You can just look at some designs."

This made me feel better and I followed him inside. There were a couple artists working on tattoos and one of them glanced up at our entrance. "Hey, Caleb, are you here for that tongue piercing?"

"Nope, Donna. This is Gianna. She's here to get my name tattooed on her ass." He said it with a straight face and I pushed him. Donna laughed and went back to the guy she was working on. She was a few years older than us, pretty with black hair to her shoulders and colorful tattoos going up one arm.

"You're a pervert, Caleb," she said. See, I was right!

"She's still thinking about what to get, Donna," he informed her.

"Okay, just let me know if you have any questions."

I thanked her and we looked through books. Too curious to resist, I asked Caleb, "Do you have any tattoos?" I'd avoided looking at his body when I'd seen him in a towel and I was regretting it now.

"Yes, and if you're lucky, you might just get to see them someday."

I rolled my eyes at his cockiness. "I think I want to design my own and I already have something in mind."

"And what's that?"

"Maybe if you get lucky, you might just get to see it," I mimicked him. "How do you get tattoos without a parent's consent?"

"Oh, Donna used to live in the same apartment building as me, so she doesn't care," he explained. "Are you ready to get one today?"

"No way, I want to work on the design a little first and mentally prepare myself." I wasn't looking forward to it hurting either.

"Let's go then." Caleb called out a goodbye to Donna and told her that we'd be back.

We were heading to his car and I wondered if we were finished for the day. Surprisingly, hanging out with Caleb hadn't been as bad as I'd thought. "What now, boss?"

"You got that right. Actually, I was wondering about number six. Why haven't you done that before?"

"Well, sometimes there are b-boys dancing on the street at the 16th Street Mall. I'm sure you've seen them, having lived down here. Even my crew does it every once in awhile, but I'm too afraid someone my mom knows will be there shopping or eating at a restaurant. If they see me and tell her, she'd freak."

"I think it's more important that you're happy. Sometimes you have to take risks. If she finds out, we'll deal with it then. You should ask about the next time the crew is planning on going and we'll meet them there." A group of guys our age were about to pass us on the sidewalk and I was surprised when Caleb steered me to the right of him so they'd pass near him.

"Okay, I'll talk to Jared," I told him, still thinking of what just happened.

"How about you talk to Cece?" he suggested, looking irritated.

"Jealous?" I teased him.

"I don't get jealous," he said smoothly. "Other guys have never been much competition for me."

"Your ego is ridiculous!" True, he looked good, especially in the striped t-shirt and jeans he wore, but an ego like that couldn't be healthy.

"Nope, just honest."

When we got back to his car, he drove to the parking garage near his mom's apartment. We had to go back to the apartment for my bag. I followed him to his room where it sat on his bed. He had a lot of band posters and drawings on his walls.

Remembering what I'd forgotten to ask him this morning, I said, "Are these yours?"

"Yes, I guess I got the gene from my mom."

Turning away from the drawings, I smiled at him. "They're really good. I should have you draw the design I want for my tattoo."

"Sure, no problem." His expression changed to something

indecipherable. "You know, I don't usually let girls come to my place. It usually results in stalkers. You should feel lucky."

"Jeez, that's the most romantic thing anyone has ever said to me," I replied sarcastically. "No wonder you don't have a girlfriend."

"You shouldn't say bad words."

"I didn't just say a bad word." His serious demeanor was confusing me.

"Yes you did. You said the G-word," he whispered. "*Girlfriend.*" His fake shudder was over the top.

"You're horrible, do you know that? A complete player."

He put his arms around my waist, pulling me into his body. "I know, but if I *did* want to enter the form of slavery called being in a relationship, it'd be with someone as hot as you."

I glared up at him. "Wow, that was the second most romantic thing anyone has ever said to me. You're on a roll, Caleb. Anything else?"

"Yep," His lips came crashing down onto mine.

Responding, I went into this kiss with my eyes wide open. I knew he was a player and developing any real feelings would be a disaster. I'd just have fun with it while it lasted. We moved over to the bed with me on top. My lips roamed from his lips to his neck. Instinct told me to mark him. I sat up laughing.

"What?" he asked, brows drawn together.

"I gave you a hickey!" I declared triumphantly.

"Are you trying to mark your territory?" he asked, gripping my hips to grind me against him. He didn't seem bothered at all.

"No, it's just that you're a player. You should look the part. It was either that, or write *Player* on your forehead with permanent marker while you sleep tonight."

"If you do that, I'll write my name on your forehead while *you* sleep." One hand moved up my waist and was just under my breast.

"That wouldn't be a good idea. Someone might make the mistake of thinking you had a girlfriend. I couldn't imagine anything worse happening than that!" My mock horror made him chuckle.

"Very funny, princess." Caleb rolled me over onto my back

with him on top and *damn* did he feel good there. We started kissing again and I slowly inched his shirt off.

"What are you doing?" he mumbled against my lips.

I quickly tugged his shirt over his head, so just his arms were still in it. "I want to see your tats!"

He leaned back, pulled his shirt over his head and gave me a good look. Maybe that wasn't such a good idea. He looked so fucking hot! It made a girl want to give up her virginity. I guess I should've known since he had one eyebrow pierced, that both his nipples were pierced too. His body was ripped. I'd never noticed him going to the gym, but he must fit it in sometime with abs like that.

On his chest was a really cool Chinese dragon tattoo done in red and black. I touched it and he asked, "Do you like it?"

"Yeah, do you have any other ones?" He started to unbutton his jeans and I put my hands over his. "Wait! I don't want to see that one!" I don't, right? I'd probably faint and never be able to face him again.

He laughed and said ambiguously with a strange glint in his eyes, "I'm just kidding. Maybe."

Now I had to wonder if he really did have a tattoo somewhere under those jeans. Damn him! The idea of getting a little payback popped into my head. I leaned up to lick his nipple, flicking the ring. He shuddered as I sucked his nipple into my mouth.

"Gianna," he moaned. "*Fuck.* We should stop before this goes too far." He didn't sound as if he really meant it.

"That won't happen," I told him confidently. "My first time isn't going to be with a player."

He sprang away from me so fast I swore I felt a whoosh of air. "Whoa, first time? You're a *virgin*?" The way he said it, you'd think I'd just told him I had the clap.

"Yeah, so what? Why's that so bad?" Anger was building in me at his attitude.

"I do *not* mess around with virgins." He picked his shirt up and yanked it back over his head.

"You're an asshole," I told him, not believing his attitude. "Peace out, motherfucker!" I snatched my bag off where it'd fallen on the floor and left the apartment. My whole point had been that

I'd never have sex with *him*, but the way he'd acted you'd think I threw myself at him.

As I walked to my car, I was thankful I didn't have to drive home with him. I'd have probably followed through with number one on the list and punched him in the face. I was pissed on the way home, until I realized the best way to handle how he just treated me was to get a little payback. Now, I just had to figure out how to do it.

CHAPTER TEN

"In youth and beauty, wisdom is but rare!"
-Homer

CALEB

After Gianna stormed out of the apartment in a huff, I laid back on my bed. Crap! I almost had sex with a virgin. Crap! I almost had sex with my stepsister! We may not be blood-related, but I still thought us hooking up was something most people would frown upon.

Besides, Julie may have liked me, but I didn't think she'd like me banging her daughter. That woman had some serious issues when it came to her child and trying to live through her. She saw Gianna as her perfect little angel. No wonder she'd never caught on to Gianna's Saturday night activities. All Julie could see was perfect looks and pom-poms.

Speaking of pom-poms, I hoped Gianna realized she'd seen the end of those. I did have to admit, though, that I loved seeing her in her little cheerleading outfit at the football game Friday night. It gave me lots of school spirit. *Go Team!*

I wondered again what number thirteen on her list meant. Since I was blackmailing her, I was sure I could make her tell me. It was probably some stupid girl thing. Back to the blackmailing thing, shouldn't I have been getting more out of it? I guess I was having fun messing around with her life. Plus, I got the satisfaction of being in control.

Maybe we didn't just almost have sex. She did say she had no intention of giving it up to a guy like me. That she didn't want her first time to be with a player. It was like she was asking me to prove her wrong. *No! Don't think like that!* I didn't sleep with virgins. They were too emotional about sex.

What kind of tattoo did she want? Probably a butterfly or daisy. Chicks always got stuff like that. Speaking of chicks, it was hilarious when Gianna got jealous of that girl at the diner. What was her name again? All I vaguely remembered about her was the weird sounds she made during sex. I probably shouldn't have mentioned to that girl the night we hooked up that I always ate at the Rocky Mountain Diner.

When I was back at my dad's house, I parked out front. I hoped it wasn't awkward between me and Gianna, but I mostly hoped she wasn't still pissed. From the foyer, I heard Julie and my dad talking in the kitchen. In the living room Gianna sat in front of the television playing video games with Chance.

"Hey," I cautiously greeted.

Their heads turned around almost as one. "Caleb! Watch me play!" Chance demanded.

Gianna smiled sweetly at me and I wondered what that was all about. "Hi, Caleb."

"Hi?" I repeated, confused. Wasn't she still the least bit pissed at me? Wasn't she the one who said *peace out, motherfucker*?

I sat down on the couch behind them and watched them play. Chance was whooping Gianna's ass at Mario Kart. I'd hooked up my Wii the other day and he was now obsessed with the game.

Gianna turned around and whispered to me, "Caleb?"

"Yeah?" I answered warily. What was with the whispering? I leaned forward and so did she.

"You remember what we were talking about earlier?"

"Yes," I replied, not exactly sure what she was referring to.

"Well, I think you were right," she whispered.

"Right about what?" I asked, still confused.

"We'll talk about it later," she said on a conspiratorial wink. "Come to my room later."

That sounded like an invitation for more than talking.

"Dinner's ready!" Julie called from the dining room. Okay, not sure what Gianna was talking about, but I guess I'd be finding out later.

We sat down to eat the spaghetti and garlic bread Julie made. Gianna was acting oddly happy, which was making me wonder what the hell happened between her leaving my mom's apartment and her coming here. After dinner, I went upstairs and turned on my laptop. I felt weird going over to Gianna's room, but eventually I found myself knocking on her door.

"Come in!"

I shut the door behind me, almost bracing myself for whatever it is she wanted to talk about. She sat at her desk in front of her computer, watching a music video online.

"You said you wanted to talk about something I was right about earlier?" I said slowly.

"Caleb, the way you acted about me being a virgin, well, you were right."

"I was?" Where was she going with this?

"Yes, you were, and I've decided it's time I lost my virginity." She was serious about this from her earnest expression.

"Gianna, I told you I don't mess around with virgins," I reminded her.

"No, not you. Jared." she blithely blurted out.

"What the fuck, Gianna? You're not having sex with Jared!" I yelled.

"Shh! Do you want my family to hear? And why not Jared? He's one of my best friends and from the kiss he gave me last night, I can tell we have some chemistry. He isn't a jerk like Josh or a player like you. He's perfect!"

Okay, I didn't see any of this coming. She was technically right. If she was going to lose her virginity, she should lose it to a guy like Jared. That didn't mean I'd allow it. "When do you plan on this happening?"

"I figure the sooner the better. I'll see Jared on Saturday, so probably then."

Good to know when I needed to be prepared to stop this mistake. I would stay informed of her plans and stop them. "Why are you telling *me* this?"

"Duh! I need your help."

"You need my help to lose your virginity . . . to Jared?" I asked skeptically.

"Of course, you're the biggest manwhore I know. You can give me pointers and help me out with what lingerie to wear. We'll go to Victoria's Secret together. You know, you may as well add this to my list. Lose my virginity, number fourteen."

"All right," was all I could manage to choke out.

What the hell had I done? I wanted to be a bad influence on Gianna for the right reasons, not the wrong ones. Sure I'd had sex with a lot of girls. I'd be the first to admit I was a manwhore who loved easy girls, but I couldn't let that happen to Gianna. She was too special to turn into me *or* one of those easy girls. She deserved her first time to be special, too.

Most of all, I didn't want anyone else touching her. Not that douche Jared, not that date-rapist Josh, no one. Since I couldn't have sex with her, the best plan was for Gianna to stay a virgin. If I couldn't touch her, she'd just have to be happy staying untouched. I wondered how she'd take it if I tried blackmailing her into staying a virgin.

GIANNA

After Caleb left my room, I buried my face in a pillow and let all of my pent up laughter out. That was the funniest thing ever! I had a hard time controlling my laughter when he was here, but I did. That was what he got for treating me like a leper for being a virgin. And I meant it when I said earlier today I'd never lose my virginity to a player like him. I had no intention of having sex with Jared on Saturday night. I mean, I was in no way against the idea of sex, but I figured it'd happen when it was meant to. It just hadn't happened yet for me.

The look on his face, or I should say the many looks on his face were hilarious. Shock, jealousy, irritation, anger all flashed over his handsome mug. Oh, it was a beautiful sight! He probably thought he'd kept his cool too, but I was looking out for it. I was deciding how far I should take this revenge. I thought I'd take it as far as I could without actually having sex with Jared. Caleb deserved it for blackmailing and insulting me.

I knew this would work. I had to deal with Josh's jealous and possessive ass for long enough to know that no matter what Caleb felt about me or my virgin status, the thought of me having sex with Jared would bother him. Caleb may not want to be with me, but being territorial just came naturally to guys.

CHAPTER ELEVEN

"The world's biggest power is the youth and beauty of a woman."
-Chanakya

GIANNA

Waking up the next morning with a feeling of anticipation, I felt better than I ever had on a Monday morning. I hurriedly dressed for school and went downstairs. Grabbing a breakfast bar and Gatorade, I sat at the kitchen table, tossing my backpack on the chair next to me.

My mom snatched the Gatorade from my hand and replaced it with a bottle of water. "Honey, do you realize how many calories are in just one Gatorade?"

"No, mom." The bottle of water got a scowl from me. My mom got another one as she left the kitchen.

Caleb walked in and awareness coursed through me. Did he have to be so hot? His body was freaking ridiculous. He was obviously irritated. This wouldn't happen to have anything to do with our little chat last night, would it? I hoped so.

"Good morning, Caleb!" I said cheerfully.

"Morning," he grumbled while pulling the Gatorade I wanted back out of the fridge.

"So when are we going shopping?"

He finally looked at me, eyes wary. "Shopping? For what?"

I leaned forward and whispered, "For Operation Pop My Cherry."

He was in thc middle of taking a drink and spewed red liquid all over the countertop. I turned my head to the wall, holding back laughter.

"Are you serious, Gianna?" he asked, his eyes flaring wide.

"Of course I'm serious. You're a dude. You'll be able to help me pick the sexiest outfit for Jared." I thought my patient tone was a nice touch.

"You want me to go with you to pick out an outfit for you to lose your virginity in?" His own tone of disbelief and horror was priceless.

"Well, I probably won't be losing my virginity in the outfit.

The goal is to drive Jared so wild he rips it off me first," I explain coyly.

"Please someone save me," he muttered distractedly.

"What was that?" I pretended not to hear.

"Nothing, we'll go later this week, I guess," he agreed reluctantly.

"Thanks, Caleb. You're the best stepbrother ever!" This revenge stuff was fun. Picking up my backpack, I slung it over my shoulder.

"Wait, Gianna, I'll drive you today."

"Why?"

"Just do what I say," he barked out irritably.

"Um, okay," I said quietly. Why would he want to drive me?

We drove to school in silence. I couldn't help noticing how handsome he looked in a white Henley and dark blue jeans. The Henley was tucked in only at the front, showing his belt, which added a bit of sexiness.

He managed to get a close spot in the school parking lot. I grabbed the door handle but he put a hand out to stop me. He was about to say something but changed his mind, shaking his head. People approached both of us as we got out of the car. If you put a camera in their hands, they'd be paparazzi.

I zeroed in on Josh standing by the front doors, staring our way. God, I'd totally forgotten about him. I glanced over at Caleb to see him glaring back at Josh. I was surprised Josh didn't come up to me. Maybe he was taking this breakup better than I thought he would. Well, that was a relief. I had been worried he'd do something crazy or embarrassing.

People crowded us as we entered the front doors. I mostly ignored them and nodded my head here and there. My gaze met Josh's when I passed by him. "Hi, Gianna."

"Hi, Josh." Deciding that was polite enough, I kept walking.

Some girl I'd never seen came up and touched Caleb's arm, hanging on as if she were afraid to let go. He smiled charmingly at her and she giggled like an idiot. I had the urge to pull her bleached hair. At least my naturally dark blonde hair didn't look like straw. I couldn't believe I was getting jealous again over a player. It defied logic. A guy like him shouldn't even be taken seriously.

I ignored their flirting and walked to my locker. So much for Hannah, I guess she was last week's flavor like I'd thought. Speak of the she-devil; she was waiting by my locker.

"Hi, Hannah." Turning the dial, I unlocked my locker and unloaded a book from my backpack to replace it with another. Finding a Gatorade I'd left there on Friday, I opened it and took a big gulp. What my mom didn't know didn't hurt her.

"Do you know what your stepbrother did to me on Friday night?" Hannah hissed angrily.

I thought to myself, *do I want to know?* But I instead said to her, "Nope."

She stomped her foot, and I thought, *oh my god did she just stomp her foot?* "I asked him if he was going to ask me to be his girlfriend!"

Oh no, the G-word. That was taboo with Caleb.

"And do you know what he did?" she asked insistently.

"Nope," I repeated, hoping she would just go away.

"He laughed and told me, 'As long as you're okay with an open relationship.' What the hell is that, Gianna? I can be his girlfriend as long as he's allowed to be with other girls. That defeats the whole purpose of being his girlfriend!" Hannah screeched, oblivious of the attention she was drawing to herself. Two sophomore boys were her rapt audience.

I managed to hold back my laughter, but at the same time I thought, *what a creep Caleb was*. But then, it'd been his whole purpose, to discourage Hannah from thinking relationship-type thoughts.

Before I had to suffer any more of Hannah's whining one of Josh's friends came up to me. "Hey, Gianna, can I talk to you for a minute?"

I gave him a grateful smile. "Sure, Seth, do you want to walk with me to class?"

His green eyes lit up. "I'd love to." I'd always liked Seth. He was such a sweet guy. He was kind of cute, too, with brown hair and green eyes. He played on the football team with Josh and we'd chatted in the past.

While we were strolling down the hall, he cleared his throat nervously. "Josh told me about you two breaking up. I'm sorry."

"I'm not," I told him. Truthfully, I really wasn't sorry at all. Josh suffocated me with his attention and possessiveness. It felt as if a weight had been lifted off my shoulders, the weight of a smothering ex-boyfriend.

His expression transformed from nervous to relieved. "I know this is kind of soon, but I was wondering if maybe you'd want to go out with me after the game on Friday night?"

Hearing an obnoxious giggle, I turned my head around to see Caleb and that idiot girl leaning into each other in a flirtatious manner. I spun back to the guy next to me. "That sounds like fun, Seth."

His shocked face made me smile. Seth reached out for my hand. "Thank you."

"What?" I asked, laughing. Did he just thank me for agreeing to go on a date with him?

"Oh, I mean, I'll meet you in the parking lot after the game," he rushed to say, blushing.

"Okay, see you later," I responded, entering my first class. I'd never thought of Seth in a romantic way before and I hoped I didn't regret going out with him. I hadn't foreseen him asking me out, being Josh's friend and all. I probably would've said no, but seeing Caleb flirting with another girl after the weekend we just had made me jealous as hell. So, I figured, why not?

My first few classes were a nightmare. News spread fast about me and Josh breaking up. I'd had three more guys ask me out already. I declined by saying I was already dating someone new. Hopefully news would spread just as fast about me being off the market again. A lot of girls liked Josh so he was probably going through the same thing.

Hurrying to third period across the building, I felt someone grab me from behind and pull me out of a set of doors leading to football field. As I was pushed up against the brick wall, I saw it was Josh who'd yanked me out of the building.

"What are you doing, Josh?" I yelled at him, getting scared at the hostility in his eyes.

"I should be the one asking that," he gritted out. "What's this I hear that you're already dating someone new, Gianna? Since when? Were you cheating on me the entire time?"

I fought against his hold, but he was too strong. "No, of course not. And I'm not really dating anyone else yet. I have a date Friday night, that's all."

He pushed his body harder against mine. "With who?"

"None of your business!" I tried pushing back against him, alarm flashing through me, but couldn't move.

He squeezed my jaw roughly with one hand and planted his lips onto mine. His tight grip was hurting my face and I couldn't help crying. "Shh, don't cry, baby. I'm sorry. It's just that I love you so much and the thought of you with someone else drives me fucking insane. Tell me you won't be with anyone else, baby."

Not wanting to antagonize him, but refusing to get back together, I told him, "We're not getting back together, Josh."

His face turning red, he grabbed me by the shoulders and slammed me against the wall. I cried out from the pain of hitting my back and head against the brick. "Don't say that!" he screamed at me.

I started crying harder because he was still hurting me. "Please let go of me, Josh!"

He swooped in for another kiss, but I turned my face to the side and his lips met my cheek. Enraged, he slammed me against the wall again, but the doors suddenly opened and a P.E. class filed out. He released me at once and I took the opportunity to run away from him and around the building. I didn't stop until I reached Caleb's car in the parking lot. Checking the doors, they were locked, so I circled around to the other side of the car and crouched down against the side of it. I was worried Josh would come looking for me and I didn't want him to find me if he did.

I pulled out my cell from the front of my backpack and sent Caleb a text.

Me: *Can you give me a ride home?*

I was relieved when he answered immediately.

Caleb: *Right now?*

Me: *Yes PLEASE!*

Caleb: *Ok meet me at my car*

No problem, I thought to myself. I still sat against the side of his car when he showed up. "What are you doing down there?"

I quickly wiped my face with my hand and said nonchalantly, "Just waiting for you."

"Why were you crying?"

"I wasn't crying," I denied, then changed the subject, "Hey, if you don't want to miss class, I can just take your car and pick you up after school."

"When did you get the impression I gave a fuck whether or not I missed class?" His hazel eyes still roved over my face, taking in what I was sure were red eyes and blotchy cheeks. "Come on, get in the car."

I had to circle the car again to the passenger side. Once we were out of the parking lot and on the street, he demanded, "Tell me why you were hiding on the side of my car, crying."

CHAPTER TWELVE

"Beauty in distress is much the most affecting beauty."
-Edmund Burke

CALEB

When Gianna ignored me, I repeated, "Tell me why you were crying."

"It was nothing," she stalled.

"If it was nothing, then why do you need to go home?" I continued to interrogate her ruthlessly.

"I just had a fight with Josh," she finally admitted, leaning her head against the window dejectedly.

I'd met plenty of guys like Josh before. I knew the type and I wanted a full explanation. "Tell me, Gianna, or I'm just going to turn this car right around, pull him out of whatever class he has right now and beat the shit out of him."

She looked alarmed by my threat. "You can't do that!"

"I can and I will, if you don't tell me." I made sure to look her straight in the eyes so she could tell how serious I was.

She sighed in resignation. "Fine, I was walking to third period when he pulled me outside and demanded to know if I was seeing someone new."

Her eyes avoiding mine gave her away. "Gianna, what are you leaving out?"

She glanced down at her hands and said softly, "Um, he yelled at me and kissed me a couple times and slammed me against the wall a of couple times." She lifted her head with new tears in her eyes and her bottom lip trembling.

I screeched over to the side of the road and she jumped in her seat in alarm. Unbuckling her seatbelt, I pulled her in for a hug. She rested her head against my shoulder and I reached up to feel a bump on the back of her head. He was going to pay for this.

"It's okay now. I'll make sure it doesn't happen again."

She drew back to look into my face. "What are you going to do?"

"Beat his ass next time I see him."

"What if he wins? I don't want you to get beat up." She was so cute.

"Don't worry, I won't. What did you tell him when he asked if you were seeing someone new?" Brushing the hair back from her forehead, I kissed her red nose.

"I told him I wasn't actually dating anyone new yet since our first date isn't until Friday."

Shit! Did she think we were dating? "Who exactly are you going on a date with?"

"Seth."

"Who the hell is Seth?" I practically yelled at her, making her flinch.

"Seth Nichols. You've met him, right? He sits at the same table at lunch as you do. Just at the other end by where Josh and I usually sit."

I finally realized who she was talking about and had to admit myself it was jealousy I was feeling. "What about your plans to have sex with Jared?"

Her expression turned guarded. "Oh, Jared is Saturday night. Seth is Friday night."

"Will you be fucking Seth also?" I asked through clenched teeth.

She pinched my stomach hard. "Don't be an ass, Caleb, of course not. I mean, at least not yet. But you never know what will happen in the future. I figure, once I lose my virginity and get that out of the way, everything will change." The sly look in her beautiful blue eyes worried me.

"What do you mean?" I asked her, not knowing if I wanted the answer.

"Well, look how miserable I've been in the past and look how happy you are with the way you live your life. I want to be a player like you. From now on, I don't even want to hear the word *boyfriend* because it's a new bad word in my dictionary, the B-word. Just think of me as your protégé!" She seemed delighted at the prospect.

Jesus Christ, what had I done? I'd turned an innocent girl into a female player! There had to be a way to prevent this all from happening. But who was I to scold her about it? She was just following my example.

GIANNA

Oh my god! This was hilarious. I could totally tell Caleb was freaking out in his head. His eyes weren't even focused anymore. I couldn't believe he was buying it! Like I was just going to go whoring around for the fun of it! When I finally had sex for the first time, I wanted it to mean something. Maybe his way of thinking about sex was so ingrained that he could easily imagine someone else adopting the same attitude.

Without a word, he buckled me back in and drove us home. The house was quiet with my mom and Scott at work and Chance at school. Fortunately, we wouldn't have to answer any awkward questions about what we were doing home in the middle of the school day.

Caleb finally spoke again when we entered the house. "You know, this is number ten on the list, ditch school. This isn't really your first time ditching is it?" The way he said it, he made me sound lame.

"It's the first time without my mom's permission," I informed him. "But, I'll probably have her excuse this one. I'll tell her I wasn't feeling good."

"It doesn't count if you do that. Plus, to ditch school and only go home is lame. Some other time we're going to do it right."

"Should we go back to school then?" I asked, not keen on the idea.

"No, we'll stay here and watch a movie or something."

"Sure, but I get to pick it," I announced and headed over to the DVD collection in the living room. I took out *28 Days Later* and put it on.

After I pushed play on the remote, Caleb asked, "You like zombie movies?"

"I love zombie movies, but this isn't a zombie movie. The people in this movie have The Rage virus."

"Whatever," he replied indifferently.

I glared at him. "You don't have to sound so excited."

"Okay, I won't." He grinned at me in a way I was starting to like. "What if I get scared, Gianna? Are you going to hold me?"

My first thought was to call him a wimp, but then I thought

better of it. I was supposed to be playing the part of player protégé. Instead, I scanned his body and finally settled my eyes on his crotch. “Where exactly would you like me to hold you?”

His mouth dropped open in shock. He was about to say something but closed it. Caleb’s gaze took in my own body. “Princess, you’re asking for trouble.”

I blanked out my face. “Would it be like a lesson of some sort?”

His eyes clouded over for a moment as if he was going through some sort of internal debate. “I don’t think that’s a lesson you need to learn yet.”

I shrugged carelessly. “Whatever, I guess I’ll learn it soon enough.”

Going into the kitchen, I searched for something for us to eat and drink. When I returned to the living room, Caleb was laying down on the couch, so I sat in front of him on the floor, with my back against the couch.

Soon after the movie started, Caleb began playing with my hair. I couldn’t help remarking, “I wonder what my mom would do if I dyed it black.”

“Probably dye it back to dark blonde while you’re sleeping. Don’t dye it, though, I like it this color.” The compliment made me all happy inside, which was stupid.

I turned around to ask him why he liked the color and he leaned forward to capture my lips with his. As usual, I kissed him back, prompting him to pull me up onto the couch with him. Sucking his bottom lip into my mouth, I luxuriated in his taste. He groaned, pushing his hips up against mine. His own lust fueled mine. I was kissing his neck when I got to where I gave him a hickey yesterday. A giggle slipped through my lips.

“What’s so funny?” he asked playfully.

I sat up, looking down at him. “I guess the hickey didn’t work. It didn’t stop that slutty girl this morning from throwing herself at you.”

“No it didn’t. Actually, I have a date Friday night, too.”

“What?” I shouted while jumping off of him. I was incredibly pissed now. Maybe I didn’t have a reason to be mad, since I had a date also, but he started it! He was flirting with that girl before I agreed to the date with Seth. If he hadn't been, I may have turned Seth down.

"What's wrong? Jealous?" he taunted.

"No, I would *never* be jealous of a guy like you. Who was that girl anyways? What's her name?"

His eyebrows drew together in concentration. "You know, I actually can't remember her name. She did put her number in my phone, so I guess it's in there."

"You know you're horrible, right?" I was in twisted awe of him. It was incredible what a player he was. I'd think the guy deserved a medal if it didn't irritate me so much.

"Hey, I thought you wanted to be just like me?"

Dammit, I'd forgotten about that. "You know what? You're right. Jeez, I suck at this player thing." An idea came to me. "I have a great idea! How about we all go out on a double date Friday?"

"A double date?" he repeated skeptically.

"Yes, a double date. How better for me to learn from the master?"

"A double date?" He appeared to be having trouble with the concept.

"Just say yes," I ordered him.

"Um . . . yes?" His gorgeous face showed evident pain at the idea.

Good, I thought to myself. I was going to ruin his stupid date. He thought he could keep kissing me and still mess around with other girls. I didn't think so. I mean, what the hell? He kissed me and then was like, *oh by the way, I already have plans to be kissing some other girl on Friday and I don't even know her name.*

Screw that!

CHAPTER THIRTEEN

"Love is the attempt to form a friendship inspired by beauty."
-Marcus Tullius Cicero

CALEB

Seething over Josh attacking Gianna, I was in my room later that night drawing a comic strip of me hitting him with my car. The impact was hard enough that his body parts were strewn across the road. As I drove away in the last picture, my back tire went over his head, squashing it. He obviously hadn't learned his lesson Friday night, so I'd have to teach him another one. I didn't ever want to see Gianna hurt again and I couldn't be with her all the time at school, so the lesson would have to be a good one.

I needed to learn a lesson of my own and stop kissing her all the time. I couldn't seem to help myself with her. She was so beautiful and fun to be around. Too bad she was a virgin *and* my stepsister. That made her double off-limits.

The double date she'd talked me into for Friday seemed like a bad idea. Who did that other than cheesy people on sitcoms? How was I going to get any action with Gianna there? I especially didn't want to be around her and that Seth guy while they were on a date. I hadn't talked to him yet, but if he was Josh's friend maybe I wouldn't approve. Maybe it was a good thing we'd all be hanging out on Friday, so I could keep an eye on him. It was unreal that she already had a date with another guy. She just broke up with Josh this past weekend.

As for her plans to sex with Jared on Saturday, that wouldn't be happening. I'd stick by her side and not let her out of my sight all weekend. It was no hardship hanging out with her anyways.

With music playing, lying back on my bed, I got an idea for the first part of Josh's lesson. Eager to make him pay, I changed my clothes and slipped on shoes. Leaving my room, I lightly knocked on Gianna's door. She opened it wearing just boy shorts and a tank top. Damn, I wanted to fuck her. Gianna deserved to be made love to and I didn't think I had it in me.

She snapped her fingers in my face. "Caleb! What do you want?"

With great effort, I dragged my gaze away from the bit of skin showing above her waistband. "Oh, um, get dressed."

"Where are we going?"

Trying not to leer at her cleavage, I told her, "On a field trip, my apprentice. Wear black."

She shut the door on me and emerged less than a minute later wearing black leggings and a hoodie. We quietly went down the stairs and out the front door.

In my car, I asked her, "So, where does Josh live?"

She twisted in her seat, her eyes wide. "What are you going to do?"

"You mean, what are *we* going to do?"

"We're going to beat him up together?" she guessed, eyes going impossibly wider.

"As romantic as that sounds, princess, we aren't even going to see him. Now, where does he live?" She supplied me with directions and I parked my car a few houses down from his ten minutes later. Reaching into my backseat, I picked up the shopping bag which still had the cans of spray paint. There would be just enough left.

"Oh my god, we aren't going to do what I think we are, are we?"

"See, you're already learning from me." Opening my glove compartment, I took out a black beanie. I placed it on Gianna's head, hiding some of her dark blonde hair. "There, now you look like an adorable little robber."

Josh's truck was black, so we only used the white, aqua blue and hot pink paint. The truck was parked in the driveway, with the driver side closest to the front door, so we painted the passenger side. When he got into his truck the following morning, he probably wouldn't even see what we'd done. We gathered up the cans when we were finished and put them back in the shopping bag.

Once we were back in my car and driving away, Gianna busted up laughing. "I can't believe we did that! He's going to freak! Oh no, what if he figures out it was us?"

"Don't worry, princess, I'll take care of him," I assured her, turning up the radio.

High on adrenalin, I took hold of her hips before we went through the front door and kissed her. She must've felt as exhilarated as me because she matched my enthusiasm. Her arms twined around my neck. God, I loved her mouth. I kept telling myself to stop before I became addicted, but already nothing was better than kissing Gianna. As long it didn't go any further, I figured no harm done.

Gianna was the one to end the kiss. "Thanks for the fun, Caleb."

"Glad to be of service." I watched her ass as she went inside and upstairs ahead of me.

*****

The next morning, I drove Gianna to school again. Eating the breakfast burritos Julie made us, we waited in my car in the parking lot for Josh to arrive. When he did, last night's efforts proved to be well worth it. Everyone who caught the show laughed along with us. Josh exited his truck, still obviously clueless. He had a bewildered look on his face until he rounded the back of his truck to the other side where a crowd was gathering.

Since my car windows were rolled down his, "Who the fuck did this?" was loud and clear.

Written along the side of his truck was his first and last name, but that wasn't all. For each letter of his name, coming down from that letter, Gianna and I had added a word to describe the wonderfulness that was Josh Larsen.

J*ackass*
O*bsessive*
S*hithead*
H*ater*
L*imp-dick*
A*sshole*
R*apist*
S*leaze*
E*vil*
N*ecrophiliac*

We'd run out of room on the last word, but he'd get the gist of it. I was itching to go over there and beat the shit out of him for hurting Gianna, but I realized he would know then Gianna and I had vandalized his truck. I didn't want him going after her for it. A target on my back wouldn't have bothered me, but Gianna couldn't fight back. I still owed him a beating. First chance I got, he'd meet my fists. Until then, I'd keep a close eye on Gianna at school.

Still sitting in my car, I warned her, "Gianna, I want you to be careful at school from now on. Go everywhere with at least one other person and wait at your locker for me after school. I'll drive you to and from school for awhile."

Shifting in her seat, she looked worried. "Okay, I guess." Then with an impish smile, she added, "Do you think we should offer him the can of black spray paint we didn't use to cover it up?" She laughed so I knew she wasn't serious.

Picking up her backpack along with mine, I said, "Come on, princess, I'll walk you to first next class."

I had second and fourth periods with Gianna and I actually found myself eager to get to them. Last week she ignored me like a stranger, but this week she smiled at me when I came into class. I always sat in the back of my classes, so my view was of the back of her head in second period and her profile in fourth. I was so pathetic, acting like all the other guys at this school who worshipped Gianna.

I definitely needed to get laid on Friday night. That'd clear my head of her. During fourth period, I browsed through the contacts in my phone to figure out my date's name on Friday. Desiree was her name. Such a gentleman, making sure I knew the name of the girl I'd be screwing. Gianna would be proud.

Catching up with Gianna at the end of fourth period, I took her backpack off her shoulder and carried it. "Princess, we're going to work on number eleven now."

She looked at me quizzically. "Number eleven?"

"Yep, make new friends."

"I can't do that," she breathed out.

"Why the hell not?"

"Because I belong with the popular group. The other kids always treat me weird, like I'm so above them. They won't have a real conversation with me or anything. They just agree with whatever I say and stare at me." Her face was so sad I couldn't resist putting my arm around her and bringing her close. The situation was ridiculous and it just showed how silly kids my age could be.

"Well, that's where I come in." Confidence mixed with humility always worked.

"What do you mean?" she asked suspiciously. As if I'd ever steered her wrong!

I smiled knowingly at her. "You'll see."

We went through the lunch line. "So, being brave, where'd you like to sit?"

She scanned the lunchroom before her blue eyes settled on a table. "Do you see those people over there?"

Following her gaze, I spotted a group of guys and girls near the windows. "Yeah, why them?"

"Well, I was friends with a couple of them in elementary school. Do you see how they don't all dress the same? From looking at them, you wouldn't even think they had a lot in common, but they're friends. That tells me they all accept each other for who they are, not for what they look like or what they wear. I've always thought it'd be cool to hang out with them." From her pink cheeks, she was embarrassed about opening up about something she'd obviously given a lot of thought to.

Not wanting to discourage her, I ignored her embarrassment. "Wise choice, let's go introduce ourselves."

Her nervousness was cute as we walked to their table. It was funny that the most popular girl in the school was afraid of not being accepted by what looked like a group of misfits. I liked them for that alone. Taking an empty seat at their table, I pulled Gianna down onto the seat next to mine.

I start eating my food as if sitting with them was an everyday occurrence, but Gianna sat there looking down at her food. Swallowing my food, I glanced around the group of shocked faces. "What?"

A petite Asian girl with red streaks in her hair whispered shyly, "Why are you guys sitting here? Shouldn't you be over there, with your friends?"

"And what if we want to sit here?" I challenged her, taking

another bite.

A guy with a face pierced like a pincushion said, "That'd be cool, I guess," but he was looking at Gianna as he said it. That, I hadn't anticipated. If he hit on her, perhaps we'd find a new group of potential *real* friends.

My eyes met Gianna's to see her staring nervously back at me. Breaking the ice apparently wasn't her forte. "I'm Caleb, I started here last week. Do you guys all know my stepsister, Gianna?"

A kid with spiked blonde hair and black Buddy Holly glasses answered for the table, "Everybody knows who Gianna is. She's like a *celebrity* here." His sarcasm wasn't appreciated.

Gianna stiffened next to me and I sensed her disappointment. I quickly blurted out, "Celebrity?" and laughed derisively. "That's ridiculous! Besides, she's sitting right here, so you shouldn't speak as if she isn't here."

"Sorry," the blonde kid mumbled.

I nudged Gianna and she finally spoke to the Asian girl, "Hey, Kara, do you remember when we used to walk home from school together in elementary school?"

"Yeah, I remember," Kara answered shyly. Then she laughed abruptly. "Do you remember that one time we raced and you fell into a puddle of mud in that dirt field?"

Gianna joined her laughter. "I remember that. My mom was so mad at me for ripping a hole in my jeans."

The rest of lunch was more relaxed and we got to know the other kids at the table. They were actually pretty cool. Definitely cooler and less fake than the *friends* Gianna had before. The entire lunch period, I saw kids from other tables staring and whispering. Thankfully Gianna was oblivious to it. It was the first time I'd seen her like this at school, happy. By the end of lunch, Gianna had talked about tattoos with a guy whose brother was a tattoo artist and she'd invited all of them to come watch her and her crew on Saturday at a battle. They were pretty surprised to find out Gianna was a breaker.

Leaving the lunchroom, Gianna spontaneously hugged me. "Thanks, Caleb." I watched her walking to her locker, feeling good I'd had a hand in her joy. As much as I appreciated her gratitude, when she hugged me, I couldn't help thinking about how hot her body against mine.

After school, I waited for her by her locker. As she dumped some books in it, she said, "I missed cheerleading practice yesterday. I can't miss today or they're gonna bitch."

"Well that'd be number seven on the to-do list. Quit cheerleading," I stated unbendingly.

That brought a frown to her face. "My mom would be so mad. She loves cheerleading."

"That's been established, but do you love cheerleading?"

"Well, at first I loved it, especially the dance routines, but after a while, my mom made me feel like it was a duty. Since then, I've sort of resented it. She would seriously freak if I quit, Caleb."

"How about this then, you quit temporarily. Just to show to your mom it's your choice to make. Then, if you want to go back to it for the fun of it, you can."

She bit her lip, considering my suggestion. "Um, okay. I guess I could try that. But, I'll have to stop by practice to let them know I won't be there for awhile."

"Fine, but I'll go with you," I told her, thinking Josh could be waiting around practice to try and get her alone again.

We entered the gym and Gianna approached the squad to let them know what was up. A couple of them looked kind of pissed, but I wasn't concerned. What I was worried about was Josh, who stood off to the side as if he'd been waiting for Gianna to show up. He stared Gianna's way with an intense expression on his face. Lucky for him, he didn't try confronting her, probably because I was there.

Taking the opportunity, I stalked over to him. "Do you remember what happened Friday night?"

He scowled back at me and bit out, "Yeah."

"Now that you two are broken up, I'll expect you to stay away from her."

"And if I don't?" he asked, his eyes darting around.

"I already owe you a beat down for hurting her yesterday which believe me is still coming your way. If you do it again, I'll put you in the hospital while I'm at it." With that parting line, I walked to where Gianna waited for me, shifting nervously from one foot to the other.

She gave me a questioning look and I offered her a reassuring smile as we left the gym. Now, if only I could threaten every other guy who was interested in Gianna, I'd feel much better. Starting with Jared and Seth.

Gianna had a mischievous gleam in her eyes as we got in my car. "Since I'm not going to practice, I know what we can do!"

Reaching over to buckle her in, I asked. "What's that?"

"We can go shopping for the lingerie and outfit I'll be wearing on Saturday when I lose my virginity!"

CHAPTER FOURTEEN

"It's sad when girls think they don't have anything going on expect being pretty."
-Keri Russell

GIANNA

Walking across the parking lot to the mall entrance, I asked Caleb, "What should we do first? Lingerie or dress shopping?"

His jaw was clenched and his eyes were hidden behind sunglasses. He took a long time answering with, "Dress first."

We shopped my favorite stores and I tried on the sexiest dresses they had to offer. I made Caleb wait outside the dressing rooms, coming out to model each one. At the third store, I found a slutty black dress that covered my butt and the top of my thighs only. It also showed off an abundance of cleavage.

I snickered before coming out of the dressing room to show Caleb. "So, what do you think?" Spinning around, I gave him the full effect.

Caleb got a burning look of lust in his eyes while taking in my showing. After a long moment of silence, he rasped out, "It looks like shit."

"You liar!" I exclaimed. "I look damn right fuckable in this dress. Maybe you're gay. Are you gay, Caleb? You can confide in me. As your sister, I accept you for who you are."

"Stepsister," he corrected me. "And, no, I'm not gay. Do you want me to prove it to you?" Amazingly, the burning lust in his eyes went a few degrees hotter.

Hell, yes, a big part of me wanted him to prove it to me. Unfortunately, Caleb was a player and I'd be one of many girls who'd hooked up with him. I sighed. "No thanks, I'll leave that to your harem of skanks."

I shouldn't care who the sexy bastard spent his time with, but I did. At least I'd ruin his good time Friday night.

"Jealous?" he taunted, one pierced eyebrow raised. He probably practiced that look in the mirror until he'd perfected it.

"Yes," I admitted and his jaw went slack in surprise. "I'm jealous that my harem of men is so much smaller than your harem of skanks. But I'm just getting started in this player gig. It won't be long till I have so many men that I'll start forgetting their names, too." Then, as if the idea just popped in my head, I said, "Hey, what do you think about me dating older men?"

I saw his sour look reflected back at me in the mirror I faced. "I think I'd have to call the cops on them."

"Have you dated any older women?" I couldn't resist asking.

The self-satisfied smile on his face made me want to slap him. "Of course I have."

Why did I even bother asking? *Of course he had*, I thought miserably. Now I was not only jealous of girls my age, but females *not* my age. He definitely deserved all of the revenge I dished out.

"Enough talk of the dirty old women you've fooled around with. I've decided on this dress. I can totally picture Jared ripping it off me on Saturday." Strutting back to the dressing room, I said over my shoulder, "Time to go shopping for what he'll see after he rips this off."

Caleb wore a disgruntled look on his handsome face the whole time we were walking to Victoria's Secret. I told him as we went inside, "I hope you'll be more help here than you were dress shopping."

Trying not to show my embarrassment at lingerie shopping with Caleb, I snatched up the first items I saw. I was irritated at every stupid older woman and teenage girl Caleb had ever slept with. He was so stupid. Didn't sex mean anything more to him than getting off?

I put on the first item, a tight black halter babydoll with a plunging neckline. I'd never worn anything like it before. I'd never had a reason to. I had to admit, it looked sexy.

A blush formed on my cheeks at the thought of coming out of the fitting room and showing Caleb. How humiliating. I needed to remember why I was playing this game. He was an insensitive jerk when he found out I was still a virgin. The thought of me becoming the female version of him disturbed him. Any mental stress I caused him was just a little bit of justice. Not only for me, but for all the girls he'd used for sex.

I stepped out of the fitting room and moved to where Caleb sat leaning back in a chair. His eyes flared as he shifted in his seat.

Yep, the embarrassment was worth it.

"So, Caleb, do you think Jared will want me when he sees me in this?"

The fierce expression mingled with the possessive gleam in his hazel eyes alarmed me as he stood up and closed in. I backed up a few steps towards my fitting room, wishing a sales associate or someone would show up. I was almost to the safety of the dressing room when he pushed me inside.

"Caleb, what are you doing?"

He locked the door and dragged me to him. The kiss was far from gentle and when it ended, I was practically panting. "I guess this one's a winner. Too bad you don't mess around with virgins, huh?"

"Maybe you'll get lucky and I'll make a temporary exception for you," he purred, coming in for another kiss.

His arrogant remark reminded me that every girl was *temporary* for him. Temporary for as long as it took to get in their pants. I reached around him to open the door and push him back out. "No thanks, I'll pass!" With that, I slammed the door in his face.

CALEB

I couldn't believe Gianna just did that. She'd pass? She'd pass over me for what, that douche Jared? I didn't think so. I'd kidnap her Saturday night if I had to, to keep her from sleeping with him. She'd looked so hot in the dress she bought earlier. Jared wouldn't be the only guy having sexual thoughts about her after seeing her in that scrap of fabric. Not to mention the lingerie she just tried on. Jared didn't deserve to see her in any of it.

She came out of the dressing room and paid for the lingerie. I'd have paid for it if she were planning to wear it for me. She purchased the first one she tried on that made me hard as rock.

We left the mall in silence and I burned with jealousy at the thought of Jared touching her and the fact she'd chosen him to give her virginity to. It almost made me wish I were the type of guy to commit to a girlfriend. Then Gianna would be mine. I'd make sure of it.

Julie opened the front door when we got home. "Where have you two been?"

Gianna shuffled in place, hiding the pink shopping bag behind her back. Taking pity on her, I told her mom, "We were just spending some quality time together shopping."

Julie's demeanor shifted from suspicious to delighted. "How fun! How was cheerleading practice, honey?"

"Um, great," Gianna mumbled, running past both of us and upstairs.

"Dinner will be ready in thirty minutes, Caleb, so go wash up!" Julie ordered me before heading to the kitchen in her ruffled apron.

Wash up? I'd never get used to this wholesome family routine. My mom didn't care whether or not I came home for dinner and if I did we usually ordered in or ate out. Even when she was married to my dad she wasn't the homemaker type.

I followed Gianna upstairs and knocked on her door. "Come in!"

She sat cross-legged on her bed, texting. It bothered me to think she was exchanging cutsie little messages with Seth or Jared. "We need to talk."

Her fingers stilled on her phone and she looked up at me. "About what?"

"About you telling your mom you quit cheerleading."

An unsure expression flashed over her features. "I guess I should. She goes to most of the football games to watch me so she'll notice me missing from the squad this Friday."

Her phone beeped and she looked down to read the text. Her laughter put me on edge. "Who's that?"

Her fingers moving over the screen, she answered while responding to the text. "It's Cece. She's being a weirdo."

Annoyed for no good reason, I stepped out of her room to go next door to mine. I couldn't believe what a spaz I was becoming. I felt like a jealous boyfriend ready to throw down with any dude who flirted with her. I refused to become pathetic like Josh or Jared.

At dinner that evening, World War C began. Gianna brought up the subject of quitting cheerleading soon after everyone had dug into their tacos and rice. She was right, her mom freaked.

Her mom started off by trying to cajole Gianna into compliance. "Honey, why would you want to do that? You were meant to cheer. Just look at you. You're beautiful, popular and so talented in dance." Was this lady serious? The only part of her argument that made sense was the part about Gianna being a good dancer.

I finished off my first taco and waited for Gianna's response. "But mom, it's not fun anymore. I don't want to do it." Gianna plate was still full, her food ignored.

"Cheerleaders are hot!" Chance interjected through a mouthful of rice.

Surprisingly, I was the only one who laughed. My dad threw me a look as if to blame me for the kid's wisdom. I gave my dad an innocent look back and his attention returned to his wife.

Julie was too focused on Gianna's submission to care about her son's inappropriate comment. "Honey, I got pregnant with you when I was sixteen years old and had to give up cheerleading. I missed out on so much. I couldn't be a pregnant cheerleader." Persuasion was turning into a guilt trip. How great of Julie not to abort Gianna so she could hop around with pom-poms.

Gianna wore a stubborn expression, leaning forward in a move of defiance. "Mom, I don't care what you did or didn't get to do when you were in high school. It's not my fault you got pregnant with me. I shouldn't have to do something because you wished you could have. This is my life and I'm not cheering anymore!"

My dad shifted in his chair, obviously uncomfortable with the scene, but unwilling to interfere.

Julie slammed her fist on the table. "Gianna Hilary Thorpe! You will *not* quit cheerleading and that's final!"

"If you don't let me, then I'll go live with dad!" Gianna shouted, storming out of the dining room.

I swallowed down the last bite of rice and gathered my dishes to rinse them off in the kitchen sink. As I stepped through the doorway, I heard Gianna's Jeep screeching out of the driveway.

That went well.

*****

The remainder of the week flew by. Gianna and her mom weren't speaking to each other except to bicker. Every day Gianna and I sat with who I liked to call *the misfits* at lunch. Josh stayed away from Gianna, probably because I kept close to her.

Desiree, the girl I had my upcoming date with, visited our lunch table on Friday and plopped herself on my lap. "Hello there," I flirted.

She flipped her straight blonde hair over her shoulder. "Where are you taking me tonight, Caleb?"

Flicking a look at Gianna sitting across from me, I leaned in to whisper something dirty in Desiree's ear. Gianna's eyes narrowed in either jealousy or disgust when Desiree giggled. "You're so naughty, Caleb."

By her response, I could tell Desiree was naughty, too. Unrepentantly, I grinned. "You'll find out."

Glancing around, I noticed we had the attention of the rest of the table. Gianna rolled her eyes and turned to say something to Kara. Once my target audience was no longer rapt, I had the urge to move Desiree off my lap. The perfume she wore was fruity and she'd pumped one spray too many.

I nixed the idea of sending her on her way when Seth came over to finalize plans with Gianna about their date. When he stroked her cheek, I had a new urge to snap his finger. Gianna moved her backpack. "Sit down, Seth."

"Thanks, babe."

Babe? They hadn't even had a first date yet.

I checked Seth out while he gazed at Gianna. His mom obviously dressed him and his hair had too much product in it. I was definitely better-looking. Cooler, too, but that was a given. Was it just me, or did his voice squeak a little? No contest, I'd be able to take him in a fight.

A hand creeping up my thigh turned my thoughts back to Desiree. Her hair wasn't very healthy-looking; it didn't have the shine Gianna's did either. Her nose wasn't cute like Gianna's was. I didn't have the urge to kiss her. She wore a lot of dark eye makeup and dressed to school like she was going clubbing. Girls shouldn't try so hard and I liked it when they were more casual. There was a time for a miniskirt and there was a time for jeans.

"Caleb!"

My head snapped Gianna's way. "Yeah, what?"

"You've met Seth, right?"

The guy hadn't done anything to piss me off yet, so I offered my hand. "Sort of. You're friends with Josh, right?"

Seth shook my hand. I thought his grip was weak. "We're on the football team together." I hoped he gripped a football better than that.

"Well, he's on my shit list," I informed Josh's teammate.

Seth shifted uncomfortably on his seat and changed the subject. "So, you're Caleb, Gianna's brother."

"*Step*brother," I corrected. "We're not really related."

"Oh," was his cautious response. I could so take him in a fight.

"Anyways," Gianna interrupted, "I was just telling Seth we'll be doubling on Friday after the game."

A smile popped on my face when I spied Seth's disappointment at the prospect. Fucker had obviously looked forward to getting one-on-one time with Gianna.

I knew Desiree didn't care about the double date when she whispered in my ear that we'd have to get some alone time afterwards. I smiled a different type of smile then. The unwanted thought of whether or not Seth was thinking the same thing about Gianna entered my head. This whole situation with Gianna was starting to aggravate the hell out of me. I mean, how was I supposed to enjoy getting laid when I'd have to worry about Seth trying to get in her pants?

GIANNA

Desiree was such a slut! If she touched Caleb one more time, I was going to pull her away from him by her stringy hair. Dammit, she just touched him again. I needed to calm down. I'd have to get used to seeing girls touch him. Caleb was a manwhore and would likely be both that and my stepbrother for years to come. I was so going away for college. My dad would welcome me with open arms in Houston.

I sat miserably at the football game Friday night with Caleb and Desiree. After the game, we were meeting Seth in the parking lot and going out to eat. Until then, I'd have to sit here in the bleachers, trying to ignore Desiree grope Caleb like a bitch in heat. Her skirt was so short I was sure anyone sitting down below could turn around and see her panties, if she were even wearing any.

As much as I wanted to say something snide to Caleb, I couldn't because I was supposed to be his protégé. The more convincing move would be to high-five him. Caleb pulled out his phone and started texting someone. My phone beeped a couple seconds later. It was from the man himself. What was he up to?

Caleb: *Why do you keep dogging us? Jealous?*

I immediately answered his taunt.

Gianna: *Just watching the master work. Taking notes for Seth later. Can't wait to put my hands all over him!*

His clenched jaw gave me immense satisfaction.

Caleb: *That'd make you a slut like Desiree, not a player like me.*

Gianna: *I'm confused, aren't you a slut too? What you're saying is I should be the one with Seth's hands all over me?*

Caleb didn't text back again. He just rolled his eyes as if I were an idiot and put his phone back in his pocket.

CALEB

How was I to convince Gianna to remain a virgin and not be a player like me without sounding like a hypocrite? If Seth laid one sausage-fingered hand on her, I was going to break it. If I saw her put one hand on him, it'd be my own hand landing hard on her cute ass. Actually, the idea of spanking Gianna turned me on so it'd be no hardship.

After the game, we met Seth in the parking lot and decided to take separate vehicles to the restaurant. Desiree rode with me and Gianna went with Seth in his car. Desiree was starting to get on my nerves, but I still planned on screwing her tonight. I figured the whole problem with Gianna stemmed from me going too long without sex. Obsessing and lusting after her was a result of not getting laid in awhile.

Our booth was large at the restaurant. It was already past nine o'clock, so the place wasn't full. Desiree slid up close next to me and Gianna eyed the lack of space between us. Desiree's hand found its favorite spot on my leg under the table. If we didn't have company, I'd be checking out what was beneath her skirt.

Seth was pathetic in his admiration of Gianna. She wasn't exactly discouraging him, responding politely and smiling when he sucked up to her like a little bitch. The whole scene was pissing me off. I kicked my leg out under the table.

"Ow!" Gianna cried. Crap, I meant to kick Seth, the little bitch.

"Sorry, leg spasm," I lamely apologized.

"Are you alright, Gianna?" Seth asked in exaggerated concern. I wondered if they'd believe my leg had another spasm.

She gave him a sweet smile that he didn't deserve. "I'm fine. Thanks, Seth."

Obviously something had to be done about Seth. Any good stepbrother would do the same. "So, Seth, how good of friends are you with Josh?"

Seth appeared both wary and uncomfortable, as he should. "We hang out sometimes."

"Are you a date rapist like him?" I blurted out, earning a gasp from Desiree.

"Caleb!" Gianna scolded through her embarrassment.

I gave them the innocent look that stopped working with my mom years ago. "What? I just want to know if I'm going to have to pull him off you and beat his ass like I did Josh."

Gianna's blush darkened, but I was guessing it was also from anger. Seth turned to her in shock, taking hold of her hand. "Babe, did that really happen? Is that why you broke up with him?"

Gianna glared at me as I took a sip of soda out of my straw. "Yes, last Friday."

"I'm sorry, Gianna, that's horrible. I'd never try anything like that." His earnest expression seemed sincere, but I wasn't ready to give him the benefit of the doubt. To be safe, she shouldn't either. In fact, she would be better off not dating at all for awhile.

Gianna, unfortunately, wasn't of the same thought. She gave him the sweet smile *again*. The smile that should be reserved for a guy more worthy. "I know, Seth, you're a good guy." *Agree to disagree.*

In my opinion, Seth was coming out too good in this

conversation. A guy shouldn't earn brownie points for simply stating he wouldn't force himself on a girl. Desiree rubbed higher up on my thigh. Instead of being able to enjoy it, thinking about what I'd be up to later tonight, I had to worry about what the couple across from us would be up to later that night.

GIANNA

Caleb was such a jerk to blab to these two about what happened with Josh. What the hell did he do that for? At least Seth was a gentleman. Caleb should be taking pointers from Seth on how not to be an ass. Why was I even attracted to Caleb? He didn't want me because I was a virgin. He didn't feel guilty about loving and leaving girls if another guy had been there first. Like it was okay to use girls if they'd already slept with someone else.

Seth was the type of guy worth my time. He was handsome and sweet. He hadn't given any indication he was expecting me to have sex with him tonight. And if I told him I was a virgin, I was sure his response would be a lot nicer than Caleb's had been. Not that I would've slept with Caleb anyways. Not that I was planning on sleeping with Seth.

From the way Desiree was acting she definitely planned on spreading her legs for Caleb tonight. Being a hotshot player, he wouldn't pass up the offer. The thought of it was driving me crazy. Stupid sexy player, the way he kissed me all the time and made me want him. Stupid slut Desiree, being the kind of girl he wanted.

The whole point of the double date was to ruin Caleb's date with Desiree. "So, Caleb, why'd you and Hannah break up?" I asked out of nowhere.

Caleb threw me a suspicious look. "Hannah and I didn't break up because we were never technically together."

"Oh yeah, that's right. You don't do relationships. What was it you said again? That the word *girlfriend* is a bad word."

Desiree's head jerked at my words. "Did you really say that?"

Caleb glared at me before answering her. "What does it matter, I'm here with you now, aren't I?" His logic sucked, but Desiree must've been some sort of idiot because she smiled as if satisfied with his answer.

I spoke to Desiree, turning her attention away from Caleb's neck. "Yeah, maybe Caleb would be willing to have a girlfriend. He told Hannah he'd let her be his girlfriend as long as she was okay with sharing him with other girls."

Desiree put her arms around his neck in a possessive way. "Probably because he didn't like Hannah. But he likes me." The face Caleb made said otherwise, but with her head on his shoulder she missed it. Caleb's silence told me he didn't plan on enlightening her and ruining his chance to get laid.

Frustrated, I scooted out of the booth. "I'm going to the restroom."

Desiree popped up immediately. "I'll go with you."

Washing my hands at the sink, I glanced at Desiree in the mirror as she came out of the stall. "So, Gianna, have you fucked Caleb yet?"

"What?" I asked, surprised by the crude question.

Desiree shot me a dirty look in the mirror as she smoothed down her hair. "I know you want him, you're practically gagging for it. But he doesn't want you back does he? That's why you were out there trying to make him look bad in front of me. What's the matter? The perfect Gianna Thorpe finally met a guy who doesn't worship her?"

"You don't know what you're talking about," I denied while contemplating pulling her hair.

"I think I do. And you know what? After we ditch you two, Caleb told me we're going to be spending some alone time together, if you know what I mean. And if you don't, I'll spell it out for you. We're going to be fucking each other's brains out." Her smirk made me what to sock her. She spun on slutty stilettos toward the door, saying over her shoulder, "Have a good night with Seth." If I took both her kneecaps out, she'd have a hard time wearing shoes like those.

I studied my own reflection in the mirror. The jean shorts and cute tank top made more sense than her fancy getup. She was pretty, but her outfit screamed desperation. Unfortunately, my hurt feelings didn't care about how pathetic Desiree acted. I stood there for a minute gripping the sink, trying to hold back the stupid tears. *That bastard.* I wasn't good enough for him, but that slut Desiree was? I needed to get out of there. I left the bathroom in a rush and strode back to our booth. I didn't even bother sitting down.

"Seth, do you think we could go now?"

Despite his confusion, he readily agreed, "Sure, babe."

We'd only ordered drinks so far, so Seth dropped some money on the table and, without even looking at Caleb, I walked out of the restaurant holding Seth's hand. I forgot about trying to ruin Caleb's good time. He could do whatever and whoever the hell he wanted for all I cared. Hopefully he'd catch something from the nasty bitch.

CHAPTER FIFTEEN

"Beauty and folly are old companions."
-Benjamin Franklin

CALEB

I slapped my alarm off when it woke me up at eight o'clock Saturday morning. What the fuck? Oh yeah, Gianna, Saturday. I dragged my ass to the shower and dressed quickly. Catching up with her as she was going downstairs, I ignored her unhappy frown. What was her problem?

"Hey, Gianna, I'm taking you downtown today."

She turned to face me where I stood on the steps. "Like hell you are!"

Julie walked in on cue from the kitchen. "Gianna, watch your language. I think it's a wonderful idea for Caleb to drive you. I get worried, you going down there by yourself."

Gianna dropped her bag on the floor and asked her mom, "So now you're talking to me again?"

Julie hugged Gianna, patting her on the back. "I just think you're going through some sort of teenage rebellion thing. You'll regret quitting and go back to it in no time."

Gianna's only reply was to grunt. "Come on, punk, I don't want you to make me late."

So it was back to punk again, was it? As we got into my car, I checked out the large duffel bag she threw into the backseat. Did she have the dress and lingerie in there? Should I chuck it out the window while on the freeway?

As I started the car, Gianna switched it to a Top 40 station, turning it up full blast. Reaching out, I turned it back down. "What's the matter, princess? Did you get your period this morning?"

"Nothing's the matter. How was the rest of your date?" she asked then turned her head to stare out the window.

"Fantastic," I enunciated slowly. "How was the rest of yours? Did that loser kiss you goodnight, or was he too much of a gentleman to kiss on the first date?"

"How was the slut? Did you knock her up?" she retorted,

sounding peeved.

I didn't see Gianna after leaving the restaurant last night. Desiree and I stayed to eat and Gianna didn't respond to my texts later on. When I got home, Gianna was already in bed. "Why'd you rush out of the restaurant?"

"I couldn't wait for dessert." Leaning one elbow against the door, her smug face and words insinuated that more than a kiss goodnight happened.

I gripped the steering wheel tightly and turned the music back up. A popular boy band sang about a girl being beautiful but I didn't care. Thinking about Gianna making out with that loser made me wish I'd drug her out of the restaurant myself last night. Kissing better be all they'd gotten up to.

We neared downtown and I turned down the music to ask Gianna which exit to take. She continued giving me directions all the way to the ballet studio. When I found a parking spot a couple buildings down from the studio, she jumped out without even a thank you.

I stepped out of the car and yelled after her, "What time do you get done?"

She didn't turn around, calling out, "Noon!"

"I'll be here to pick you up!"

"Whatever!" she shouted back and disappeared into the building. *Ungrateful brat*. And here I was taking time out of my Saturday to chauffeur her, time I could be happily asleep.

"Hey, Caleb!" I turned around to see Cece running down the street from a bus stop.

"What's up, Tiny Dancer?"

She giggled at the nickname. "Just going to class. Hey, Gianna told me what you guys did to Josh's truck. Freaking hilarious. He really deserved it. So, how'd the double date go last night?"

"Alright. Do you think Gianna likes that Seth guy?"

"Well, I haven't met him, but she texted me last night saying he's really nice. But, I don't think she has any real romantic feelings towards him. I think she likes someone else, but she won't tell me who it is," she said in a frustrated tone.

Did she mean Jared? Is that why she wouldn't tell Cece? I hated that prick.

"I don't know who it could be," I lied.

"Well, we'll find out eventually. The guy would have to be an idiot not to want to go out with her. She's a sweetheart. See you later, Caleb."

Jared *was* an idiot, but I knew for a fact he wanted Gianna. As Cece too was about to disappear through the large wooden doors, I called out, "I'll be here at noon to pick up Gianna if you need a ride!"

Cece spun around, holding the door open. "Don't you mean 11:30? That's when we get done."

"Yeah, that's what I meant," I corrected. Satisfied, she simply nodded and went in.

So, Gianna told me the wrong time to try to ditch me? *Nice try, princess.* That gave me two hours to kill, so I drove over to my mom's apartment to see her. Since she was out of town last weekend I hadn't seen her in forever.

When I walked in the door, my mom was making coffee in the kitchen. "Hey, mom."

"Hi, sweetie. What are you doing here so early?" Still in her robe, her black hair pulled into a messy bun, she came over to give me a hug.

"It's already 9:45, mom. It's not that early." The coffee smelled good and I planned on chugging at least two cups.

"It's early for you. You never wake up before noon on Saturdays."

Feeling weird, I told her, "I gave my stepsister a ride to ballet class."

"That's right, you have a stepsister around your age. What's her name again?"

"Gianna," I said nonchalantly. Why did I feel strange talking to my mom about her?

"So, how's everything going, living with your dad? Is his wife nice?" she asked, aiming for the same casual tone. I gave my mom a knowing look because she'd taken my dad remarrying pretty hard three years ago. My mom noticed my concern. "It's okay, Caleb. I'm over it."

"She's alright. She's the exact opposite of you and the Martha Stewart type. She has a little boy also. He's pretty cool and especially entertaining when he's misbehaving."

"Have you been staying out of trouble yourself?" She has a concerned look on her face, as if bracing herself for disappointing news.

I thought about the tiny bit of trouble Gianna and I had caused together. It didn't count because we didn't get caught. "Yes, mom, I've been a good boy. I haven't even had detention yet. It's so boring in the suburbs. I don't know how I'd even find any trouble to get into."

Letting out a relieved sigh, she beamed at me. "I'm proud of you, sweetie. Maybe living with your father was just what you needed."

She patted me on the cheek like she always did when I pleased her. I'm not sure I agreed with her about living with my dad. Since meeting Gianna two weeks ago, it seemed like everything had gone to hell. I didn't feel like myself anymore.

My mom wasn't in the mood to cook, big surprise, so we went to breakfast at the diner. Avoiding any conversation about Gianna, I told her about my new school and classes. We talked more about Julie and my dad. My mom really did seem okay now about it. I almost asked if she was dating anyone, but chickened out because it would be too weird to talk about.

I was back at the dance studio on time to pick up Gianna. When she stepped out of the building with Cece, I stood out front, leaning against my car. Holding back laughter at her scowl, I opened the door to the passenger side.

She approached me with Cece by her side. "Caleb, I usually go to Cece's house right after class and the crew comes by to practice."

"No problem, I'll drive you guys there."

Before Gianna could argue, Cece was climbing into the back seat. "Thanks, Caleb!"

GIANNA

I told Caleb the wrong time on purpose so I could get rid of him. Unfortunately, he showed up thirty minutes early to pick me up and now he was giving me and Cece a ride to her house. I didn't want to be around him. I was still so pissed about him sleeping with Desiree last night.

Okay, so maybe I was more than just pissed. As much as I didn't want it to, it hurt. I cried myself to sleep last night over stupid Caleb! It was dumb to be upset about it. He was just being himself, doing what he normally did, easy girls. It wasn't as if any girl, including myself, would ever be special to him. It took a special girl to tame a bad boy and he hadn't met her yet.

I'd stood there like an idiot in the bathroom last night while Desiree got her digs in. Since then I'd come up with a ton of comebacks I should've said to her. Now it was too late. What a whore she was. Ugh, I didn't want to think of what they did last night. I'd start crying then Caleb and Cece would think I'd lost it.

Pulling up in front of Cece and Jared's house, I was about to say goodbye and good riddance to Caleb, but he turned off the engine and got out too. "What are you doing, Caleb?"

"I want to watch the crew practice. That's okay isn't it, Cece?" he asked, smart enough to look to her for backup.

"Sure, that'd be fun. Friends or the guys' girlfriends sometimes come by Saturday afternoons to watch." Cece and her super-friendly attitude would be the death of me. What could I say? *No, I don't want Caleb to hang out with us because I'm unreasonably hurt over him screwing Desiree last night.*

Key word: unreasonable. I had no right to be hurt and Caleb was nothing more to me than a sometimes-friend, sometimes-enemy and sometimes-confidant. Oh, and I couldn't forget the stepbrother thing.

Inside the house Jared sat on the couch. The memory of the kiss we'd shared last Saturday popped into my head and I didn't know if it was going to be awkward between us.

It wasn't. Jared acted completely normal. "Hey, Gigi, are you ready for tonight?"

I let out a relieved breath before answering. "Of course, we're going to kick ass."

Cece and Caleb walked into the house behind me. Caleb must've heard our conversation because he said, "So, you guys have some sort of battle? Like a break dancing dance-off?"

Jared rolled his eyes, but sounded friendly when he explained,

"Something like that and don't call it break dancing. That's what the media calls it. We either call it breaking, street dance, popping or locking, depending on the style. You can also call it b-boying."

"Thanks for the lesson," Caleb joked irreverently. "So, where's this happening tonight?"

I wanted to blurt out not to tell him, but didn't want to sound like a spaz.

"At a warehouse not far from downtown," Cece blabbed. "It's going to be awesome. There will be other crews there competing."

"Who decides who wins?" Caleb asked, appearing more interested.

"There are judges. This is an organized competition, so it's all pretty fair." Jared got up off the couch, brushing by me on his way to the kitchen. "Anyone want something to drink?"

"Water, please," Caleb answered, sitting on the couch himself.

Wanting to get away from Caleb, I told Cece, "Let's go get changed. The guys will be over soon."

I should've seen it coming. Cece pounced on me as soon as her door shut. "So, Gianna, Jared told me about the kiss you guys shared last weekend."

"What about it?" I played dumb.

"Just about how great it was. You know, he's liked you for a long time, but you've always had a boyfriend. What do you think of him?" Shouldn't she shun any conversation about her brother's love life?

I liked Jared, but the attraction I had towards Caleb was much stronger, which didn't bode well for a relationship between me and Jared. Did I even like Caleb? I didn't know. When he wasn't being a player, he was great to be around. He seemed to genuinely care about me, in a stepsister sort of way. Of course, he did kiss me all the time, but maybe it was just what came naturally to him. He probably kissed any cute girl he was around long enough.

"I like Jared, I guess. I don't know if we should date, though. I don't want to lose him as a friend."

"But if you're really into someone, you have to take a chance," Cece practically pleaded.

Maybe she was right. Maybe I should give Jared a chance and it'd help me forget about any attraction I had for Caleb. I opened my bag and peeked at the dress and lingerie I'd bought for the trick I was playing on Caleb. Maybe I *should* give my virginity to Jared. He was one of my best friends and there was some chemistry between us. Either way, tonight after the battle, I'd put this dress on just to teach Caleb a lesson. Let him think I'd had sex with Jared.

The guys show up for practice psyched for the battle tonight. We'd won a few in the past and had mastered some new moves since the last one. Cece's parents let us practice in their garage as long as it wasn't too early in the morning or too late at night. Caleb sat on a couch against the wall with a couple of the guys' current girlfriends.

We practiced for the next few hours and the guys all went home to eat and change before the battle tonight. Cece, Jared, Caleb and I ate at Cece and Jared's parents' Mexican restaurant, Las Delicias.

Their parents' came out from the office and kitchen to take our orders themselves and baby Cece. She was so spoiled, especially by her dad. Being little and cute had their benefits. They let Cece and Jared know they wouldn't be home till around two in the morning, after they'd closed, cleaned up and prepped for the Sunday morning breakfast rush.

Their parents were pretty cool about everything. They knew Cece and Jared were good kids who got good grades, so they were okay with the crew using the garage and coming over Saturday nights.

I tried to ignore Caleb at the restaurant, but it was impossible with him sitting right next to me. Jared had made a move to sit next to me when we got to our table, but Caleb had smoothly slid in first.

After eating, we returned to their house to change. Tonight the crew was wearing black track pants, white tank tops, white sneakers and different colored neon hoodies. Cece and I both decided to wear hot pink hoodies and did our hair and makeup crazy. I scolded myself to forget about Caleb for now and focus on the battle ahead.

The four of us rode in Jared's car to the warehouse to meet the rest of the crew. I still couldn't get over the fact that Caleb had known Taye for years. With him being best friends with Taye's cousin, Dante, I wondered if we would have eventually met even if our parents hadn't married.

CALEB

I'd stuck close to Gianna all day. However, I could tell she was pissed at me about something and didn't want me around. I wasn't sure what her problem was, not that I'd ask her. Girls were irrational. I figured, if I didn't let her out of my sight, how was she going to go through with her moronic plan to sleep with Jared?

The crowd at the warehouse was insane. The amount of hot chicks in skimpy clothing made me realize I should've been attending these battles sooner. Did Dante know about this? Taye was evil for not telling us about the massive amount of hot chicks that attended these events.

I could see where the judges were, because they had a table set up. From all the coordinated clothing, I counted five crews besides Gianna's. Three crews performed before theirs and two would go after. When Gianna's crew danced, they were awesome. Gianna and Cece left most of the more athletic breaking to the guys, but they did plenty of their own moves.

After all the crews had their turn, the judges decided it came down to Gianna's crew and another crew. Each crew did a routine thing together then some of the individual members stole the spotlight to do their own routines.

Gianna looked so hot when she and Cece popped to a remix of Salt-N-Pepa's "Push It." Cece was so damn little it was hard not to find her adorable. Her serious face while she danced made me laugh. In her head, she was a little badass in that moment.

The judges finally decided to call it, naming the other crew the winners. Maybe I was biased, but I thought DCK were the better dancers.

When we left, Gianna didn't appear disappointed at all. She actually seemed really happy.

Starting my car, I had to wait for another car to clear out of my way before I could pull out. "Are you guys bummed out about losing?"

Cece leaned forward from the backseat. "No, we know we can't always win. As long as we do sometimes, we're satisfied. Plus it's just fun to compete."

"So, did you have fun Caleb?" Jared sat next to me up front since Gianna had turned down the spot.

"Yep, you guys were awesome. Plus, I got like three chicks numbers," I bragged. With the radio off, I could hear Gianna mumble something under her breath from the backseat.

Some of the crew and their girls beat us to Cece and Jared's house. I would've invited one of the girls I met tonight, but I didn't want to be distracted from keeping an eye on Gianna and Jared.

The party was small, less than thirty people total. Gianna and Cece had been shut in the room for quite a while. Anxiety was clawing at me as I sat on the couch talking to Taye. I tried to pay attention to what he was telling me about his college plans for the following fall, but I was too agitated about Gianna's own plans for tonight to listen.

When the girls finally came out of the room, changed from their earlier outfits, Cece wore a pink dress with a flared skirt and Gianna had changed into that damn black dress she'd bought earlier this week. Gianna spotted me staring at her and winked impishly. It couldn't help visualizing what she was most likely wearing beneath the dress. It turned me on simply imagining it.

She wasn't really going through with this, was she? No, she definitely wasn't. That was why I was here, watching her every move. Jared wouldn't get the chance to touch her. As if to mock my determination, Jared came up to her and casually put his arm around her shoulders. He probably thought he had a shot because they kissed last Saturday. Well, I'd kissed her several times since then.

Leaning down, Jared whispered into her ear and Gianna nodded. Coming to some sort of agreement, they walked out of the room together and back down the hallway where she'd just been with Cece. But it wasn't Cece's bedroom they went into. Oh hell no.

GIANNA

Way less confident than I hoped, I'd come out of Cece's room wearing my slutty black dress. I'd feel better about the whole Caleb situation once I'd gotten a little payback. Coming into the living room, I'd rejoiced at the dark look in Caleb's eyes. Just to annoy him, I winked. *Are you worried, master player?* Caleb's broody expression turned broodier when Jared put his arm around me.

"You look hot," he whispered in my ear, making me shiver. "Can we go somewhere to talk about what happened last weekend?"

This was working out better than I'd planned. Nodding my head in agreement, I let him take my hand and lead me to his bedroom. Pretending Caleb didn't exist, I never glanced back. Jared sat on the foot of his bed, gently pulling me down next to him

"I'm just going to get straight to the point, Gigi. I've liked you for a long time and I want to be more than just your friend."

Caleb's face flickered through my mind for a brief second. "I like you too Jared, but I don't want to lose you as a friend."

"You won't. No matter what happens," he promised before kissing me softly.

I returned his kiss like before, feeling unsure and thinking my plan may end up blowing up in my face. Without breaking the kiss, Jared maneuvered us so we were lying back on the bed on our sides. Jared had skills and kissing him was nice, but not as explosive as kissing Caleb, which only fueled me to put more into kissing Jared. He placed his hand on my bare thigh and moved my leg up over his. The position made me feel vulnerable, but I trusted him. His warm lips moved across my neck.

The door slamming open, letting in the light from the hallway like a spotlight, came as shock. Jared yanked his head up and I peeked around to see Caleb standing there like he was about to kill someone.

CHAPTER SIXTEEN

"You can take no credit for beauty at sixteen.
But if you are beautiful at sixty,
it will be your soul's own doing.
-Marie Stopes

CALEB

I debated for about one minute whether or not to follow them down the hallway. Was Gianna planning on giving her virginity to Jared right now? Maybe so, and that was enough for me. I followed them to what I figured was Jared's room, the sly fucker.

Standing outside the closed door, my fists were clenched and I felt pumped like I was about to get in a fight. After all we'd shared over the past week, Gianna was going to fuck some other dude? It didn't matter how long she'd known Jared, it wasn't happening. Thinking I might have to break it down, I swung the unlocked door open with more force than I needed to.

On the bed making out, Gianna's leg was propped up over Jared's hip. He had one hand on her thigh, stroking the smooth skin. Jared's head whipped up and Gianna's eyes slowly met mine. Coming closer, I pushed Gianna's leg off of him.

He held up both hands in a placating gesture. "Hey, man, I know she's your sister, but I only have good intentions towards her."

"*Step*sister," I corrected him. "And I don't give my blessing."

Gripping her arm, I drew her off the bed and away from Jared. "What are you doing, man?" Jared asked. He made a move to get up, but I put a hand to his chest and pushed him back onto the bed.

"Family emergency, don't interfere." Ignoring his confusion, I guided Gianna out of the bedroom, shutting the door behind us. I took a detour into Cece's room to grab Gianna's bag of tricks. A few weird looks were thrown our way in the living room as I pulled her behind me and out of the house.

I'd parked my car in front of the house next door, so in seconds I was ushering her into the passenger seat. "Get in."

I was surprised by her immediate compliance. She didn't put up the slightest argument. Maybe she was going with the silent treatment as she stared out the window while I drove down the street. Passing a park, I pulled into the parking lot.

She was still turned away from me as I turned off the engine. "What the hell, Gianna? Are you turning into a fucking whore?" In the quiet of our isolation, my words sounded harsh.

She flipped around in her seat and even in the dark I could see the flash of anger in her eyes. "Me? I'm just following your example. Why do you care who I have sex with?"

"I don't!" I shouted back at her on a big fat lie.

"If you don't care, then why don't you drive me back so I can fuck Jared!" she yelled at me. It was like she wanted to rile me up.

"Like hell!"

Grabbing her shoulders, I brought her close, meaning to forcefully plant my lips on hers. Instead, I teased her mouth with mine, planning to persuade her to see things my way. It was driving me crazy that Jared had put his hands on her. She didn't know what he got up to during the week. He could be sleeping around with the nastiest of chicks. Yes, soon she'd be seeing things my way.

She jerked back before I'd given her the good stuff and smacked me across my left cheek. "No, you don't get to kiss me and then go around screwing every girl you meet!" She was breathing hard, but not worked up in the way I'd intended.

Where did that come from? "I don't want to fuck anyone else." Why did girls have to be so unreasonable?

"Yeah, at this very moment you don't. But you screwed Desiree last night and you'll be screwing a new chick as soon as you meet the lucky girl. How do you think that makes me feel after you kissed me?" A sheen of tears in her eyes glistened in the dark, which made me enormously uncomfortable.

"I don't see any other girls in my immediate future and I didn't fuck Desiree last night." Thank god I could honestly say that.

Gianna opened her mouth to say something then closed it, blowing out her breath. In a calmer voice, she finally said, "She told me in the bathroom that *you* told her after you ditched me and Seth, you were going to take her somewhere to have sex." Her suspicious tone made it clear she didn't believe me.

"Actually, that was all Desiree's idea," I gladly informed her.

She made a skeptical sound. "So you didn't plan on having sex with her?"

I was almost home free! If only she hadn't asked that question. "Well, I did plan on it."

She interrupted me before I could smooth things over. "See! Don't kiss me ever again. You can't play these games with me, Caleb."

Trying to soothe her temper, I brought up my hand to the back of her neck and started rubbing circles. "Let me finish, princess. I didn't have sex with her, and trust me she was more than willing, because I didn't *want* her." Her shoulders relaxed as my actions and words began to work. "I thought if I had sex with her, I'd stop obsessing and wanting to be with you, but it didn't work. I couldn't even get past kissing her. I took her home and, believe me, she wasn't happy."

Gianna's teeth gleamed in the dark as she smiled. "You're obsessed with me?" Just like that, her mood changed from pissed to pleased.

I let out a disgusted sigh. "I must be. I don't know what else to call it. I spend most of my time with you and when I'm not with you, I'm thinking about the next time I'll spend time with you." A chuckle escaped from my throat. "It's pathetic. I've never spent so much time with one girl and we're not even having sex."

She shook her head slowly and I moved my hand to allow the movement. "Caleb, only you would think liking a girl for more than just sex for one day is pathetic. It's too bad though, because even if we like each other, it does no good. I'm still a virgin and you still think *girlfriend* is a bad word." She paused then continued in a defeated tone, "Might as well take me back to Jared. Neither one is a problem for him."

Was she trying to make me angry again? "Fuck that! He's doesn't get to have sex with you or call you his girlfriend."

"Oh," she said in a way that warned me her temper was also rising. "So I'm supposed to remain a boyfriend-less virgin because you say so?"

"No," I responded slowly. I couldn't believe the words were about to come out of my mouth. It was like watching a car wreck in slow motion. "You're going to be . . . *my* girlfriend."

I could almost hear her mouth dropping open and her giggle sounded a little hysterical. "What if I don't *want* to be your girlfriend? I mean, why would I want a boyfriend who'd be flirting with other girls and probably cheating on me?"

"Gianna," I said her name sternly. "I would never cheat on you. You mean more to me than that." Deciding on persuasion again, I told her, "Look, if I'm willing to commit to you, I obviously don't plan on cheating on you. I couldn't even fuck another girl last night, when you weren't even my girlfriend yet. Do you think I'm going to be messing around with other girls now that you are?"

"You sound like you resent not wanting other girls."

More confident now I'd get what I wanted, I pulled her into my arms. "I don't resent it as long as I have you. Now say you'll be my girlfriend."

"I'll have to think about it. You haven't exactly been romantic about it." What did I know about romance?

"I guess I'll just have to convince you." When I kissed her again, I gave her the good stuff, starting out gently with a slow build to a hot climax.

Her efforts to pull away this time were weak because she didn't really mean it. Her lips were so sweet, her willing response even sweeter. Dragging her onto my lap, so she was straddling me, I fingered the hem of her dress.

"Caleb, what are you doing?" she mumbled against my mouth.

"Convincing you." Using the hem of her sexy dress, I quickly peeled it up and off her body, tossing it over my shoulder into the backseat.

"What the heck, Caleb?" she squeaked, trying to cover herself with her arms.

"Why aren't you wearing the babydoll you bought?" I pouted in disappointment. She wore a lacy black bra and matching panties, a suitable consolation prize.

She made an exasperated sound. "I wasn't going to actually have sex with Jared. I was just messing with you."

"Oh really? And why would you do that?" I asked, feeling absurdly happy as I wrapped my arms more tightly around her. With her wearing practically nothing, I had access to a lot more nakedness than if she were wearing the babydoll. Suitable consolation prize, indeed.

"Because you pissed me off, treating me like something was wrong with me because I was a virgin. Plus, I knew it'd make you jealous to think I was going to have sex with Jared. And it did," she finished smugly.

Running my hands over silky skin, I thought on her words. "I'll owe you for that one. I've been stressed out about it all week. I'd be expecting some payback for that, if I were you." For now, her hot body could start making it up to me.

Despite her words, she didn't try to stop my exploration. "I already think you're going to have sex with every willing girl you meet, so I guess we're even." Hitting a sensitive spot, I had her moaning and squirming in my lap.

I cupped her jaw to look her in the eyes. "Gianna, I only want to be with you. Now say you'll be my girlfriend."

Her nervous wiggling was torture. "Caleb, I'm not sure. I mean, I don't know if I could trust you. Plus, what will people think? Our parents are married. Even though we're not actually related, they'll think it's weird."

"Just give me a chance, Gianna," I pleaded softly. "I'll prove to you how much I care about you. Forget about what everyone else thinks. If you want, we can wait to tell them."

She still looked doubtful as she nodded her head. "Okay."

I never thought I'd beg a chick to be my girlfriend. It was always the other way around, girls thinking just because we'd had sex I'd commit to them, eager to claim me as their boyfriend.

With Gianna, it strangely felt good. Only because it was her that would call me boyfriend. Finally able to do what I liked without restraint, I got lost in her taste, touching her wherever I had access. My fun came to an end when headlights flashed into the parking lot from a car pulling in.

"Crap!" I searched for her dress in the backseat. Sliding it over her head, I regretfully helped her smooth it back over her body.

The other car didn't park anywhere near us, but we still lacked complete privacy. Reaching over to buckle her seatbelt, I felt a sense of possessiveness. She was my girlfriend now, belonging solely to me.

After we'd pulled out onto the street, Gianna asked, "What

about the problem of me being a virgin?"

I gave her my patented panty-melting look. "Trust me, it won't be a problem for long. And I'll be expecting to see you in that babydoll real soon."

In response, she rolled her eyes.

CHAPTER SEVENTEEN

"Even I don't wake up looking like Cindy Crawford."
-Cindy Crawford

GIANNA

Was I stupid enough to agree to be Caleb's girlfriend? I was kind of freaked out about the future. Dating a guy like him was like serving your heart up on a platter for him to devour.

One hand still on the wheel, he reached with his free one to hold my own. Brushing aside worries of an unknown future, I asked, "Where are we going?" It was pretty late and it'd be more than a little awkward going back to Jared's house.

"We're going to my mom's."

Not a better idea. "Won't she mind?"

"No, she's cool about most things as long as I'm not getting into trouble." He drove into the same parking garage from the last time we were here. Taking the keys out of the ignition, he said, "Wait there!" I sat in the car as ordered, watching in the side mirror as he came around to open my door for me. He smiled proudly as I stepped out of the car. "See, aren't I a good boyfriend already?"

In a condescending manner, I patted his cheek. "You still have a long way to go, master player."

He scowled at me and took my duffel from me after I grabbed it from the backseat. Throwing it over one shoulder and taking my hand, he locked the car door. "Come on. My mom is going to freak, me bringing a girl home. It's unheard of." His sneaky grin hinted at anticipation.

We walked the distance to the apartment building and waited for the elevator. Entering the place, all the lights were off with the glow of the city coming in through the blinds.

Halfway to Caleb's room, a bedroom door opened and a woman stepped out. "Caleb, sweetie, is that you?"

Sweetie?

"Yes, mom, it's me and Gianna."

His mom flipped a switch, turning on the hall light. She was a pretty older woman, in her late thirties with dark hair like Caleb.

"Oh hi, that's right, Gianna, the stepsister. It's nice to meet you." Her eyes glanced down at where Caleb was still holding my hand before coming back to rest on my blushing face.

"You too," I responded awkwardly. It felt weird and scandalous to be spending the night at a boyfriend's house. Would she tell Scott?

"Wow, Caleb didn't tell me how beautiful you are," she complimented. My face grew warmer and I wanted to elbow him for forcing me into this embarrassing situation.

"Thank you," I mumbled, not having anything better to say.

"She's also very tired, so we'll just be going to bed now," Caleb cut in, making me want to murder him! It sounded so bad when he said it aloud.

"Okay then, goodnight, sweetie. Goodnight, Gianna." As she closed her door I knew I should tell her goodnight, but I couldn't get it out. She must've thought I was the biggest slut.

"Oh my god, Caleb!" I whispered harshly. "Did you have to say it like that? I can't believe your mom is okay with this. My mom would totally freak if you stayed the night in my room!"

Inside his room, he shut the door and locked it. "Who says I'm staying in here with you? Maybe I intend to sleep on the couch to protect my virtue."

"Oh please, I'm the virgin here. You're practically a gigolo. You lost your innocence a long time ago." I wonder how long ago that was.

He faked hurt. "You make me feel so dirty and used."

"You said it, not me." Mentally worn out from everything that'd happened I laid down on the bed thinking about the last time I was on here. Did Caleb really have a tattoo somewhere under those pants or had he been messing with me?

"I'm not the one in the hooker dress," he teased.

"It was for a good cause." What the heck did his mom think when she saw my racy dress? Probably that I was a slut! Mortified, I kicked off my heels and grabbed my bag. "I'm going to change in the bathroom. I think you and your mom have seen enough of this dress tonight."

"I really didn't mean it about the dress. Come back . . . please," he trailed off dramatically as I quietly padded down the hallway to the privacy of the bathroom.

I changed into very unsexy sweats and a tank top. For modesty's sake, I covered up more skin with my hoodie. When I returned to Caleb's room, he was already down to boxer briefs. Holy crap, a girl could get knocked up just looking at him. Switching off the lamp to give my hormones a rest, I got under the blanket, sensing him doing the same. He wrapped his arms around me and my head naturally rested on his chest.

"Is this where you try to get into my sweatpants?" I asked him, feeling nervous about sharing a bed with a guy.

He laughed softly. "There would be no trying involved. If I wanted in them, they'd already be on the floor."

"Oh, so now you don't want to have sex with me?"

He grabbed my hand and I was startled as he placed it on his crotch. "Believe me, I do. Just not with my mom in the other room."

I yanked my hand away. "You are such a pervert!"

"Thank you," he said. "Now, I'm going to sleep. I know I'm irresistible, but please try not to molest me again, Gianna."

Determined to block out the memory of the feel of him in my hand, I shifted position to lie on my side, facing away from him and his massive ego. "Whatever."

He pulled me into his arms again, spooning me from behind and laughing into my hair. "I'm sorry, princess."

"No you're not. Goodnight, Caleb," I said grumpily.

Not denying it, he whispered sweetly, "Goodnight, beautiful girlfriend."

That was the problem with players. They always had the charm to go with the good looks.

CALEB

Gianna's breathing slowed down as she fell asleep. It was so insane that I now had a girlfriend. Doomed from the start, she had me at *get off me, asshole*! Well, that and her hot body. If I had to have a girlfriend, only someone as awesome as Gianna would do. She wasn't only beautiful, but also cool and fun to be around. Even if she was mad at me half the time. Not that I didn't sometimes deserve it. Not that I'd ever admit to deserving it.

I'd never cuddled with a girl before without sex being involved and usually not even then. I liked holding Gianna in my arms. I liked knowing she was mine. Josh, Seth and Jared were suckers! I'd never felt protective of a female before, besides my mom, and this was the first female I'd been possessive of. This thing between us could go somewhere serious but I could also manage to keep it to having fun. We were too young to worry about forever.

The player in me was screaming for his freedom, but I couldn't stand to let her belong to anyone else. The only way to prevent that was for her to belong to me. The idea of not messing around with other girls was surprisingly acceptable. It helped to have the most beautiful girl in the world as my new playtime partner.

How would my dad and Julie take this? Probably not very well. My mom noticed us holding hands, but she didn't say anything about it. She was cool like that, but Gianna wasn't her daughter.

I was nervous about having sex with her. She wouldn't be my first virgin but I stayed away from virgins for a reason. Girls put a lot of importance on their first time and I didn't want the pressure of not fucking it up. I ached to have sex with her now, but I had to wait until she was ready. It also needed to be special for her.

Kissing her head through a silky cloud of hair, I let go of my worries and joined her in sleep.

*****

When I woke up at eleven the next morning, Gianna was still asleep. I quietly got out of bed and went to the kitchen. My mom was in there at the stove. "Mom, why are you making breakfast?"

"For you and Gianna. Which reminds me, what exactly is going on between you two? I saw you holding hands last night and she slept in your room. I don't think stepbrothers and stepsisters normally do that."

"No, but boyfriends and girlfriends do."

"What? *You* have girlfriend?" My own mother was laughing at me! "Don't get me wrong, she's gorgeous, Caleb, but do you think it's the best idea to break your own stepsister's heart?"

"Why would you say that? Who says I'm going to hurt her?"

She looks at me seriously. "Caleb, you're my son and I love you, but I know how you are with girls. I'm just trying to be realistic here. Besides, how do you think her mother is going to feel about this?"

"Her mom is sort of intense when it comes to Gianna. She had her in high school and feels she missed out, so she wants everything in Gianna's life to be perfect, including Gianna herself. But I don't care what her mom says about it," I said defensively.

My mom twirled a spatula in the air. "Like it or not, Gianna is only sixteen years old. Her mom still has a lot of say in what she does or doesn't do."

"We aren't going to tell her or dad yet. When we do, they'll just have to get used to it."

"Well, I'm here for you two if you need me," she offered doubtfully.

"We appreciate that, Mrs. Morrison." a voice said from behind me. I turned around to see Gianna standing in the doorway. How long had she been there? Hopefully she didn't hear the part where my own mother called me a player.

"Morning, Gianna. Come sit down, I made you guys breakfast."

"Good morning." Gianna yawned and took a seat at the table. Her hair was all messed up from sleep, but she looked cute like that.

"What are you two going to do today?"

"I don't know, mom, whatever Gianna wants to do." My mother raised her eyebrows at my comment. Jeez, why was she so surprised? Was I usually that selfish?

Gianna bit her lip. "Cece and some of the guys were going to check out 16th Street and see if there anyone was up for a cypher. I thought maybe we could go."

"What's a cypher?" my mom asked, handing us both plates full of omelet and fried potatoes.

Gianna looked from me to my mom. "It's when a bunch of breakers get together and freestyle."

"Gianna's a b-girl," I told my mom in between bites of omelet.

"Oh, that sounds like fun! You two be safe today."

I could tell she liked Gianna, despite any doubts she had about me or Julie. She probably hoped having a girlfriend would keep me out of trouble. Little did she know, Gianna was more of a partner in crime.

Since my mom was using her bathroom, Gianna and I took turns getting ready in mine. My mom hugged us both as we left, which brought a smile to Gianna's face. Getting off the elevator, Gianna called Cece to find out what their plans were.

Those of the crew not busy or working were already there. I assumed Jared would be there, but didn't ask. It was funny that I stole Gianna right out from under him, almost literally. By this point, the dumbass had either figured it out and was pissed, or he was dumb enough to buy the protective stepbrother act and was going to suck up to me to get my permission to date my stepsister. After last night, he'd be asking to date my *girlfriend*. That was a big fat negative.

I paid for parking near the 16th Street Mall and we walked several blocks before finding the group. The outdoor mall was packed, with the MallRide shuttle buses transporting people up and down 16th Street. A crowd of mall-goers were already gathered around the street dancers. I recognized a few breakers from the crew.

When we circled around to where Cece and Jared stood, he gave me a weird look and asked Gianna, "Can I talk to you for a minute?"

"No," I told him, feeling that was clear enough.

He both looked and sounded annoyed as he said, "Caleb, I know you're her stepbrother and all, so I don't blame you for trying to protect her, but I've been her friend a lot longer than you've known her."

"I don't care how long you've known my *girlfriend*," I corrected him with a triumphant smile.

Jared's face fell and he looked to Gianna. "Is this true? Are you two together?"

"Uh, yeah," she said guiltily, staring at the ground.

"What are you thinking, Gigi? You can't date a guy like him. I asked Taye about him and do you know what he told me?" Jared's appalled face was overly dramatic.

"No, and I don't want to know!" She yelled, finally looking

him in the eye.

"Fine, then I'll tell you this. I love you and I have for a long time. He doesn't love you and he never will. He'll get tired of you and throw you aside like he has to all the girls before you!" Jared's raised voice was drawing the attention of those around us. Poor Cece looked ready to cry.

And she said *I* wasn't romantic. Bitching a girl out while you declared your love for her was a fool's move. Gianna was stunned but I'd had enough of his crap. Taking Jared off guard, I pushed his chest, making him stumble backwards. "Fuck off, man! I don't care what you've heard. You don't even know me."

Jared didn't seem ready to back down. "I don't need to know you. All I need to know is she should be with me, but instead she's wasting her time with a loser like you. I've looked out for her the best I could for years and you just come along and decide to make her your next conquest."

"She means more than that to me," I argued through clenched teeth.

"Yeah, for how long?" Jared sneered. Obviously there was only one way to shut him up. I punched him in the face, drawing gasps from the girls. I heard Gianna call out my name, but he'd recovered quickly and punched me in the gut. From there it escalated and we went at it for a few minutes before some of the guys dragged us apart because some police officers are jogging down the street towards us.

We all got the hell out of there. Jared and I were both pretty roughed up, but I was pretty sure I'd won the fight.

Jackass.

Gianna and Cece were long gone.

CHAPTER EIGHTEEN

"Do not confuse beauty with beautiful. Beautiful is a human judgment. Beauty is All. The difference is everything."
-Matthew Fox

GIANNA

When Caleb and Jared started fighting, Cece and I hadn't stuck around to watch. *Stupid boys*. I still reeling from the things Jared had said. Cece was walking next to me down 16th Street and for once she was quiet.

"Cece?"

"Yeah, Gigi?" she asked, nervously looking at me from the corner of her eye.

"Did you know how Jared felt about me?"

"Um . . . kinda." She was playing with a curl in her hair now, pulling it straight.

I stopped at a bench and yanked her down to sit next to me when she just stood there. "Why didn't he tell me before?"

"He wanted to, but you were with Josh and for a long time and before that, he was just too nervous. He's my brother, so of course I want you to give him a chance." She took a deep breath, turning to me with a serious expression. "But, I'm also your best friend and I have to tell you to do whatever you feel is right." She visibly relaxed then blurted out, "I think you should choose Jared!"

Despite feeling crappy about the whole situation, I laughed. Cece *always* made me laugh. "What do you think about Caleb?"

"He seems nice enough and he's protective of you," she said carefully.

"No, I mean, do you agree with Jared? That Caleb will only hurt me?"

"Gigi, I honestly don't know him well enough, but I was there when Jared asked Taye about him and he does have a bad past when it comes to girls. *Lots* of girls," she explained with obvious pity. Did everyone have to keep emphasizing how many girls there were in Caleb's past?

"I know, but people can change and he's trying to prove it to me," I stubbornly defended.

Then she dropped the bomb. "What do you think your mom is going to say about you dating Scott's son?"

"She's not going to say anything because I'm not telling her." Cece was shocked, but she already knew the secrets I kept from my mom, so she shouldn't have been surprised.

My phone started playing "Good Girls Go Bad" by Cobra Starship. I rolled my eyes at the ringtone Caleb put on my phone for when he called. The stupid boys were done proving how tough they were and now they were wondering where the ladies had gone off to.

"Hello?"

"Where the hell are you?" Caleb demanded.

"Where the hell are *you*?" I mocked him.

"You're not funny, Gianna. Why'd you take off like that?"

"Because maybe I didn't want to see my boyfriend and best friend beat the shit out of each other."

"He started it." What was this, the third grade?

"Do you always get into a fight when you don't like what someone has to say?"

"Not always. Where are you, Gianna?"

"In front of the movie theater," I finally told him.

"Okay, I'll be there in a few minutes."

"Whatever." I hung up without waiting for him to answer.

"He's coming?" Cece asked.

"Yep, he'll be here in a couple minutes."

Cece laughed at my displeasure. "Act like that all you want, Gigi, you're totally in love with him."

"Am not!" I shouted and ignored her scoffing.

Caleb came strolling up, acting as if he'd done nothing wrong. Brushing his hair off his forehead, he asked Cece, "Hey tiny dancer, do you need a ride home?"

She leaned against the back of the bench, crossing her arms. "Are you sucking up to me because you tried to beat up my brother?"

Caleb got a smug look on his face. "There was no trying involved. I kicked his ass."

Scanning his disheveled appearance and the red mark on his cheek, I copied Cece's pose but added a smirk for effect. "From the looks of you, Jared must have held his own."

He took in my body language, shaking his head. "He looks much worse."

Cece stood up and I did the same. "No thanks about the ride. I'm going to go find my brother and some band-aids." She hugged me tight and glared at Caleb before waving goodbye.

Caleb and I stood there, gauging each other for a moment before I spun on my heel and started in the direction where his car was parked. Catching up with me, he wrapped his arms around my waist, stopping me in my tracks.

"Are you mad at me, princess?" he purred into my neck.

"Very," I informed him and pushed his hands off my waist before walking away. Unconcerned, he strolled alongside me in silence. If he started whistling I was going to kick him in the shins. We reached his car and I made sure to buckle my own damn seatbelt. My phone played a different song when it began ringing again, "I'm Real" by Jennifer Lopez and Ja Rule.

Nervously answering it, I managed to say in an even tone, "Hey, Jared."

Caleb made an irritated sound from next to me while pulling out of the parking lot.

"Gigi?" Jared asked hesitantly. I hoped this wasn't going to get awkward. What I needed was alone, non-Caleb time to think over Jared's declaration of love.

"What's up?"

"As much as I want you to choose me, I can tell it isn't going to happen right now. He's manipulated you into thinking he's a good guy. Just promise me I won't lose you as a friend."

"I promise, Jared." We had history so losing him would royally suck.

"Okay, Gigi, that's all I needed to hear. I'll talk to you later."

"Bye, Jared."

What the hell had happened to my life? Things weren't this complicated a few weeks ago. My best friend was in love with me and my stepbrother was now my boyfriend. It was like some freaky alternative universe.

While I was trying to get my head on straight, Caleb must've been fuming over Jared's phone call. "What the fuck, Gianna?"

At this point, I was in no mood to put up with any boy's bullshit. "What the fuck what, Caleb?" Maybe I should've just stayed single, like forever. Boys were pains in the asses. First Josh, then Caleb and now Jared.

Taking his attention off the road, he shot me an exasperated look. "What the fuck are you promising him, Gianna? And what the fuck is up with that ringtone?"

I shot him back a look like he was retarded. "Just that we'd stay friends no matter what happened and that song is mine and Jared's song."

"You two have a fucking song? I don't know if I like my girlfriend hanging out with a guy who wants to take her away from me."

"Too bad you don't get a choice. You knew how close Jared and I were before you asked me to be your girlfriend. He and Cece have been the most important people to me, besides my family, for a long time now."

"Way to make me feel special," he muttered peevishly.

"Caleb, should we be fighting like this already? I mean, our relationship is only a day old."

A worried expression flashed over his handsome features. "I'm sorry, Gianna. I think I just need to get used to this boyfriend thing. I'll try harder. I'm just not used to being jealous over a girl."

He was saying the right things and I didn't actually want to break up with him. Figuring a few bumps in the beginning of a relationship were normal, I brushed aside all thoughts of ending things with Caleb. I wasn't sure I had much of a choice anyways. I was drawn to him in a way that drugged my mind, preventing logic from winning out.

I rubbed the back of his head, running my fingers through his hair. "Oh, poor baby, getting jealous over a girl."

He did a mock pout. "I know. I'm going to need some cuddling to make me feel better." By cuddling he probably meant groping each other in our underwear.

He looked so cute, how could I deny him? "Later, hot boyfriend."

Caleb brought my hand up to his full lips and kissed it. "Gianna, I have to know how you feel about Jared. Do you have feelings for him?"

To be fair, I went over it in my head for a moment before answering. "I don't know. Before he kissed me last weekend, I'd never thought of him in that way. He's always been my rock, one of the few people who acted real with me. He tells me the truth, good or bad."

"How do you feel about him saying he loves you?" Jeez, I could practically hear Caleb grinding his teeth.

"I haven't had time to digest that yet. I'm trying not to think about it. I don't want things to change between me and him." I'd think about what Jared said later, when I was alone. Jared deserved that much.

Caleb didn't look completely satisfied with my answer, but nodded his head. I noticed he still kept my hand in his.

A change of subject would be best. "So we did go down to 16th Street, does that mean I've completed number six?"

"I'll consider it completed. I definitely don't feel like doing it over again." Good to know he wasn't eager to fight Jared again.

The Sunday afternoon traffic going north was bad due to a car wreck up ahead, so it ended up taking almost an hour to get home. Not that I was looking forward to being home. I didn't want to tell my mom and Scott about us, but we shouldn't have to hide it. Walking in the front door, we could see through a back window that Scott and Chance were in the backyard.

From the sounds coming from the kitchen, it was easy to guess where to find my mom. Caleb followed me into the kitchen where my mom was cooking. "Hey, mom!" I chirped like an idiot.

"Hi, honey. Caleb, dinner will be ready in a little bit. Why don't you wash up?" As she turned back to the stove, Caleb threw me a *what the hell* look. I was used to my mom's personality but to an outsider she probably came across as fifties housewife throwback.

My mom was still busy stirring something in a pot when I was suddenly pulled out into the hallway. Caleb pushed me up against the wall, kissing me like he was starved for it.

Half-afraid and half-excited, I whispered against his mouth, "Are you crazy?"

"Uh-huh," he responded, not stopping. Caught up in him, I

forgot about my mom on the other side of the wall. We continued making out until someone cleared their throat.

Turning our heads in unison, we saw Caleb's dad, Scott, standing there.

Less than a day and our secret was out.

CHAPTER NINETEEN

"All the freaky people make the beauty of the world."
-Michael Franti

CALEB

Shit, my dad caught me making out with his stepdaughter. In my opinion, we were doing nothing wrong, but I understood he and Julie might not see things the same way. Hell, they definitely wouldn't. From the look on my dad's face, I couldn't tell what he was thinking, besides what a shock it was to find us like this.

My dad's face turned from shock to seriousness once he'd composed himself. "Caleb, in the study. *Now*." Expecting immediate compliance, he turned around and marched into his study.

Staring down at her face as she nervously gazed back at me, I had one thought in my head, *fuck 'em*. Something new was happening here and if we couldn't stop is ourselves there was nothing anyone else could do.

I gave Gianna a reassuring smile then pulled away from her to follow my dad. Shutting the door with a click, I stood defiantly instead of taking a seat. Having no need to defend myself, I waited for him to break the silence.

My dad began with, "Gianna is a good girl."

"I know."

Maybe that wasn't the response he'd expected. He didn't say anything for a full minute. "How serious are you about her?"

How serious? She meant a heck of a lot more to me than all the girls in my past combined. "Very." I could see Gianna and I being together for quite a while.

He obviously didn't expect that answer either. He'd practically cringed at my response. "You have to end it."

"No."

My dad sighed. "Caleb, if it was up to me, I'd leave the two of you alone. But Gianna isn't my daughter. She's Julie's daughter and I know Julie wouldn't like the two of you dating."

I scoffed at that. "Too late, we already are."

"What am I supposed to do about this? You're my son and

she's my wife. I also care about Gianna and Chance and how they're affected."

"We aren't doing anything wrong."

"But if you hurt her. . . ." he trailed off.

"I won't."

"Does she plan on telling her mother?"

"Not yet," I told him. "We wanted to give ourselves time to adjust to the relationship ourselves."

My dad gripped the arms of his chair. His agitation made me feel bad. "Okay, I won't say anything to Julie yet, but this can't stay a secret forever. Her mom has a right to know. I have a feeling things may get bad when she does find out. We'll just deal with it when the time comes."

"Thanks, dad." My dad appeared surprised by my gratitude and a little pleased. We hadn't been close since he and my mom divorced so maybe sharing this secret would be a good thing.

I found Gianna in the living room and related the conversation I'd with my dad. She was relieved he'd stay quiet about it for now. They may be worried about Julie's reaction, but I hardly knew the woman and she wasn't my mother. For their sake, I'd let it be a secret for now, but not for long.

Later that night, when Julie and my dad were downstairs watching a new Disney movie with Chance, Gianna and I were in her room. I sat at her desk as she stood behind me, looking over my shoulder. Following her instructions, I'd drawn a sketch of the tattoo she wanted. She seemed kind of shy about it and I almost had to force the details from her. It was cute. She had me draw a boom box with wings.

"Where are you getting it?" I asked her.

"I'm not sure yet," she said, looking down at her clothed body. "Definitely somewhere my mom won't see it."

"All this hiding things from your mom is really getting on my nerves," I mumbled. "Maybe we should just lay it all out. She's a big girl and she has to find out eventually."

"You can't do that!"

I narrowed my eyes at her. Was this about more than me being her stepbrother? Would her mom think I wasn't good enough for her precious angel? We weren't really related! Julie would have to be delusional to protest for that reason.

"Fine," I said. "What about school? Are we going to hide it there also?"

"I'll let you decide. I don't care either way," she conceded.

"Well, that makes me feel good, you not caring either way." I turned back to the sketch, touching it up.

She wrapped her arms around my neck from behind and kissed me on the cheek. "I didn't mean it like that. I don't care because there's no one there that's important enough to me."

"What about the misfits?" I asked, mostly forgiving her.

"The what?"

"Our new friends."

"Oh yeah, we'll tell them, of course, but I could care less what anyone else thinks." When she nibbled on my ear she was completely forgiven.

"Now, about that cuddling we discussed earlier," I reminded her, making her giggle in my ear.

*****

As was our new habit, I drove Gianna to school the next morning. I'd decided she'd be coming to and from school with me from now on. Things would be unpleasant when I gave Desiree the brush off today and let Seth know to back the fuck off. Josh had better not try any shit either.

I chose a spot far out in the parking lot. Before Gianna got out of the car, I grabbed her waist to pull her onto my lap. I'd miss her lips and wanted to get my fix before the faculty's judging eyes killed the mood.

Breathless, she rested her head on my shoulder. "I'd be okay with skipping today."

"Me too, but I think we should get this over with. Give a big *screw you* to anyone who has a problem with it."

"You can give them a *screw you* attitude and I'll give them a *leave me the hell alone* attitude," she informed me.

"You do that, little badass. Come on, I'll walk you to first period"

Holding hands as we walked through the parking lot, we drew

stares and whispers right away. It was like being in a bad teen movie. Didn't they have classes to get to? We passed by Seth and Josh where they were leaning against the back of Josh's truck. Their dirty looks made my day. Perhaps Seth wasn't such a nice guy after all, at least not when it came to me. My smart-ass grin didn't help matters.

Gianna didn't seem fazed by it all. My girlfriend was so beautiful and brave. Walking past people, she acted as if we weren't the focus of their attention and conversations. But then, our classmates had gossiped about Gianna in the past.

We spotted Kara and the other misfits standing near the front doors. Kara greeted is with, "Hi," then took in where our hands were joined and shouted, "Oh my god! I knew it! Didn't I tell you guys?"

"How'd you know?" Gianna asked Kara while I wondered if they'd taken bets.

"Duh! By the way you two acted around each other," Kara explained, clearly enjoying being right.

"You don't think it's weird?" I asked her, not beating around the bush.

"Why would it be weird? It's not like you guys are blood-related."

"Well, I think it's sick!" a high-pitch voice sneered from behind us.

Desiree stood there, staring daggers at Gianna. I was about to give her a piece of my mind, but Gianna beat me to it. "Desiree, you're just mad because you threw yourself at Caleb and he threw you back."

The crowd forming around us laughed, mocking Desiree. "You bitch!" Desiree shrieked.

Gianna ignored her and turned to me. "Walk me to class, Caleb?" The sugar-sweet voice was a nice touch.

"Sure," I replied, pulling her close as we entered the building. Outside her class, teachers be damned, I went in for another kiss. Let everyone see, the sooner they got used to it, the better. "Bye, princess. See you next period."

"Bye," Gianna sighed, leaving me to go in and take her seat. I traveled to my first class with a big grin on my face.

After first period was over, I hoofed it to my second class which I had with Gianna. She still hadn't shown up yet when the final bell rang. Feeling that something wasn't right, I grabbed my backpack and didn't stop to let the teacher know where I was going. I stepped into the hallway calling her phone, but there was no answer. I didn't even know where to begin to look. Maybe it was a girl emergency? If so, wouldn't she at least text me to say she wasn't coming to class?

I first checked out the parking lot to see if she was by my car. No sign of her. Circling around the school, I was figuring out my next move when I heard from around the corner someone yelling.

"You're mine!"

I ran around the corner and saw Josh holding onto Gianna's upper arms as he shook her. Before I could reach them, he slammed her against the wall making her head bang hard against the brick.

"Hey!" I growled.

Josh turned his head to sneer at me. Releasing his hold on Gianna, she slumped to the ground. I rushed at Josh and slammed him against the wall. He punched me in my side, but I ignored it and grabbed his big head. I started banging his head against the brick until he was knocked out by the impact. As he fell to the ground, I kicked him in the stomach, putting all my strength behind it. He'd be waking up with a bitch of a headache and a gut ache to match.

I bent over where Gianna was on the ground. Enraged and wanting to go back and stomp on Josh's balls, I pushed it back so I could take care of my girl. Carefully, I picked her up and carried her to my car. She opened her eyes a crack as I buckled her in.

"I guess we're ditching after all," she mumbled and passed out again. Grabbing a sweatshirt from the back of my car, I bunched it up and used it as a pillow for her.

I didn't want to take her to the house. I was pissed at everyone in her life: her mom, Josh, the kids at school. Getting on the freeway south, I headed for downtown and my mom's apartment. At least there no one would bother us.

Gianna woke up before we were out of Broomfield, but she didn't have much to say. Knowing we both needed the quiet, I let her be. In the shade of the parking garage, I leaned my head against the steering wheel, trying to get control of my turbulent emotions.

Shaking off the need to go back and pull Josh out of whatever class he was in, I opened my door, going around to her side to help her out. She was a little dizzy on her feet, so we moved with my arm around her waist.

Once in the apartment, I stretched across the couch with my back to the armrest and her in front of me so her back leaned against my chest.

Hearing her finally cry, I was glad to hold her. "It's gonna be okay, Gianna."

She sniffled, her voice weak. "No, it's not. Everything is so messed up right now. Maybe we shouldn't be doing this."

"Yes, we should." Turning her around in my lap, I kissed her gently on the lips.

"What happened after I passed out?"

Playing with her hair, I filled her in. "I banged Josh's head against the wall until he was knocked out."

She gasped. "Are you serious?"

"Yep, and I'm not done with him either." It apparently hadn't gotten through to Josh to stay the fuck away from Gianna, so I'd be bringing in reinforcements.

Her head dropped against my chest in a trusting move. "I need to text Cece and Jared. I promised them I would let them know if Josh did anything else."

I clenched my teeth to hold back a rude remark. She'd just been through a lot and she didn't need to hear me complain about her friendship with Jared right now. It didn't mean I couldn't get things done on my terms.

I pulled my phone out of my pocket and said, "I'll text Cece for you. You just lay back and rest. You may have a concussion so I'll have to keep an eye on you for the next 24 hours."

"Okay," she agreed and turned back around to fall against me. I didn't have Jared's cell number, but Cece would most definitely pass on the information.

Me: *Josh hurt Gianna again. I took care of it. She's resting now.*

About thirty seconds later my phone beeped. Jeez, she must have had turbo fingers.

Cece: *OMG! Where is she now? Home? Jared and I will come up there after school. I'm going to do something really bad to Josh!*

Me: *No, I took her to my mom's*

Cece: *Address*?

Fuck, I didn't want Jared coming over here. Seeing no choice, I texted Cece the address and let Gianna know that they'd be over later. I could tell she was sleepy, but I made her eat some toast before she took a nap in my room.

Still wound up, I watched TV on the couch, making sure to wake her every so often in case she did have a concussion. When Gianna woke for good, I ordered a pizza and called my mom to let her know we were at the apartment.

After eating, we cuddled on the couch under a blanket, watching an action movie. Just before four o'clock my phone rang. Cece and Jared were downstairs so I rang them up and let them know the apartment number. I still wasn't happy about Jared coming over, but I knew if I didn't respect his and Gianna's friendship, she'd be upset with me. Which would only work in his favor and I couldn't have that.

To me, the knock on the door was obnoxious, so it must've been Jared's weak fists. I got out from under Gianna to let them in. Cece practically trampled over me in the doorway to get to Gianna. Jared and I just gave each other a nod, no love lost there. Right now was about comforting Gianna, not beating the shit out of each other again.

"Gigi! Tell us what happened! I'll run that jerk over with Caleb's car! What did he do?" Cece raged. *My car*? She could just leave my baby out of it.

Gianna calmly explained to them that while she was walking to class, Josh grabbed her from behind again and forced her out of the building. He went crazy finding out she was dating me and kept yelling at her, demanding she break up with me and give them another chance. He slammed her against the wall like last time, but harder, so that she was knocked out. By the end of her story, Gianna was crying again and I let Cece comfort her.

I picked up the story from there, letting them know I beat the crap out of Josh in an *eye for an eye* style. I also told them I planned on getting Dante and Taye to come with me to have a nice long talk with Josh sometime in the near future.

"I'm coming with," Jared insisted.

Grudgingly, I bit out, "Fine." I did respect the fact that he was always looking out for Gianna, but I still didn't have to like him. It was the principle of it. He wanted what was mine.

The four of us hung out for about an hour, trying to cheer Gianna up and make her forget about being attacked. It worked mostly because Cece was a little ball of hyper energy. However, Cece didn't like violence in movies, so we switched it to one of my mom's indie flicks.

It was getting late, so I told them Gianna and I had to get home before Julie and my dad god worried. We said our goodbyes and on the drive home Gianna was in much better spirits.

At home, my dad gave me a disapproving look and Julie questioned us coming home so late. I wondered if she was starting to get suspicious. They bought our excuse of an afterschool homecoming project. I'd been smart enough to call in to the school's office earlier pretending to be my dad to excuse our absences.

Upstairs in my room I called Dante. He'd already heard about what happened from Taye, who found out from Jared. The plan was for the three of them to meet me at my school sometime after they got out tomorrow. Then we'd wait for Josh at his truck after football practice. He didn't see me by myself as enough of a threat, so we'd see how he liked the threat of four of us.

CHAPTER TWENTY

"It seems like the chaos of this world is accelerating, but so is the beauty in the consciousness of more and more people."
-Anthony Kiedis

GIANNA

Caleb slept in my bed with me last night, waking me up every hour just in case I had a concussion. He slipped out of my room before dawn and went back to his own so my mom wouldn't catch us. In the morning, he drove me to school *again*. He insisted on driving me everywhere nowadays, but I didn't mind. But would I ever drive my Jeep again? Maybe I should've demanded we take my car sometimes.

Caleb told Kara and the misfits, as he'd so fondly nicknamed them, about Josh attacking me twice at school. It was kind of embarrassing. He left out the first incident before I broke up with Josh when he tried to force himself on me.

They agreed to help keep an eye on me at school which made me feel like a helpless wimp. As if knowing about my ex-boyfriend drama weren't bad enough. Even if it was pathetic, it'd make me feel safer to always have someone with me.

Josh scared the crap out of me yesterday, acting like a psychopath. Caleb was so sweet through it all, taking care of me at his mom's place, feeding me and trying to get my mind off what happened. Maybe he was capable of being a good boyfriend after all.

Caleb drove us home after school but made no move to get out of the car. "I'm going back to the school to meet Dante, Taye and Jared. We're going to wait until Josh is out of football practice then confront him."

"Do you think this is such a good idea Caleb? I mean, what if he gets crazier after this? Maybe we should just call the police on him."

"We could do that, but they'd want to speak with your mom and Josh. Josh knows we're together and it may get back to your mom. Are you ready for her to find out about us yet?"

Some choice. "I'm not looking forward to that confrontation," I grumbled. "Fine, do it your way."

"Good, we'll take care of it ourselves." He sounded so confident that roughing Josh up would work. I wasn't so sure. If I had any more problems with Josh after this, I'd go straight to the cops and risk my mom finding out about me and Caleb.

Kissing him goodbye, I said, "Be careful." Necessary or not, I didn't like the idea of Caleb fighting. Even after everything he'd done, I didn't want Josh beaten up either. But I'd like to be able to walk down the hallways at school without worrying about him attacking me.

I was going to be a nervous wreck until Caleb came home. My feelings for him were getting stronger every day, which scared me, because he now had the power to really do me damage.

CALEB

I only had to wait thirty minutes for the rest of the guys to show up in the school parking lot.

Dante strolled up to me wearing a shit-eating grin. "So, you have a girlfriend?"

I should've seen this coming. "Yeah, yeah, I've already heard it from everyone else I know. I'm a player. I'll only hurt her, blah, blah, blah."

Dante held up his hands in surrender. "Hey, man! I was just saying. You aren't exactly the boyfriend type."

"I agree," Jared butt in. "You should just stop wasting your time and let me have her now."

"Gianna isn't a possession. Even if I wanted to, which I don't, I couldn't just hand her over to you. Besides, she chose me, so stop wasting your time."

"I never said she was a possession. And don't act like you know her better than me, Caleb. Gigi and I go way back," Jared reminded me.

I mimicked him in a girly voice, "Gigi and I go way back!" His face twisted in annoyance at my mocking. "Well, Gianna and I go forward together from here on out."

Taye stepped between us with a hand on each of our chests. "Hey, we're here to beat up the guy who's been messing with her, not fight amongst ourselves."

"You don't want her too, do you?" I asked Taye. Jared was making me suspicious of all Gianna's guy friends.

He laughed. "Don't get me wrong, Gigi is beautiful, I just like a different flavor. I'm only here to hurt the guy who's been hurting my friend."

Dante pounded me on the back. "I'm just here to back up my boy, Caleb. Plus, maybe Gianna will put in a good word for me with that hot friend of hers, Cece."

"Ugh, man! That's my sister!" Jared exclaimed in disgust.

Dante grinned, nodding his chin at Jared. "You want to put in a good word for me with your sister?"

"Are you sure, Dante?" I teased him. "That girl talks up a storm."

"Again, I say, that's my sister! Just stop all conversation having to do with her!" We ignored him.

"She's a good kisser," Taye put in.

"When the fuck did you kiss my sister, Taye? Never mind, just don't do it again. And shut the fuck up about her, all of you!" Jared yelled. This was too much fun, irritating Jared.

The fun stopped when over Jared's shoulder I recognized some of the guys on the football team coming out to the parking lot. Josh wasn't amongst them. "Hey guys, football practice is over. Josh should be coming out soon. Let's go wait by his truck."

They followed me to the truck and a few minutes later Josh showed up with Seth. Seth looked confused, but by the expression on Josh's face, he knew exactly what was up.

Seth spoke first, asking, "What's going on, Caleb?"

"You can take off, Seth. We just need to speak with Josh," I told him.

"You had to bring backup, Caleb?" Josh taunted me.

"I've already kicked your punk-ass twice, Josh, all on my own. I think it's been established backup isn't required," I belittled him. "Obviously you aren't getting the message, so I brought a few friends of Gianna's and mine to help get it through your brain to leave her alone."

Seth tried to play mediator. "Okay, I think Josh gets the point."

I turned my attention to Seth, wanting him to just go away.

"That's the problem. He's *not* getting the point. He attacked Gianna again yesterday." By this time a few more guys from the team had gathered around.

Seth spun on Josh in disbelief. "You attacked her again?"

Josh narrowed his eyes at Seth. "What do you mean *again*? How'd you hear about any first time? Not that there *was* a first time," he quickly and unconvincingly added.

"Uh, I didn't," Seth evaded. If Seth wanted to be a wimp and hide the fact he took his friend's ex-girlfriend out on a date, then fine. I could've cared less.

"Yeah, the *first* time he tried to force himself on her. The *second* time, he decided to slam her against a wall. And the *third* time, which was yesterday during second period, he managed to knock her unconscious in the process." My voice was loud enough for all the guys from his team to hear. Any decent guy would have a problem with violence committed on women and I figured most of them would be appalled by Josh's actions.

"Enough talk," Jared said. "You already got a piece of him, Caleb, now it's my turn." Jared stepped towards Josh, who turned on his heel and started running.

Dante busted out laughing. "What a bitch! He's running away!" We took off after him. What seemed like half the football team followed us but I didn't know if they planned on helping him out. After all, they did just hear how terribly he treated females. Maybe, like most teenage boys, they just liked to watch a good ass-kicking.

We respected Jared's call on getting a shot at him first, so when we caught up to Josh we let Jared do his thing. Jared first grabbed him from behind in a headlock and grunted at Josh, "You'd be smart to stay far away from Gianna. We aren't the only guys that look out for her. There are lots more where we came from and next time you fuck with her, they're all invited."

By the time Jared was finished, Josh was pretty messed up, not that Josh didn't get a few jabs in. Josh was in good shape, but Jared had a street edge when he fought, like me, that these suburban boys just didn't possess. Some things, you had to go out into the real world to learn.

Josh went unconscious for less than a minute when Dante

hollered in his face, "You got knocked the fuck out, man!" Guess what Dante's favorite movie was? He quoted that line at every available opportunity. To him the joke never got old.

Before we left, Taye punched Josh and Dante kicked him in the stomach while he was down. I figured they came all this way so they deserved at least one or two good hits each. I pulled back my arm like I was going to punch Josh, then I turned it into a bitch slap at the last minute.

After smacking him, I told Josh, "I suggest you listen this time."

Driving away, I could see in my rearview mirror some of the guys from the football team helping Josh up and into his truck. I respected them for not interfering. They understood that Josh needed the violent lesson.

When I pulled up in front of the house, Gianna was sitting on the front porch. She hopped up and met me as I opened my door. Her tight hug was unexpected. "Were you worried?" I teased her.

"Of course I was! What if you got hurt?" Her arms were still tight around my waist.

"You had no reason to be worried. But I'll take the hug and anything else you want to give me."

"In front of the whole neighborhood? Come inside before one of the neighbors tells my mom we were making out in the front yard," she said, dragging me up the walkway.

"You shouldn't have to worry about Josh again. He'd have to be suicidal to try anything now."

Her face went pale. "What if this only makes him worse?"

"Then we call the cops, no matter the consequences." If things got any worse, I didn't give a damn whether or not her mom found out. "And oh yeah, do you think you could put a good word in for Dante the next time you talk to Cece?"

Her smile was full of feminine delight. "Dante likes Cece?"

"Yep."

Her smile grew wider. "If they get together, then we could double date!"

I thought to myself, *crap*.

CHAPTER TWENTY-ONE

"I do not see any beauty in self-restraint."
-Mary MacLane

GIANNA

It was so fun teasing Caleb about double-dating with Cece and Dante. The last double-dating experience was enough for me. I wouldn't want to do that again, even with friends.

Josh hadn't bothered me since the guys had a *talk* with him. Although, he did show up pretty banged up the next day at school. I almost felt guilty.

Thursday afternoon I went up to my room to do some math homework. Caleb plopped down on my bed. "What are you doing?"

"What does it look like I'm doing? Homework. You should try it," I joked.

"I already did mine," he informed me smugly.

I was surprised. "You did? When?"

"Study hall."

"I have study hall too, but I can't finish it that quickly," I told him. "I bet you get horrible grades rushing like that."

"You shouldn't assume things." He looked slightly annoyed with me. "I've never gotten anything below a 'B' in my life."

"So, you're a juvenile delinquent, who got expelled from two different high schools, but you're also an honor student?"

"Yep."

His palm running down my back and over my bottom almost distracted me. "Do you also work as a janitor and solve impossible math problems in your spare time?"

"Ha, ha, ha," he faked humor. "I saw that movie, Miss *Bring It On*."

I gave him a dirty look. "I'm not a cheerleader anymore, remember? Plus, I like that movie."

"You would," he teased.

"Can you go find something else to do? Isn't there a shed somewhere you need to burn down for fun?"

His palm landed hard on my behind. "Fine, since my girlfriend isn't going to give me any attention, I'm out of here. I'll be in my room. You can find me there when you start to miss me." He got off the bed and I couldn't help but watch him leave until the door closed behind him.

I forced myself to stay in my room and finish my homework. Since I started it in study hall, I was done only thirty minutes later. Taking my time, I checked my email and sat on my bed playing with my phone. I was *not* going to rush over to Caleb's room like some sort of lovesick girl. But, dammit, I did miss him. I waited a whole ten more minutes before knocking on his door.

"Come in!" Caleb yelled. He shut a notebook and shoved it under his pillow.

"What was that?" I asked, intrigued.

"Nothing. Miss me already?"

"Nope," I denied, locking his door.

He raised one pierced eyebrow. "Why are you locking the door? Are you here to molest me?"

"Shut up," I said, pushing him onto his back so I could lie on top of him. Hungry for him, I initiated the kiss. Not that he seemed to mind in the least bit. Wanting to see more of him, I started to yank off his shirt when there was a knock on the door.

"Caleb, I can't find Gianna! Did she come home yet?" Oh shit, my mom was home early from work!

Seeing the panic on my face, Caleb's chest rumbled from the laughter he held back. "Um, no, Julie! She was going over a friend's house."

"Okay, Caleb. Dinner will be ready in an hour, so make sure to wash up!" my mom called through the door. He made a face at that. My mom must've thought he was one dirty boy.

"I have everything I'm hungry for right here," Caleb growled in a sexy voice while squeezing my butt.

"Nice line," I said sarcastically. "But what if I hadn't locked the door and my mom had walked in?"

"Then we would've had to politely ask her to leave so we could finish," he kidded, thrusting against me.

"You are so bad." I lifted up the front of his shirt to suck on both of his pierced nipples. He groaned, grinding his hips into mine. Reaching down between our bodies, I grabbed his crotch through his pants.

He jumped at the contact. "Now who's bad? With your mother downstairs, Gianna? Shame on you!"

"So spank me." I suggested. Before I could react, he maneuvered us so he sat at the edge of the bed with me draped facedown over his lap. "I was kidding, Caleb!"

"It's too late to take it back now. I've already accepted your offer. So take your punishment like a big girl."

He smacked my ass. I started laughing so hard I had to hold a hand over my mouth to muffle it. I didn't want to try explaining this to my mom, especially the part about it kinda turning me on.

After a few hits, Caleb propped me upright on the bed next to him. "Now, if you didn't learn your lesson, I'll be more than happy to punish you again."

I straddled him on the bed and we began making out again. This time I took his shirt all the way off so I could run my hands up and down his chest and abs. He removed my shirt and I started unbuttoning his pants.

"What are you doing?" he mumbled against my skin.

"Getting in your pants," I told him. I was dying to see if he really did have a tattoo somewhere under there. If he did, I planned to lick it. Maybe I was the bad one, but my guy was so freaking hot. After I unzipped his pants, he put his hands over mine to stop me.

"What?" I huffed, frustrated.

"I am not fucking you with your mom downstairs."

"Oh, baby, you say the sweetest things," I crooned sarcastically. "Seriously, Caleb, you need to watch a few chick flicks to learn what *not* to say to girls."

"My apologies, Gianna darling. I do not wish to make love to you with your mother downstairs. How was that?"

That was a smart-ass.

"Whatever!" I announced while climbing off him. "You're lame and boring. I was planning something involving my tongue down there, but if you're too scared. . . ." I trailed off with a shrug. Putting my shirt back on, I left.

CALEB

What a tease she was. She wasn't serious about that, was she? *Damn*!

After dinner, Gianna and I pretended we were going to the library to study. My dad gave me a hard, knowing look while Julie asked us what time we'd be home. That woman was dense, lost in her la-la land of hanging curtains and pie-making.

We went for a drive to a nearby park. Going for a walk, we found a bench and sat down. Gianna leaned her head against my shoulder. How weird it was to just be with a girl like this.

"So, do you want to spend the weekend at my mom's place with me?" I asked, trying to remember what my mom said she had going on this weekend.

She squeezed my hand, cuddling closer. "I can't."

"Why not?"

She brought her head up at my abrupt tone. "I'm going camping up in the mountains."

"When were you going to tell me this?"

"Before I left tomorrow," she explained, looking as guilty as she should.

What the hell was going on? "Who are you going with?"

"The crew," she said slowly.

I was beginning to see where this was going. "Does that include Jared?"

"Of course it does, he's part of the crew." When she tried burrowing into me again, I inched away.

"So, you're telling me that my girlfriend is going to be alone for a whole weekend with some dude who has the hots for her?" I tried to keep my voice down so the guys playing a game of basketball close by wouldn't hear.

She looked even guiltier. "Well, when you put it that way, I guess it sounds kind of bad."

"It sounds really bad to my ears," I said. "That's okay. I'll just go out partying with Dante."

"Are you trying to make me jealous?" she asked, sitting up straighter.

"No, but since my girlfriend will be busy on a camping trip

with a bunch of *other dudes*, I feel like I'm entitled to a night with my best friend."

"Cece will be there too," she pointed out.

"Oh, so sorry, my bad. You each only have a few guys to yourselves," I said sarcastically.

"You know it's not like that!" she yelled. "You could come, you know."

"Yeah, you invite me as an afterthought. No, that's okay, I'll pass."

Gianna moved closer. "No really, I want you to come. And you can bring Dante, since Cece will be there!"

"I'll think about it," I told her, upset that she'd been planning on ditching me to hang out with Jared and the crew. She could keep her damn charity invite.

Since the mood was ruined, I grabbed her by the hand and took her home.

Should I go with her? It seemed like a sort of bitch move, to tag along with my girlfriend and her friends. Of course, Taye would be there and I was friends with him. Also, if I brought Dante, I could just call it doing a favor for a friend, since Cece would be there and he wanted to get to know her better.

Who was I kidding? If I went, it'd be to keep Jared away my girlfriend.

CHAPTER TWENTY-TWO

". . . Beauty is jealous, and illy bears the presence of a rival."
-Thomas Jefferson

GIANNA

At school on Friday I was feeling guilty about the whole camping thing. I'd never felt the need to explain myself when I was with Josh. He didn't even know Jared, Cece and the rest of the crew. I was with Josh for a long time but he never got to know the real me like Caleb had. It was almost as if Josh had only been a boyfriend in name and Caleb was the real thing.

We'd had this camping trip planned for weeks now. We wanted to go before the weather turned cold. For the past few weekends we'd had club appearances and battles scheduled. This weekend was the perfect opportunity to finally go. With how unpredictable weather was in Colorado, maybe even our last opportunity until late next spring.

I hadn't thought it'd bother Caleb I was going camping with the crew, since he knew they were my friends. But I guess I could see his point when it came to Jared. I wouldn't have wanted him going on a trip with a girl who wanted him as more than a friend. When I realized it bothered him, I did the right thing and I invited him along. Shouldn't that have counted for something? Cece and I told the guys they couldn't bring girls so it would be me breaking the rule.

And what did Caleb say to my invitation? That he'd *think about it*. I could tell he was still upset with me. He'd been moody all day at school. I actually did want him to come camping with us now. I didn't want to seem like the clingy girlfriend and tell him, though. I actually thought it'd be nice to cuddle next to him in front of a campfire.

Still barely talking to me on the ride home from school, Caleb hadn't given me his answer yet. Sitting in his car outside my house, I asked, "So are you coming with us?"

He looked thoughtful for a moment then turned his head to tell me, "No."

I was actually surprised. I'd thought he'd say yes but was

making me suffer. "Oh, okay. What do you plan to do all weekend?"

"I'm sure I can find something to occupy my time, Gianna. I did manage to have a life before you came along," he said sarcastically.

Ouch.

Oh, I saw how it was. He was going to play games and pay me back for hurting his feelings and probably bruising his massive ego in the process. He was pissed about me going on a trip with my friends so he was lashing out.

Opening the door and holding my backpack, I jumped out of his car. "Well, have fun having a life this weekend. I know I will." I slammed the car door as hard as I could, wishing it would damage his precious Camaro.

Running into the house and up to my room, I grabbed the bag I'd packed last night. Downstairs in the garage was my own precious vehicle. I'd missed driving my Jeep. I got in and started it, waiting for the garage door to open.

Caleb knocked on the window. I pushed the button and asked rudely as it rolled down, "What?"

"Don't I get a kiss goodbye?" He stood there arrogantly but my feelings were hurt now also.

"No, you don't."

"What are you being so bitchy about?" he asked, gripping the open window.

Oh hell no. He did *not* just call me bitchy. "I don't like your attitude, Caleb."

"Too bad. And, Gianna?"

"Yeah?" I asked, matching his arrogance.

"Don't worry. I won't be doing anything this weekend you aren't doing." With that parting remark, he turned around and walked back into the house.

What the *fuck* was that supposed to mean?

I squealed out of the driveway.

Motherfucker!

He just said that to make me worry all weekend about what he was up to. He wouldn't really go hang out with girls, would he?

Motherfucker!

Yes, he would. The whole way to pick up Jared and Cece, I stewed about what my boyfriend may or may not be doing over the weekend.

CALEB

I'd let her think about that! After Gianna took off, I went up to my room. For sure I'd be crashing at my mom's for the next couple days. I wouldn't sit here like a bitch waiting for my girlfriend to come home from camping with douchebag Jared.

The whole way down to Denver, I brooded about Jared spending the weekend trying to steal my girlfriend. I thought about changing direction and going on the damn camping trip, but it'd make me feel so fucking whipped. Tagging along with my girlfriend and her friends would turn me into every pansy-ass boyfriend I'd ever made fun of. I had more pride than that. I didn't care if Taye was there and I didn't care if Gianna said Dante could come too. All I knew was Jared better keep his grubby hands to himself.

Tense and worn out, when I arrived at the apartment, I crashed on my bed. Waking up later it was already dark, so I checked the time, nine o'clock. The night was just beginning. I grabbed my phone and read through my missed calls and texts.

Nothing from Gianna. She must be too busy with loser Jared and her friends, probably acting like a bunch of *Fame* wannabes. Stupid breakers.

I did have a text from my friend, Hailey, though. I hadn't seen her in forever.

Hailey: *How's it going, player? When are we going to cause some trouble together?*

Hailey was like my female counterpart. We'd been friends since middle school where we'd bonded over many a detention together. Hailey was the cool kind of girl that was just one of the guys. It didn't hurt that she was pretty hot, too. We'd fooled around a little freshman year, but nothing serious. She was a female player herself and never dated one guy for long. I texted her back.

Me: *I don't know. How about tonight? I'll call Dante and see what he's up for.*

Calling Dante's number, I didn't get an answer, so I left a message for him to call me back. Soon after I hung up, my phone rang and Hailey's name flashed on the screen.

"What up, girl?"

"Ugh, I'm bored and you need to find me some fun."

She sounded so put out, I laughed. "Since when is it my job to entertain you?"

"Since always. Where the fuck have you been, Caleb?"

"I moved up to Broomfield to live with my dad," I told her.

"Wow, sucks for you. Are you up there now?"

"No, I'm staying at my mom's for the weekend."

"Good, come pick me up at my house," she demanded.

I figured I had nothing better to do. "Sure, I'll be there in twenty minutes."

GIANNA

I was surprised Dante came on the camping grip. He and Taye were cousins, so it made sense he'd be invited. Dante probably came to try and get with Cece. After setting up the tents and getting a campfire started, we were all sitting around drinking and talking. A couple of the guys were trying out a new moves, which was hilarious because they were tipsy and getting dirty in the process.

Cece and I sat on a log together. "So, Cece, what do you think of Dante?"

She glanced over at Dante and said, "I think he's cute, why?"

"Because I heard he has a crush on you," I drawled, waiting for her reaction.

Cece perked up, getting excited. "Really, who told you that, Caleb?" Hearing his name made me miss him more than I already did.

"Yep, he said Dante wanted me to put in a good word with you."

"Consider the good word put in," Cece responded, ditching me to go sit by Dante. The girl didn't have a shy bone in her body.

With Cece gone, Jared took her spot. "How's it going, Gigi?"

I gave him a fake, sweet smile. "Jared, why don't you just ask what you really want to know?"

"Fine, are you still dating that loser?"

Scowling at him, I answered in the same rude tone, "Yes, I'm still dating *Caleb*."

"Why isn't he here with you then?" Jared asked, pretending to look around.

"We don't have to spend every minute together. We can have separate lives, too." Taking a drink out of my beer, I acted unconcerned.

"Uh-huh," Jared said knowingly. "So, you invited him and he didn't want to come?"

"It wasn't like that. I sort of sprung it on him at the last minute."

"If you were my girl, I'd want to be here with you, no matter how last minute the invite was." Why didn't he go find some other girl to date? Jared was hot and pretty girls were always flirting with him when we went to battles.

After Jared walked away, I drank some more and started feeling sorry for myself. I really missed Caleb. A part of me wanted to leave the camping trip early to be with him. Wouldn't that seem kind of desperate, though?

Why hadn't he wanted to come? What was he doing right now? He better not have been doing what he threatened to do and went out where there were a bunch of girls. I hated girls! They were all dirty whores after my boyfriend. I was going to drive myself crazy thinking about it.

CALEB

I woke up on Saturday around one o'clock in the afternoon at my mom's apartment. She'd had to go into work today to finish up a project. Otherwise she would've probably been questioning me right now about why I slept on the couch. I didn't want to have to explain that Hailey was sleeping in my room. She knew Hailey and I were just friends, but she also thought Hailey was a bad friend for me to have.

From a parent's point-of-view, she was right. Hailey wasn't the kind of girl any mom would want her teenage son to hang out with. Although, I wasn't exactly a *good kid* myself. Sitting up on the couch, I rubbed a hand over my face, thinking about how Hailey got us kicked out of a club last night.

After she'd gotten into a fight with some girl, she'd cussed out the bouncer who broke it up. He'd ended up carrying her out of the place and depositing her on the sidewalk outside. I'd finally got her drunk-ass calmed down and brought her here to sleep it off. As entertaining as it always was, it was hard work hanging out with someone like her.

Needing to use the bathroom, I passed by my room and peeked inside. She was still asleep face down on my bed. Shit, there was drool on my pillow. That was going in a dumpster.

As I walked back into the living room, there was a knock on the front door. No one asked to be buzzed up so it was probably a neighbor. Going over to the couch, I picked up my jeans from last night, pulling them up as I went to answer the door.

It was a pleasant surprise to find Gianna on the other side of the door. "Hey, how'd you get up here?"

"Surprise! I couldn't remember your exact apartment number, but someone buzzed me up," she explained, looking sheepish.

She threw her arms around me, putting her head on my chest. "I missed you, Caleb. I know I'm the biggest loser ever, leaving the camping trip early to see my boyfriend, but I couldn't help it. Being away from you sucked so bad. Especially with the way we left things. I don't want to fight with you. I'm sorry for being a bitch."

Enjoying having her in my arms again, I kissed the top of her head. "I missed you too, princess, and I'm sorry for being a jackass." She peeked up at me with a smile and I stroked one blushing cheek.

"So, what'd you do last night? Were you totally bored without me?" she teased, leaning into my hand.

Crap. How did I answer that question? I didn't actually do anything wrong. At least I didn't think so. Boyfriends were allowed to have female friends, right? To be safe, I'd better not mention Hailey. She'd probably be passed out for a while longer and I could get Gianna out of here quickly.

"Nothing much, just hung out with Dante."

She tensed up at my words. "You hung out with Dante?"

"Yeah," I said, leaning down to kiss her.

She turned her head to avoid my lips. "Last night?"

"Yeah," I repeated slowly.

"Dante, Taye's cousin?" she asked, sounding weird.

"That's the one," I agreed, not liking how she was acting. "What's the matter, Gianna?"

She took a couple steps away from me, staring down at the ground. When she finally looked up, I almost flinched at her expression. "If I'm acting weird, Caleb, it's because I don't understand how you could've hung out with Dante last night when he was camping with us!" She screamed the last few words.

Oh shit.

Hailey decided to pick that moment to come out of my room. "Hey, Caleb, do you have any aspirin? I have a killer headache."

Gianna blue eyes moved to where Hailey stood at the end of the hallway in nothing but one of my t-shirts. I could see shock and tears in her eyes when they returned to me.

I held up my hands, feeling panicked. "Gianna, it's not what you think."

Bitterly, she replied, "What a cliché you are, Caleb."

Spinning around, she rushed out of the apartment. I saw her go through the door at the end of the hallway to take the stairs and quickly searched for a shirt, socks and shoes to put on.

Hailey ran her fingers through the knots in her red hair. "What's going on?"

"That was my girlfriend and now she thinks I cheated on her with you," I said agitatedly.

Hailey gave me a look of mixed disbelief and hurt. "You have a *girlfriend*?" Why was Hailey acting hurt? We were only friends and neither of us had ever wanted more.

Slipping on shoes, I snatched my wallet and keys. "Yes, I have a girlfriend, who I need to go catch up with to explain."

Leaving the apartment, I ran down the stairs after Gianna. Out on the street, I didn't see her anywhere. The parking garage was my next destination, figuring she'd probably parked there. Almost to the garage, I saw her Jeep pull out and turn in the opposite direction.

I didn't have to be an experienced boyfriend to know my girlfriend finding Hailey like that was bad. How the hell was I going to convince Gianna I did nothing wrong?

CHAPTER TWENTY-THREE

"Shame, like beauty, is often in the eye of the beholder."
-Julie Burchill

GIANNA

Did that really just happen? I made a complete fool of myself over that cheating jerk! Obviously I wasn't the only girl Caleb liked to have sleepovers with at his mom's place. Why was I even crying? He wasn't worth it and I should've known this would happen. Hell, everyone else knew it would. Caleb couldn't change who he was. I was stupid falling for a guy like him. Had the whole thing been a game to him?

No wonder he hadn't wanted to go camping. He'd had a whole different recreational activity in mind for this weekend. He must've been so happy to get rid of me so he could screw around with that slut!

He'd better just stay away from me at home, because I knew where that motherfucker lived. I could do all sorts of bad things to him in his sleep. *Better sleep with one eye open, dirty dog*. I shouldn't have run away like that. I totally spazzed out and ran away instead of bitching him and her out. How pathetic! I should have stayed there and kicked his ass then yanked out both his nipple piercings.

It was smart to let the anger come. It was much better than the pain. Dammit, now they were just angry tears. I pulled my Jeep over to the side of the road because my vision was getting blurry and I didn't want to cause a crash. That would really top off an astoundingly bad day.

I'd never cried over any of the other guys I'd dated. That was probably because they'd never made me feel as much as Caleb had. I really thought he cared about me. He was so attentive to me and protective about the whole Josh thing.

What started out as him being my annoying new stepbrother blackmailing me, seemed to turn into something more. He acted like he actually gave a damn about my happiness. He claimed to be bothered that my home and school life made me miserable. I thought he saw past my looks to the person I really was.

Obviously, I was just another conquest to him. One of god knows how many stupid girls who fell for his handsome face and bad boy charm.

What an idiot he was, saying he hung out with Dante last night. I wouldn't have even known it for the lie it was if Dante hadn't gone camping with us and that skanky girl hadn't come out of his room when she did. At least I found out now instead of later when I'd look like a bigger fool. Clearly, a player couldn't change his manwhore stripes.

Where was I even going? Definitely not home. The asshole could show up and if he did, I couldn't guarantee I wouldn't kill him. But I couldn't sit on the side of the road in my jeep all day.

CALEB

When I got back to the apartment, Hailey was dressed in what she wore last night waiting for me. "Caleb, why didn't you tell me that you had a girlfriend?"

"I didn't know I needed to. You and I are just friends, Hailey," I reminded her.

"Whatever happened to players for life?" she argued.

"Things change." Not feeling like I needed to defend myself to Hailey, I tried calling Gianna but there was no answer. Even if it was pointless, I sent her a text to call me back.

"Why her?" she asked, sounding hurt again.

"Why do you care?" I countered, getting annoyed with her.

Her shoulders jerked in a shrug. "It's just that, I always thought if you were ever going to pick one girl to be with, it'd be me."

Wow, she was so far off the mark. "I'm sorry, Hailey. I don't see us that way," I told her softly. Usually I didn't feel bad about hurting girls' feelings. Now I was feeling bad about hurting two girls in one day.

"You saw me that way once," she pointed out.

"Yeah, like two years ago and that was just a fling. I didn't realize it meant more to you. I mean, you never acted like it did. You haven't exactly been the relationship-type yourself."

Her face scrunched up and I couldn't tell if it was anger or hurt now. "You know what? Never mind, I don't know what I was thinking. Maybe I'm still drunk." She didn't meet my gaze when she spoke, though.

But I wasn't one to argue when I given an easy out. "Okay, good to get that cleared up. Now, can I ask you for a favor?"

She gave me a dirty look. "As long as it involves me going home to shower and change first."

Two hours later, when we'd *both* showered and changed, I drove us to Broomfield. I had it all worked out. Hailey grudgingly agreed to explain everything to Gianna. She would tell her nothing happened and that we were only friends. Then Gianna would forgive me.

At my dad's house, Julie said Gianna hadn't been home. Where could she have gone? She still wasn't answering my calls or texts.

Three more hours later, I was driving around the campgrounds Julie said Gianna was at with her *cheerleader* friends. Little did Julie know, Gianna was with her crew. *With Jared.* Okay, maybe she hadn't come up back up here, but I didn't know where else to look.

"What's so special about this girl anyways, Caleb? Why don't you just forget about her and find another like you always do?" Hailey asked combatively.

"Are you really that jaded, Hailey? That you think any girl will do? I only want this girl. Gianna *is* special."

"Her name is *Gianna*? Sounds prissy. I didn't get a good look at her before she went running off like a baby. Is she pretty?"

"More than pretty, she's beautiful. And she went running off because I opened the door half-naked and you came out of my room half-naked. It looked like we'd been bumping uglies."

"Classy, Caleb," Hailey commented snidely.

Ignoring her bad mood, I continued, "Plus, I lied to her about hanging out with Dante last night." Which was a moronic. But even if I'd told her the truth about hanging out with Hailey last night, would Gianna have believed I'd slept on the couch?

"You're an idiot." Hailey laughed obnoxiously as if my being an idiot was the funniest thing she'd ever heard.

"You're reading my mind," I said through clenched teeth. "Finally!" I shouted, seeing Gianna's Jeep parked behind a few other vehicles. "Fuck, I thought we'd never find them!"

I parked and got out the car but Hailey wasn't getting out. Going around the back, I opened the door for her. She didn't budge. "This is stupid, Caleb. Just forget about her!"

Grabbing her arm, I yanked her out of the car. "Just be a good friend and tell Gianna what really happened. Most of all, what didn't happen. Quit being difficult, Hailey. After all the times I've taken care of your drunk-ass and gotten in fights when you've pissed people off, it's the least you can do."

Weaving through the trees, Hailey complained, "I can't believe you have me marching through the woods at night. It's like a bad horror film where the promiscuous girl gets killed first."

"Don't worry. If you're scared of the dark, I'm sure they have a campfire going." I could give a fuck how Hailey felt at the moment. I was anxious to set everything straight with Gianna.

"Well, I can hear music. Hopefully they'll have a good party going to. I could use a beer," she said, sounding chipper at the thought.

"They have a program for that, Hailey. It involves twelve steps. Bad news, though, one of them requires you apologizing to all the people you've wronged. It might take you awhile."

She slugged me on the arm. "Hey, you better be nice to me. You need me right now."

Along with hearing the music, we could see light up ahead through the trees. When we entered the campsite, I saw Cece dancing closely with Dante to the Shakira song playing.

I didn't see Gianna. Spotting me and Hailey, Dante shot us a strange look. Cece glared at me took a step in my direction but Dante held her back from confronting me. I didn't have the patience to listen to Cece right now. A few guys were doing their b-boy thing and couple others were sitting. Hailey and I circled around them.

Hailey's laugh brought my attention to the direction of her gaze. "Please don't tell me that's your girlfriend, Caleb. I take that back. Please tell me she is because she isn't acting like it."

"Shut up, Hailey." Clenching my fists, I was preparing to use them.

Jared sat in a lawn chair while Gianna stood in front of him, giving him a private dance to the Shakira song playing. I don't think I'd ever want to watch another sexy Shakira video again after watching my girlfriend do a good impersonation of her for another guy.

We had a side view of them as Jared looked up at Gianna with lust in his eyes, while Gianna looked down at him flirtatiously. I started towards them just as Jared grabbed Gianna by the waist and pulled her in between his legs. They still hadn't noticed us, lost as they were in each other.

I approached them as Jared was about to pull her head down for a kiss. Reaching an arm between them, I put a hand on Jared's face, pushing it away from Gianna's. "You do *not* want to do that."

Gianna's head tilted my way. "Actually, we do want to."

Putting an arm around Gianna's waist, I moved her away from Jared. While I did that, Jared had gotten out of the chair. "Stay away from my girlfriend."

Jared didn't appear worried. "From what I hear, she isn't your girlfriend anymore."

By this time, everyone was watching the scene unfold. Taye put a hand on both of our chests, but addressed me first, "Hey, man, maybe you should go."

"I'm not leaving without Gianna."

Gianna angrily pushed me from the side. I didn't budge from where I stood which seemed to make her angrier. "I'm not going anywhere with you ever again! And, I'm not staying here if you are!"

"I can explain, Gianna. I even brought Hailey with me so she could tell you *nothing* happened between us." I pulled Hailey forward from where she'd been quietly watching the drama. "Tell her, Hailey."

Hailey crossed her arms over her chest, emphasizing her low cut shirt. "What do you want me to tell her, Caleb?" Her sly tone implied she'd say whatever I wanted.

"The truth," I snapped.

Hailey unhappily looked Gianna up and down before saying, "We went out clubbing last night and one thing led to another. . . ."

"What the fuck, Hailey? Tell the truth," I demanded.

Hailey sighed dramatically. "Listen, *Gianna*, Caleb and I haven't fucked for a really long time."

"What the fuck, Hailey? Did you have to say it to her like that?" I roared. This was not going the way I'd planned.

Tears formed in Gianna's eyes and she turned around, heading into the trees, probably planning on escaping me in her Jeep again. Cece immediately followed after her. Hell, now I was hurting for my girl.

Before I could reach the trees, Jared stepped in front of me. "Don't you think you've done enough?"

"That's the thing. I haven't done anything." I shouted, ready to lose it. "Now get out of my way!" I snarled, pushing him to the ground.

Gianna came back and I thought I'd have to catch her when she almost ran into me. Instead she pushed me in the chest and yelled, "You know what? I'm not running away this time! You need to take your slut and leave!"

As proud of her as I was in that moment, she was frustrating the shit out of me. "Not until you listen!"

"I've heard enough already! Hell, I've *seen* enough already!" she shouted, pushing me again.

Fed up, I picked her up and carried her to where Hailey stood with an amused look on her face. I set Gianna down and held onto her. "Now, Hailey, could you please do the right thing and tell Gianna everything that happened last night?"

Hailey scowled, staring at Gianna's face. "I can see why you want her so bad, it fucking figures."

"Just tell her," I barked at Hailey impatiently.

Hailey rolled her eyes then told Gianna in a rush, "Fine! Nothing happened last night! We went clubbing and I got really drunk. Caleb let me crash on his bed and he slept on the couch." She then looked at me with big eyes. "Happy?"

Gianna crossed her arms. "And I'm supposed to believe that?"

Everyone around us seemed disbelieving too. The only thing probably keeping Cece from jumping me was Dante's arm around her waist. Jared glared at me from the other side of Gianna. Taye whispered something to him, likely to keep him from trying to hit me.

"As much as I'd *love* to tell you that Caleb and I fucked last night, it didn't happen," Hailey admitted crudely.

"But you guys *have* slept together before?" Gianna questioned her.

"Yes," I cut in, trying to think of the best way to put this, "but it's been two years and it wasn't anything serious."

Jared muttered something rude that I chose to pretend I didn't hear.

"There, I told her, Caleb. Can you take me back to civilization now?" Hailey asked.

"I need to talk to Gianna first." I glared at Jared. "In private."

"Maybe I don't want to talk to you, Caleb," Gianna said stubbornly.

"I'm not leaving until you do." I could be just as stubborn. I'd sleep in my car tonight if I had to.

She was silent for a long moment. "Ugh! Let's get this over with so you can leave!" Gianna headed for the trees again.

CHAPTER TWENTY-FOUR

"I also became close to nature, and am now able to appreciate the beauty with which this world is endowed."
-James Dean

GIANNA

I marched into the woods wishing I'd brought a flashlight with me. I kept walking for awhile and heard Caleb's footsteps behind me. His boots made a crunching sound on the dry forest floor. Trying to walk confidently, I'd had a couple drinks and was feeling a good buzz.

"As much as I normally love the view from behind, we can stop anytime now, Gianna."

I stopped but I didn't turn around. "Say what you have to say, Caleb. I want to get back to my friends."

"Will you at least face me while we have this conversation?" he asked irritably.

No, I thought to myself. If I looked at him, it'd be harder to think straight. My tipsy mind was already muddled without having to stare at his handsome face.

Unfortunately, not wanting to appear an idiot, I turned around and looked him straight in the eyes. We had almost no light because little of the campfire could be seen from openings between the trees. He took a step forward and I stood my ground. He didn't say anything, just stood there with his hands in his pockets.

"Well?" I demanded impatiently and put my hands on my hips to let him know I wasn't putting up with any of his bullshit.

"Why are you still mad, Gianna? Hailey told you nothing happened. What more do you need?"

I don't know, I thought to myself. Some female warning system was going off in my head, telling me this was a critical moment in the relationship. "Caleb, this is my first time dealing with this type of situation."

"Please explain to me, from your point of view, what the situation is," he said slowly.

I threw my hands up in the air and let out an exasperated breath. "Caleb, I've never had to deal with a boyfriend hanging out with his ex. An ex who makes it clear she still wants him."

"You hang out with Jared," he pointed out sullenly.

"Jared isn't my ex. He's one of my best friends."

"Hailey is one of my best friends," he countered, stupidly in my opinion.

"Who you've fucked!" I hollered at him.

Even in the low light I saw his wince. "That was a long time ago and she isn't my ex because we were never technically together."

Guy logic could be so stupid. "That goes for all the girls you've screwed. Does that mean you should be able to hang out with all of them while you're supposedly *my* boyfriend?"

"Hailey is the only girl I've messed around with that I'm friends with still," he explained as if that would make it all better.

"Whatever, I'm not going to tell you who to hang out with. I refuse to ever be that kind of girlfriend. You do what you gotta do and I'll do what I gotta do."

"Is that a threat?" he growled.

"No, I'm just not going to try to change you. I'm not your mother or your therapist. You are who you are, Caleb."

"You mean a player?" he asked, clearly annoyed, but also sounding a little hurt.

"I didn't say that, but you're forgetting something else. You lied to me about hanging out with Dante." My voice cracked at the end but I refused to cry again. "I can't be with someone who's going to lie to me about hanging out with other girls." The lying was as bad as him hanging out with Hailey.

Sounding contrite, he said softly, "I'm sorry, princess. I made a stupid, hasty decision, telling you I was with Dante last night. I just didn't know how you'd take me going clubbing with Hailey."

"Obviously not well," I said sarcastically, taking a few steps further away from him. "God, I don't want to be the nagging girlfriend!"

Ignoring that, he asked, "Don't you think you're being a little hypocritical, Gianna?"

I knew where he was leading with that question. "How so? I didn't lie to you, Caleb. I told you exactly who I was going camping with and I even invited you along," I reminded him.

"You're the one that chose to spend time with Hailey instead of me."

"How kind of you," he replied sarcastically. "Thank you for inviting me the day before to tag along with you and your friends. What you're being hypocritical about, Gianna, is the fact that I can't hang out with a female friend, but you can come camping with six male friends."

Okay, there was some truth to what he was saying. "But I haven't had sex with those six male friends." I ignored his aggravated sound and went on. "Plus, it wouldn't have just been you tagging along with me and my friends. Taye is your friend also and he invited Dante who is your *best* friend."

"I may have gone out with Hailey last night, but it was only as friends. When I showed up here tonight, you and Jared were acting like a lot more than friends," he accused.

"Yeah, because when I found you with Hailey at your apartment, it looked like the two of you had just rolled out of bed together. Then you lied to me, making yourself look even guiltier. You can't blame me for taking it badly."

"And running straight into Jared's arms," he added.

I looked away from him, feeling somewhat guilty about that. Not that I was about to back down. "Well, maybe before you hung out with your little friend with benefits, you should've thought about how I'd feel about it and tell the truth. Besides, we hadn't quite gotten to the point of me being in Jared's arms. Nothing happened with Jared, either. I was just dancing. It happens to be a hobby of mine."

He closed the distance between us and placed his hands on either side of my face. Feeling a jolt at his proximity, I didn't pull away. Caleb's hands were shaking. "Because I showed up when I did, nothing happened. He was about to kiss you, don't deny it. Do I get any extra points for driving all over this damn mountain looking for you?"

"No, you owed me that much." I couldn't prevent the hurt from entering my voice again.

He must've read something into it. He began placing light, gentle kisses all over my face and neck. "So, am I forgiven, princess?"

"I need time to think things over, Caleb." I tried to stay strong. He wouldn't be able to woo me with his expertise.

"What's there to think over? We had a small misunderstanding and it's been fixed." His voice had deepened and his hands on me were distracting.

"Caleb, stop doing that," I pleaded, only half meaning it.

"Doing what?" He acted innocent, but I could feel his smile against my neck.

"Stop trying to distract me so I'll forget everything that's happened. I'm serious. I need to think things over when I'm completely sober. Plus, you need to take your little fuck friend home." It wasn't lost on me that Caleb was her ride and it encouraged me not to make up with him yet.

He groaned. "I forgot about her. I suppose you're going to stay here with Jared?"

"Yes, I'm going to stay here with my *friends*, which includes Jared."

"So, are we okay?" The touch of his lips against my neck caused me to shiver in a good way.

It took me a minute to think about what he'd asked. "We're not okay, but we're not breaking up either."

"Good." He laid a forceful kiss on my mouth. "Now I need to air my grievances."

"What?" I tried pulling away but he was too strong.

"I'm very upset with you, Gianna." He couldn't be serious!

"Oh yeah? What about?"

"First, you ran off without letting me explain."

"You can't blame me for that."

"Just promise me you won't do it again," he commanded.

"Fine, next time I'll stick around to watch you and the girl put some clothes on." I'd have the image burned into my brain for a long time of them both half-naked.

"Gianna, quit being a baby and making it sound seedier than it actually was."

I was about to argue but he put a hand over my mouth to silence me. "Second, when we have an argument, or misunderstanding in this case, answer your damn phone when I call you."

"I'll try," I said noncommittally.

"You'll do it." He gave me another one of those dominating kisses. "And thirdly, if I ever catch you dancing like that for another guy again, I'm going to beat the crap out of him and put you over my knee."

"Whatever. If I find you having another sleepover with a female friend, then I get to beat the crap out of you."

"You have sleepovers at Jared's house almost every Saturday."

"Caleb, that's not the same thing! I've been doing it for years. Plus, I sleep in Cece's bed with her, not in Jared's room." It totally wasn't the same thing.

Caleb's body language changed as he drew me closer. "Really? In the same bed? Can I come next time?"

I slapped him on the chest. "Not funny, Caleb. Besides, I don't think Dante would like it."

"So, he and Cece are a thing now?"

"I think so. Now, don't you have to be going? I'm sure Hailey is anxious to get you to herself again." I was being a bitch, but the thought of the long drive where they'd be alone was making me insanely jealous. Couldn't she just hitchhike back to Denver?

He smacked me on the butt. "Jealous, princess?"

"Maybe. Are you jealous I'll be sleeping here with all those hot guys nearby?" I teased.

With his arms around me, he lifted me up off the ground. "I think I'll just tie you up and take you with me."

"I don't think so. I left this camping trip early for you once already. Look how that turned out. I think I'll just stay here and enjoy the rest of the trip. Some of the guys are getting pretty drunk and when they try to dance like that it's hilarious."

"Just as long as you're not the one dancing for them, I guess it's okay." As if he had a say in it. He laughed suddenly. "You told your mom you were going camping with the cheerleaders?"

"Yep. You'd think she'd realize that last night the cheerleaders had to be at the game, but she was just so happy at the thought of me socializing with them, and maybe joining cheer again, she didn't even think of it." I laughed with him.

Like we were starved for each other, we ended up making out for a few minutes, forgetting the world around us. Unfortunately that stupid hoe, Hailey, started calling Caleb's name from the campsite in a whiney voice.

That was one friend of his I'd never like. She made it perfectly clear she wanted Caleb. The fact they'd slept together, even if it was two years ago was really bothering me. I didn't like her sleeping in his bed last night and wearing his t-shirt. Those were just a few of the reasons why I couldn't tell Caleb everything was okay with us.

I did need to think more about everything that'd happened this weekend. I couldn't do it with him trying to kiss me into a stupor and my friends nearby. Maybe tomorrow I could spend some time alone and think it over.

Caleb groaned. "I guess I better get her home. I don't think she appreciated me dragging her around today." Like I gave a crap what Hailey wanted?

"Well, have fun driving her home. I'll see you sometime tomorrow." I took off back to the campsite worked up again about Hailey.

A couple yards away, he caught from behind. "I think you should change what you're wearing, Gianna."

I looked down at myself. "What's wrong with what I'm wearing?" I had on shorts and a short sleeve cropped hoodie.

"You need to ask? That hoodie shows way too much of your stomach. I don't like it."

I tried pulling away but he wasn't letting go so I turned around in his arms. "Well, I don't like finding half-naked girls wearing your t-shirts in your mom's apartment. So tough, unless you want me to borrow one of Jared's shirts and prance around in only that, you'll have to get over what I have on."

I finally escaped his embrace only to get a few steps away before he grabbed me from behind again. Kissing my neck, he moved his hand up to cup my breast. I leaned back against him. "Stop it, Caleb. You're not getting your way. Take your friend home and I'll see you tomorrow. Try to keep your shirt on around her this time."

Caleb didn't say anything as we walked out of the trees with his arm around my shoulders. As soon as we get back to the campsite, Caleb kissed me passionately. I knew he was partly doing it for Jared's benefit, but I didn't mind because that slut, Hailey, was also watching.

Jared walked up and cleared his throat. I turned my head to look at him and reminded myself I'd never made Jared any promises. All I did was dance in front of him.

Jared glared at Caleb before asking me, "You forgive him just like that?"

Hailey piped in with, "I wouldn't forgive him." Like I was going to take advice from her?

"Jared, you heard Hailey explain that nothing happened. Caleb and I have some things we still need to work out, but I'm not breaking up with him over a misunderstanding." This wasn't either of their business, especially Hailey.

Hailey propped a hand on one hip. "Can we go now, Caleb?"

I really didn't like her ordering around *my* boyfriend. Caleb could feel my tension and squeezed my hip as if it was going to make me feel better.

Caleb pointed a finger at Jared. "Don't try kissing my girlfriend again. We're still together, so paws off." He better say the same thing to Hailey if she tried anything on their way back to the city.

Caleb and I kissed one last time before they left and as I ran my hand through his dark hair, I yanked it gently. "Be good."

"You too, princess. By the way, since Jared got that little Shakira performance, I'll be expecting a lap dance, stripper style."

"You're so bad," I told him.

"See you tomorrow," he whispered.

As they were walking back to wherever Caleb parked, Hailey glanced over her shoulder at me and smirked. *Smug bitch.* If she touched him, I'd kill her.

CHAPTER TWENTY-FIVE

"Beyond the beauty, the sex, the titillation, the surface, there is a human being. And that has to emerge.
-Jeanne Moreau

CALEB

I wasn't happy about leaving Gianna up in the mountains with Jared there. Especially since we hadn't gotten everything completely resolved between us. Hailey did do me a favor by telling Gianna the truth, however reluctantly she may have done it. I owed it to her to get her home after dragging her around all day.

Before we reached the bottom of the mountain, Hailey started bitching. "She isn't right for you, Caleb."

"Oh really, and what makes you the expert on relationships?"

"She's just having her kicks with you. A girl that beautiful will only dump you when someone better comes along."

Hailey started messing with the radio and I slapped her hand away, turning it off. "How would you know? Have you been dumped by a girl like Gianna?" Hailey had no right judging Gianna when she didn't even know her.

"Of course not, dumbass. What I *do* know is that girls like that don't end up with guys like you. They may date them for awhile, but in the end she's going to end up with the quarterback or the class president. The type of guy who's going to go to college and make something of himself."

"Thanks a lot. I'm not exactly an idiot, you know," I told her, stung and strangely worried she was right.

She rolled her eyes. "I know you're not an idiot, Caleb, but you don't have the dedication to do things like finish college."

"Perhaps being with Gianna is what I needed to inspire me. Maybe I want to be a better person for her. I don't even want any other girls anymore, Hailey." From the glow of the dashboard, I could see a pained expression on her face. "Besides, Gianna sees me as more than just a fling. She's opened up to me in a way she does only with those people you met tonight. Maybe even more so with me and that has to mean something."

"Maybe that's so, but let me ask you something, Caleb. Have

you done the same with her?"

I realized what she referred to. "There's no reason to tell her about anything in my past."

"If you can't do it, she isn't the right girl for you," Hailey said confidently.

Tightening my grip on the steering wheel, I thought about her words. "She knows I was no angel before I met her."

"But does she know the worst things you've done? What got you expelled this last time?" Hailey questioned with a knowing look on her face.

"She doesn't need to know."

"Are you afraid she won't accept you, Caleb?" She kept talking before I could respond. "Are you worried she'll realize she can do better?"

"She wouldn't think that," I said hotly. "Let's not talk about this anymore. Turn on the radio."

She laughed derisively, but didn't talk anymore of it until I parked in front of her house. "You don't belong with a girl like her, Caleb. You belong with someone more like yourself who won't judge you for wanting to have fun."

"Someone like you?"

She grinned, taking off her seatbelt to crawl on top of me. "Now you're getting it."

I tried pushing her away gently, but she had a tight grip around my neck. "Hailey, what are you doing?"

"Let's fuck, Caleb." She swooped down for a kiss.

I dodged it, attempting to force her off my lap without breaking her arms. "This isn't cool, Hailey. I have a girlfriend." With her in that short skirt, it'd be so easy to impale her on my dick. A few minutes and I'd get physical relief after a stressful day.

But if I did, I wouldn't get the girl I really wanted.

She huffed in annoyance. "Minor detail. It's not like you haven't two-timed girls before."

"None of them were actually my girlfriend," I pointed out, getting pissed.

"Is she that great in bed?" Hailey asked disdainfully.

"I wouldn't know."

Hailey laughed. "You aren't even getting laid?" She ground

down on my crotch. "I'd be happy to help you out, Caleb. It's been two years since we last fucked and I've only gotten better at it."

Even after several weeks of abstinence, the offer wasn't tempting. I pushed her roughly off my lap, causing her to bump her head on the passenger window. "Someone has a high opinion of herself," I joked.

She tried climbing on top of me again. "Why don't you find out for yourself?"

I held her back before she could get on me again. "Hailey, quit acting like a slut. I don't want you. I'm only interested in sex with my girlfriend and refuse to cheat on her. People change and I don't have to be like that anymore."

She made a frustrated sound and opened her car door. "Good luck with Princess Barbie. Don't come crying to me when she dumps you for Ken!" Slamming the door shut, she took off for her front door.

Wow, did she really just say that? That was the stupidest line I'd ever heard. What the hell did Barbie dolls have to do with anything? It must have been a girl thing.

It was late but I drove all the way back to my dad's house because I wanted to be there when Gianna got home tomorrow. I wasn't in the best of moods with my girlfriend camping with that douche Jared. Now that I'd taken Hailey home, I was tempted to drive back up into the mountains to bring Gianna home. I'd just have to trust her like she trusted me to drive Hailey home.

I didn't even want to think about Hailey right now. What she tried tonight changed our friendship. She wasn't the cool female friend anymore. She'd turned into the other girls I'd slept with and now had to avoid.

She was also wrong about Gianna. Josh was the type of guy Hailey thought Gianna would end up with but Gianna was never happy with him. That type of guy was all wrong for her. She needed someone who wouldn't bore her out of her mind.

Gianna wouldn't break up with me if I told her the bad stuff I'd gotten into trouble for and all the stuff I'd never got caught for. She'd still want to be with me. It wasn't like I did any of those things anymore. Not since I'd met her, anyways. To stay on the safe side, I wouldn't go into detail for her. She understood I'd been a troublemaker in the past and that was all she needed to know.

Walking through the front door, the house was quiet. Everyone was already in bed. Up in my room, I took out the drawing I'd been working on. I finished it and started a new one before falling asleep.

I woke up the next day to the sound of a lawnmower running in the backyard. Lifting my head enough to look out the window, I saw my dad pushing it around the backyard. It was past eleven and Gianna could already be on her way home. The thought woke me up the rest of the way.

After getting showered and dressed, I tried calling Gianna's phone but it went straight to voicemail. I left the message, "Hey, this is Caleb. Just wondering when you're going to be home. Call me." Jeez, I hoped I didn't sound as pathetic as the girls who left voicemails on my phone.

Having nothing better to do, I went downstairs to see what the food situation was. Chance played video games as usual. I found Julie in the kitchen making pies. Every time I encountered this woman she was doing some stereotypical housewife thing. Even when she watched television she had knitting needles in her hands.

Julie chided me while I made a bowl of cereal, "Caleb, you should've told me you were hungry. I could've made you chocolate chip pancakes."

Chocolate chip pancakes? "Uh, no thanks, Julie. You seem pretty busy there, with that pie."

"Are you sure? It'd really be no problem." Her smile reminded me of the freaky housewife in that Soundgarden "Black Hole Sun" video.

"I'm fine with cereal," I assured her. Was this woman on happy pills or something? She was like a Stepford wife.

"Have you talked to Gianna? I've been calling her all morning but her phone isn't on." Julie asked while rolling out dough.

"No," I answered, feeling like I was doing something wrong. Could she just stop talking to me?

"Those cheerleaders she went camping with are good girls, so I know she's safe with them. I wonder if that nice Josh boy went with them. I still don't understand why they broke up. He's the type of guy who'll really make something of himself."

"Yeah, he's wonderful," I agreed bitingly. It went right over her head. How would she react when she found out the truth about me and Gianna?

"I hope she comes home with the good news that she's back on the squad." Julie was delusional. Gianna used to love cheerleading but Julie was the one who ruined it for her. Gianna's old life and old boyfriend were the last things she needed.

"I'm going to go play video games with Chance," I muttered, escaping her company.

That evening, it was getting late and still no word from Gianna. I'd called her several more times and her phone was still off. I hadn't left any more voicemails, but did text her twice. It wouldn't do to come off as obsessive or possessive. The lack of communication had better not have anything to do with Jared. Maybe she was avoiding me on purpose. Maybe she'd changed her mind and planned on breaking up with me.

For the next few hours I continued to play video games then watch a movie with Chance while pathetically waiting around the house for my girlfriend to show up. I never thought I'd be in this situation. Finally, at eight o'clock, Chance had to get ready for bed. I was starting to get really worried about Gianna and a little pissed. Either something happened to her or she'd dumped me for Jared.

I went upstairs and grabbed a six pack of beer I'd hidden in my closet. Sneaking past everyone, I exited the house through the front door. I drank my warm beer while sitting on the side of the garage.

Gianna had better have a good explanation for not being home yet. Lots of horrible images ran through my head. Gianna dead on the side of the road somewhere. Gianna kidnapped by bikers. Gianna doing another dance for Jared, this time without clothes.

Many dark thoughts, three beers and an hour later, I spotted headlights coming from down the street. Gianna pulled her Jeep into the garage and I slipped inside before the garage door closed. As she climbed out of her Jeep I grabbed her from behind, making her yelp.

"Where the hell have you been?" The three beers had only fueled my anger.

With her back to me, she said, "I told you I needed time alone to think."

"You haven't been with Jared this whole time, have you? Why haven't you answered your phone?"

"Because my phone died last night and I didn't have my car charger because it's in *your* car. And, no, I haven't been with Jared this whole time. I dropped him and Cece off at home hours ago."

"Then where the hell have you been?" I was no longer angry, just annoyed.

"Here and there, nowhere special," she answered vaguely.

Her evasion pissed me off all over again. "Did Jared try anything last night after I left?"

She turned around slowly, giving me a guilty look. "Caleb, I have to tell you something." Taking a big breath, she continued, "I'm not a virgin anymore."

I grasped her shoulders and yelled, "What? I'll fucking murder him."

She started laughing. "Oh my god, you should have seen your face. Of course nothing happened with Jared. He may be all for making moves if you and I aren't together, but he's a good friend. He waited until I broke up with Josh to kiss me for the first time and he'll respect our relationship as long as we're together."

"Do we still have a relationship?" I asked warily. "While you were getting your thinking done, here and there, what conclusion did you come to?"

She looked thoughtful, tilting her head in an adorable manner. "I don't know. I need an answer about something from you first."

Crap, what could she want to know? "What's the question?"

Her gorgeous eyes studied my face. "When Hailey threw herself at you last night, what did you do?"

"How the hell did you know about that?"

She rolled her eyes. "Quit looking at me like I'm psychic. It was so obvious she was desperate and going to try something to steal you from me. You didn't answer the question, Caleb."

She should be happy with my answer. "I pushed her off me and told her I didn't want any girl but you. I'm not sure that we're even friends anymore."

Gianna threw her arms around my neck. "Then I totally forgive you!"

"I don't know if I forgive *you,*" I told her sternly.

She pulled back with her mouth open. "What did I do?"

"You worried the crap out of me, not coming home or calling all day." I gave her a fake glare, making her giggle.

"My mom!" she squeaked. "I need to go inside and let her know I'm home."

Before she could move away I grabbed her arm. "Your mom thinks you're with the cheerleaders. You could come home next week and she wouldn't care. I, on the other hand, need to kiss my girlfriend." My kiss was filled with the relief of finally having everything fixed between us.

"What did you do all day?" I asked when it was over.

She took a step back from me. "You know, this and that."

"No, I don't know. Why don't you explain it to me since I don't speak cryptic?"

She smiled mischievously. "I hooked up with some street dancers down on 16th street. Then I went to see Donna."

"What'd you go to see her for? Your design is still upstairs."

Gianna took another step back. "Oh nothing, I just got a piercing."

She quickly lifted up her shirt, flashing a pierced belly button. When she brought her shirt back down, my eyes went to her face to see her enticing grin. I reached for her, but she dodged me and ran into the house.

The little tease.

How long did it take for a navel piercing to heal? I'd have to look it up on the internet because I was gonna need to lick her there. Soon.

CHAPTER TWENTY-SIX

"I think beauty comes from within, and society paints a ridiculous picture."
-Rachel Bilson

GIANNA

"Caleb, stop!"

"Come on, just one more time," he begged.

"Ugh, fine! I should've known you'd have some sort of fetish, with all the piercings you have." I lifted up my shirt for the hundredth time so Caleb could look at my navel piercing.

Dropping my shirt, my stomach was covered up again. "Was that so hard?" Caleb joked.

"No, but it was so annoying," I teased him back.

"Admit it, baby. You got the piercing just for me to see, so don't complain." He wrapped his arms around my waist, kissing me sweetly.

"Not everything is about you, Caleb. I got it for me." I acted annoyed, but gladly kissed him again.

We were in the kitchen after school on Thursday, making popcorn for the movie we were going to watch. "Everything about you is about me now, too," he said as he grabbed two cans of soda out of the fridge.

How did I argue against that kind of charm?

"Whatever, sweet talker. Let's go watch zombies eat people who can't run fast enough."

We watched *Dawn of the Dead*, so romantic. Caleb couldn't keep his hands or mouth to himself during the movie. "Caleb, we may as well turn the movie off. You aren't even watching it."

"I'd rather watch you do a little dance for me." He grinned wickedly. "Why don't we go upstairs to my room?"

"Okay."

His surprised face made me laugh. I took off like a shot. As I ran up the stairs, his pounding tread close behind made my heart race faster. He entered his room at my heels and I yelped as he picked me up in the air and tossed me onto his bed. In a move that rivaled dancer-like gracefulness, he landed gently on top of me. Threading my fingers through his hair, I urged him on.

I let one hand drop down beside my head where it landed on something sticking out from under the pillow. Twisting my head off the pillow, I yanked it out. Caleb didn't notice because he was busy on my other side, making a trail of kisses along my jaw and down my neck. I lifted the notepad over his head.

Gasping at what I saw, it spurred Caleb to catch my lips with his. The boy could kiss, making me forget about the notepad in my hand. It dropped from my hand onto his back.

"What's that?" He stopped kissing me to see what hit him.

"Your drawing pad."

He shot up straight, snatching it out of my hand. "I'll take that."

Smiling as I guided him down for a kiss, I told him, "It's too late. I already saw it."

"It's not supposed to be you," he said, looking uncharacteristically embarrassed.

"Uh-huh, sure," I agreed unconvincingly. "Can I see the picture of me again?"

"No." He reached over to drop it in his nightstand drawer. I laughed inwardly. Like I couldn't find it there when he wasn't around.

Actually, I'd just get it now. I quickly opened the drawer, dug it out and rolled to the other side of the bed onto my stomach. I stared down at the still opened page. There was a picture of an angel that bore a remarkable resemblance to me. The angel wore a long flowing white dress and had thick white feathered wings. "I think it's beautiful."

He grunted, taking it away from me again to put it back in the drawer. "It's nothing."

That was the thing, though. It wasn't nothing. It was *everything*. Being told you're beautiful your whole life was one thing. Actually feeling like you were, inside and out, was something else. Until I met Caleb, I wasn't sure beauty existed on my inside. With him in my life, I not only saw that beauty to my core, but also in my world around me. This drawing proved he saw that beauty in me.

I could tell he wasn't comfortable with me finding the sketch, so I sort of changed the subject. "You're a really good artist,

Caleb. Why don't you take art class at school?"

"High school art class is for pansies." He laid on his side next to me with one elbow propping up his head.

I rolled my eyes at his assessment. "Art class is for artists and you should be in it."

He gave me a look like I didn't know what I was talking about. "I'm not taking art."

"Fine, don't take art at school, but how about a class outside of school? Come on, you might even get to do a nude drawing. Of a woman," I hastily added.

He raised one eyebrow. "Really, naked chicks? Sign me up."

Realizing he was only teasing me, I smacked him on the chest playfully. "Yeah, well won't you be surprised when I volunteer to be the nude model."

The chest my hand still rested on shook as he laughed. "It won't be much of a surprise now since you've already told me." He gave me a stern glare. "I'd drag you right out of there before you had the chance to drop your robe."

"You're not the boss of me," I teased.

"No, I'd never pretend to be that. But, I'm your boyfriend and I say who can and can't see you naked." He kissed me on the tip of my nose. "And I say only I can."

Typical boy, not willing to share his toys, not that this particular toy wanted to be shared. "Well, *boyfriend*, I have homework due tomorrow. I suggest you do the same. I'll be in my room and you're not welcome." I was so glad tomorrow was Friday.

"That reminds me. Don't make any plans for tomorrow night. We're going to do number twelve on your list."

"Number twelve?" I repeated, trying to remember which one that was.

"Yep, I'm taking you out clubbing and *you*, young lady, are allowed to get as drunk as you want but not so drunk you throw up in my Camaro."

"I'll say it again, Caleb. You have a way with words. You have to be the most romantic boyfriend ever."

"I'm romantic," he pouted.

Thinking of the drawing, I conceded, "I guess the drawing was pretty freaking romantic."

"Damn straight, girl. Now tell me why you've never gotten drunk while you were out clubbing."

"The only times I've gone to a club have been with the crew and I can't get drunk if I need to perform. Afterwards, we always go to someone's house to drink." I shrugged. "I sometimes get tipsy then."

"Is that the only reason?" he asked.

I don't want to think about the most important reason I don't drink at clubs. It was a year ago and I'm over it now, but not inclined to share. However, this was Caleb and I was beginning to believe I could tell him anything.

"Not the only reason. About a year ago, I went with some of the cheerleaders and football players to a club downtown. Some older guy I danced with bought me a drink and I was too dumb back then to realize what a mistake that was."

Caleb's unhappy expression made to want to stop the story there. "What happened after that?" he prompted.

"Don't worry. Someone stopped him before anything bad happened. My drink was obviously drugged and he almost got me out of the club, but one of the football players stopped him."

"Josh?" he guessed.

"Yeah, how'd you know? You have to understand Josh wasn't so bad back then. He was a really nice guy. He'd been asking me out for awhile and after he saved me from being raped by that creep, I finally gave him a chance."

Caleb made a disgusted face. "And that turned into a year-long relationship?"

"My heart never skipped a beat around him, but I was comfortable with him. It wasn't until we were together for awhile that I started to notice he was becoming obsessive." I didn't like to think about Josh. "Anyways, that's why I don't drink at clubs. I don't trust it."

"At least the psycho did something right in his life. Don't worry about tomorrow night. I'll be there and we'll have a good time."

I liked the promise of that. "Okay, but who's going to protect *your* virtue?"

"You can tread all over my virtue if you want," he offered while squeezing my hip.

"Um . . . *nah.* I'll pass," I teased him.

He pounced on me, caging me between his arms. "No girl can pass up on all this."

"Ugh, like I need the reminder. Get off, I have homework to do." Squirming out from under him, I escaped out of his room.

It was a good thing I'd left when I did because my mom was going up the stairs. Crap, I hadn't even heard her come home. "Hey, honey, how was your day?"

"Fine," I told her cautiously, recognizing from her tone she had something on her mind.

"Will you be cheering at the game tomorrow night?"

I should've known. "No, mom," I replied in a harassed tone. I was tired of her asking the same question.

My mom put the false smile on her face that I hated. "You know I only want what's best for you, honey. And I think-"

I cut her off before she could finish. "I know what *you* think what *you* want. I don't have time to hear it again, so if you don't mind, I have homework to do." I quickly shut myself in my room before she could say anything else.

Checking the time on my phone, I saw it was after six o'clock in Houston. My dad should've been off work by now. Calling him, I hoped he'd pick up.

He answered with, "Gianna?"

Just hearing his voice made me feel better. "Hi, dad."

"How's my baby girl doing?"

"Good, except mom's being a pain."

"Cheerleading still?"

I exhaled a big breath. "Of course. At least she isn't bugging me about quitting pageants anymore."

"You don't need judges to tell you if you're beautiful or not."

"Thanks, dad. That means a lot coming from a plastic surgeon," I joked.

"Brat," he said on a chuckle. "Now, when are you going to come down here to check out colleges? We never got around to it when you and Chance were here in July."

Remembering, I laughed. "Yeah, because we let Chance decide

what we'd do every day. I think I gained five pounds from eating so many donuts and cookies."

"I get you guys for Thanksgiving this year," my dad reminded me. "Your grandparents will be here from Florida and can watch Chance while we take off by ourselves."

"Okay, dad, but I don't know if any of the colleges down there can woo me away from Colorado."

"Houston and I will give it a good try, Gianna. I'd like to spend more time with you."

"You could always move back," I suggested for the millionth time.

"Perhaps," he said sadly. "I don't like missing out on so much of Chance growing up."

"He has Scott," I blurted out without thinking and added, "Sorry, dad."

"It's alright. I know he's close with Scott."

"You really could move back, though."

"Your mom," he began and left it at that. She'd never forgiven him for divorcing her, even after she married Scott. Whenever he came to visit she acted hostile. "I guess it'd be worth dealing with her to see my children more often."

"We are so worth it," I boasted, wanting to put him in a happier mood. "Guess what?"

"What?" he played along.

Dying to tell him about Caleb and me, but not enough to risk my mom finding out, I only told him, "Scott's son came to live with us."

"The delinquent?" he asked.

Play it cool, Gianna. "He's not so bad," I said lightly. "He's actually really nice to me and Chance." I couldn't resist tacking on, "But mom creeps him out."

My dad started laughing so hard I was afraid he'd have a stroke. Not that my dad was old enough for that. He was still only in his mid-thirties and, in my opinion, the coolest dad ever.

I got off the phone with my dad feeling much, much better.

CALEB

Friday after school, Gianna and I stopped by the house to each pack a bag for the weekend. She asked if we should invite any of our friends from school or any of the crew, but I wanted it to be just me and her. So often when we were together other people were around. I wanted her all to myself tonight.

It was embarrassing when she found the drawing yesterday, but I was over it now. I had trouble telling her how important she was to me, so hopefully seeing that drawing clued her in. She let me know a few times how unromantic I was, so maybe tonight I'd work on that.

The plan was to drive to my mom's place and get ready there. Then we'd go out and have a good time. She couldn't miss ballet tomorrow since she skipped last week to go camping. After ballet, she was going to practice with the crew and they'd do their thing tomorrow night.

Instead of her spending the night Saturday night at Jared and Cece's house, I planned on talking her into staying at my mom's with me. If she still insisted on keeping with tradition and staying at their house, I hoped Cece's bed was big enough for three. No way in hell was I letting her stay in the same house with Jared if I wasn't there. She claimed he'd respect our relationship, as long as I didn't fuck it up, but if he got desperate enough he'd probably try something.

I knew I sure as hell would try to steal her right out from under another guy.

Going into Gianna's room, I found her zipping up her duffel bag. I took it from her just as she was throwing it over one shoulder. "Let's go."

After I put the bags in the trunk, Gianna ran around to the driver's side before I climbed in. "Can I drive, Caleb?"

"No, we're taking my car," I told her.

"I know that and I want to drive your car." She clasped both her hands together. "Please?"

"No way, princess. I don't let anyone drive my car."

"Pretty please," she wheedled.

In answer, I moved her out of the way, pointing her in the

direction to go around the front of the car and smacking her ass to get her going.

"Oh okay," she said pathetically with her head down. She walked around the car and got in on the passenger side. She sat in her seat dejectedly as I started the car.

She looked so adorable when she was sad that it was making my chest tight. "Fine! You can drive! But if you even fail to use a blinker, you're pulling over and I'm driving."

She clapped her hands together. "Yay! Best boyfriend ever!"

Instead of getting out of the car, she climbed to my side as I opened the door. I thought she would maybe give me a reward for being the best boyfriend ever, but all I got was a push to help me out of the car.

"Get out and go around," she ordered excitedly. That was all the thanks I got for letting her drive my baby?

Feeling weird, I sat in the passenger seat for the first time. She had a big grin on her face as she hit the gas. I grabbed the dashboard. "Slower, Gianna."

She glanced sideways. "Slower? Really? I always took you for a harder and faster kind of guy." Now she flirted with me, when I couldn't touch her for fear she'd crash my car.

"Don't try to distract me with your naughty words, seductress. I'm watching the speedometer and I better not see you go a mile over the speed limit."

She turned the radio up to drown out the end of my lecture. By the time we reached the parking garage near my mom's place, I was relieved Gianna respected all road signs and speed limits. However as soon as she parked, I snatched the keys out of her hand.

I retrieved our bags from the back. "I hope you enjoyed that, because it won't happen again."

She pressed her body against mine and licked my bottom lip. "Are you sure?"

"Very," I managed, staying strong.

She rubbed her chest against me and repeated, "Are you sure?"

"Mostly." I was getting so turned on now.

She grabbed my hand and put it on her chest. "Can I please drive your car again, sometime?"

"Oh hell yeah," I practically moaned as her hand went to the front of my pants.

She laughed and darted away. "That's what I thought, master player. You're too easy."

"Only around you," I mumbled to myself, watching her ass as she walked ahead of me.

CHAPTER TWENTY-SEVEN

"There's beauty to wisdom and experience that cannot be faked. It's impossible to be mature without having lived."
-Amy Grant

CALEB

My mom was out of town again so I told Gianna she could use my mom's bathroom to get ready for tonight. After a shower, I took more thought in getting ready than usual. In a pair of black dress pants and a blue dress shirt and skinny tie, I stood in front of the mirror styling my hair with a little pomade.

I'd been on lots of dates before, but this was different. Tonight was about more than meaningless flirtation and a good time in bed. This was about romance. What the fuck did I know about romance? Obviously not much from what Gianna's teasing indicated.

I did feel romantic towards Gianna, I supposed. The problem was my inability to show it with actions and words. I was going to work on that tonight. I wanted her to know how much she meant to me. In the short amount of time I'd know her, she'd become the person my world centered around. That person used to be myself. I'd left behind a life that now disgusted me by finding something special with her.

God, I hoped I didn't turn into one of those pathetic guys who held their girlfriend's purse while watching her shop. I felt like I was becoming pussy-whipped without actually getting to enjoy the pussy. Shaking my head, I shoved aside those kinds of thoughts. Tonight was supposed to be about romance, not about my lack a sex life in recent weeks.

All in good time.

When I was ready, I waited in the living room on the couch. As I sat there, flipping through channels, Gianna strutted out from my mom's room. My mouth dropped open and I snapped it shut. She wore a dark blue dress that covered only the tops of her thighs and some black heeled ankle boots.

"What?" Gianna scanned the front of her body as if something might be out of place.

"Nothing." My first instinct was to throw her over my shoulder and carry her to my bed. Instead, I walked over and kissed her lightly on the lips, not wanting to ruin her lipstick. "You look beautiful."

She smiled up at me. "So, do you."

"Not exactly what I was going for, but as long as you're dying to rip my clothes off, I'm satisfied," I teased.

"I so didn't say that and you know it." She tried for a stern expression but it melted away when she giggled.

"I could tell by the look on your face you were thinking it. I recognize that look on a girl's face when I see it." As soon as the words left my mouth, I wished I could take them back. It was another example of the unromantic things I said to her which reminded her of what a manwhore I'd been in the past.

"You know, Caleb-" she started to say and I could easily guess the rest of it.

I cut her off before she could finish, "Forget what I just said. All other girls are ugly dogs and you're the most beautiful girl in the world."

She smirked. "That's more like it."

I cleared my throat and looked at her pointedly. She returned my look with a confused one. "What?"

"This is where you compliment me back. The romance goes both ways in a relationship."

She raised two perfect eyebrows. "Oh really? You want to be romanced? Since you're such an expert on relationships, what should I say?"

This playful banter was fun. Stroking my chin, I pretended to think really hard. "Well, you could say, wow, Caleb, you look so sexy I just want to rip off your clothes and lick you all over. A guy couldn't hear sweeter words than that."

Gianna rubbed her forehead like dealing with me was taxing, but I could tell that she was trying not to laugh. "A guy would think that was a romantic thing to say, wouldn't he?"

"Very."

She took the hand I held out. "Well, I wouldn't want to be unromantic, so I'll say this. Caleb, you look very sexy, handsome and lickable."

I locked the door behind us and put my arm around her waist. "Now, that wasn't so hard, was it?"

"I never said it was, but now that you've had your ego stroked, can you tell me where we're going?"

"Gladly. First, I'm taking you out to a nice romantic dinner. Then, to a club where you'll be free to drink girly drinks and dance to your heart's content, while I stand sober guard."

Gianna entered the elevator before me, turning around. "Caleb?"

"Yes?"

"You don't have to try so hard to be romantic. I like you for who you are, despite the very unromantic things you say." She wrapped her arms around me, leaning her cheek into my chest.

In a millisecond I'd processed her words. "Thank god," I breathed out, relieved.

Grabbing the back of her thighs, I lifted her up to wrap her legs around my waist. Her gaze found mine, her blue eyes startled. I pushed her back against the wall of the elevator and went to town on her with my mouth.

"In that case, can I just say that you look so fucking hot in this dress? Every time I look at you in it, I want to peel if off you and use it to tie you to my bed."

She laughed in delight. "There's my special guy."

The elevator doors opened and I reluctantly placed her back on her feet. On the way to my car, I asked her, "Does this mean you'll be happy if I don't take you to the fancy restaurant I book a reservation at?"

She squeezed my hand. "I'll be happy no matter where you take me."

"Where I'd like to take you is to bed. But I haven't been to the diner in forever and I'm also starving for food. We'll go there, if you don't mind." I opened the passenger door for her when we reached my car. I may not have been the most romantic guy, but I could still be a gentleman.

"This time can I order for myself?" she asked once I got behind the wheel.

"Only if it's something I like, so I can eat your leftovers."

"You're horrible," she scolded.

"No, I'm sexy, handsome and lickable. You said so yourself." I pulled out of the parking garage in the direction of the diner. It wasn't far from the apartment, but far enough not to want to walk.

Gianna leaned over to squeeze one of my cheeks. "Yes, you're those things too, babe."

We sat at one of Jean's tables at the diner and she squeezed my other cheek. What the hell? Was I that adorable today? Her smile was motherly. "How's the new school, Caleb?"

"Great." I gestured to Gianna. "You remember my stepsister, Gianna?"

Jean gave her the same smile but left her cheeks alone. "Yes, nice to see you again, Gianna. What can I get for you two?"

I ordered my usual and Gianna ordered something I wouldn't mind eating the rest of. We managed to finish our meal without any girls from my past showing up. After I paid for our meal, we walked back to my car and drove to a club where I knew the bouncers. I had a fake ID, but I wasn't sure Gianna did.

On the way there, I finally thought to ask her, "Do you have a fake ID?"

"Yep." She took it out of her purse and handed it to me.

I read off the name. "Gigi Ramirez. Isn't that Jared and Cece's last name? Funny, you don't look Hispanic."

"Jared got it for me." She put it back in her wallet.

"He gave you his last name? Remind me to get you a new fake ID," I muttered. I'd let her keep that one for now. It figured the douche would do something so cheesy.

We didn't have to wait in line outside the club since Ned was manning the door. I joked around with him before we went inside. Ned was a nice guy despite appearances. He shaved his head and wore a tight black t-shirt that showed off his huge biceps and two arms covered in tattoos.

I introduced them, "Ned, this is my girlfriend, Gianna."

"Girlfriend?" Ned repeated skeptically. "You mean, you actually claim this one out of the bedroom, Caleb?"

Gianna put out her hand. "Nice to meet you, Ned. Where did you and Caleb meet? In prison?"

Ned looked at me, still holding onto my girl's hand. "I like this one."

"I'm flattered," Gianna said sarcastically.

"And I'm charmed," Ned complimented, totally ignoring the line waiting to get in. "Actually, Caleb and I met when he was twelve. He showed up here with a shitty fake ID. When I called him on it, he tried to talk me into letting him in. He told me that middle school boys needed to get laid too. I told him to get his scrawny ass to the mall if he wanted somewhere to hang out. When I didn't let him in, he started showing up every so often with his friend Dante. They would hang out at the door with me. Once they started growing some fuzz on their faces a few years later, I started letting them past the front door."

"And now I get to benefit from their hormones' hard at work. Do you need to see my fake ID?" Gianna asked like a smartass.

"No, you two kids have fun inside." Ned waved us in, shaking head big head.

"Thanks for telling my girlfriend an embarrassing story, Ned. See you on the way out." Holding her close, I guided Gianna inside.

Ned called after me, "I've got more where that came from!"

Maybe I'd take her to a different club next time. Somewhere where the bouncers hadn't carried me out drunk or broken up catfights I'd unintentionally caused.

The music pounded inside and I led her to the bar. Ordering us both a drink from the bartender I sat Gianna down on an empty stool. The stools on both sides of her were taken, so I stood behind her with one arm around her waist. That was a sure way to keep other guys away. Once we were both finished with our first drink, Gianna pulled me onto the dance floor. After two songs, I pulled her back to the bar for drink number two.

Still working on our second drinks, someone I really didn't want to see showed up. Actually, I'd been hoping to never see this fucker again.

He shouted over the music, "What's up, Caleb? Still on probation?" I could see Gianna's eyes dart to his face. I really hoped she didn't hear that.

Holy shit, I wanted to beat this prick's ass. "Fuck off, Ian!"

"Is that any way to greet an old friend?" His expression was of mock hurt.

"We were never friends. By the way, how's Jackie? Are you two still together?" I asked him. His pissed off face made me smile evilly. He'd really liked Jackie. Unfortunately, she'd cheated on him with me. Stupid prick had asked for it.

"What school are you going to now, Caleb? Gotten expelled lately?" I was thinking about whether or not I should be punching anybody while on a date with Gianna when she stood up to step between us. It wasn't lost on me the way Ian's eyes roved over her face and body.

"Aren't you going to introduce us, Caleb?" She a placed one hand on my chest and I put one of my own over it, a gesture which Ian didn't miss.

"No," I replied stubbornly.

The prick introduced himself, "I'm Ian Crenshaw. Caleb and I go way back. What can I call you other than beautiful?" With lame lines like that, no wonder Jackie preferred me between her legs.

One side of Gianna's gorgeous lips twitched. "I'm Gianna, Caleb's girlfriend."

"Girlfriend?" he mouthed in astonishment just to be an ass. "What school do you go to?" The nosy prick wouldn't be asking without a reason.

"Don't worry about it-" I began.

"Broomfield," Gianna answered innocently.

Ian's grin was predatory. "Do you like it there? I'm thinking of switching schools." Fucker probably got expelled and was on the prowl for new stomping grounds.

"It's alright, especially since Caleb showed up." That was my girl. As if Ian hadn't been eating her up with his eyes, she turned to me. "Let's go dance!" She grabbed my hand. "See you later, Ian."

Yeah, peace out, you fucking douchebag.

On the dance floor, I yelled in her ear. "If that guy ever comes near you when I'm not around, don't talk to him."

"Don't worry. I have a good idea of what it's like between you two!" Her body melted into mine as we got lost in each other and the music.

Ian stayed away from us the rest of the night, but I did spot him from afar. By the time we left, I could definitely cross off number twelve on the list. Gianna was adorably drunk. Helping her to my car, I buckled her into the passenger seat. She stopped me from shutting the door to lay a big one on me, almost missing my mouth.

I put her hands on her lap and told her to behave before closing the door. Back at the parking garage, I made her sit in the car until I could help her out. "Gianna, I don't think you're going to make it to ballet tomorrow."

"I don't think so either," she said, sounding forlorn. "But it was worth it."

"So you had a good time?"

She would've stumbled if my arm weren't anchoring her. "Yep. Caleb?" Her eyes were glazed over as she looked up at me.

"Yes, princess?" I kissed her on the cheek and she giggled.

"Why are you on probation?" Damn, she did hear that bigmouth.

"Because I'm a juvenile delinquent," I answered simply while holding open the door of the apartment building.

"Oh." She looked confused but not coherent enough to follow it up with another question.

I pushed the button for the elevator and changed the subject. "Are you hungry?"

"I don't think so."

"Well, I'm going to feed you anyways. It'll help prevent a killer hangover in the morning." Holding onto her, we waited for the elevator to hit the right floor.

In the apartment, Gianna unexpectedly pushed me onto the couch to straddle me. "Let's have sex, Caleb."

I groaned in torment. "Gianna, why couldn't you suggest this when you were sober?"

"Who cares when I say it?" she said airily as she unbuttoned my shirt.

"I care and so should you, bad girl. You might be too drunk to even remember it in the morning." I moved her off my lap to her displeasure and escaped into the kitchen. "I'm going to make some you something to eat."

"You suck," I heard her mumble.

I'd never been the type of guy to take advantage of a girl while she was drunk. I was sure pricks like Ian did that crap all the time.

Because of his big mouth, I wasn't looking forward to Gianna interrogating me about being on probation once she was sober.

Gianna only ate half her sandwich before declaring herself stuffed. Yawning, she was turning into a sleepy drunk. I gave her two aspirin and held the cup of water as she swallowed them down. "Ready for bed?"

"Yeah," was her answer but she didn't move.

Carrying her to my bed, I set her down on it and took off her boots. I found her pajamas in her bag and helped her change while keeping my eyes mostly on her face. I didn't need any more temptation tonight.

"Caleb?"

"Yes, princess?"

"Why don't you want to have sex with me? Is it because I'm a virgin and I'll be a bad lay?" She climbed under the covers and was having trouble keeping her eyes open.

I chuckled at her ignorance. "Of course not. I just don't think we should rush it. I want you to be sure."

"I think I'm sure," she mumbled.

"Goodnight." I kissed her on the mouth long and hard because it was all I'd get tonight.

She laid her head back on the pillow with her eyes closed. "I love you," she said softly. She didn't open her eyes again.

Jolted, I sat on the edge of the bed watching her sleep. Did she mean that? Did she say that because she was drunk or because she was tired? Did she even realize who she was saying it to? If she did mean it, did I feel the same way? I really doubt she'd remember saying it in the morning.

If she didn't remember, I'd just pretend it never happened.

CHAPTER TWENTY-EIGHT

"I find beauty in unusual things, like hanging your head out the window or sitting on a fire escape."
-Scarlett Johansson

GIANNA

When I woke up the next morning my mouth felt dry. I must've been dehydrated from drinking so much alcohol last night. Slowly opening my eyes, I stared at the ceiling. Not too bad, I didn't think I was going to throw up or anything. Wondering if I'd missed ballet, I turned my head to find out the time.

"You missed class," I heard Caleb say.

Rolling my head the other way, I found Caleb propped up on one elbow, staring down at me. Had he been watching me sleep?

Pushing the thought aside, I groaned. "My instructor is going to be so mad."

Caleb shrugged one shoulder. "What can she do to you? Take away your favorite tutu?"

I laughed, placing one hand over my eyes. "We don't wear tutus in class, only in performances and only sometimes then. Besides, you've never experienced the wrath of a little old Russian lady. She could even whip you into shape, Caleb."

Caleb was silent, so I removed my hand from over my eyes to look up at him. He had a thoughtful look on his gorgeous face. "How do you feel?"

"I haven't sat up yet, but I don't feel nauseous. I'm very dehydrated though."

He pushed me back down as I try to sit up and hopped out of bed. "Wait here. I'll get you some water."

"Thanks," I sighed, glad not to get up yet. While he was gone, I thought back on last night. The last thing I remembered was leaving the club.

After that, *nada*.

Caleb returned and handed me a glass of water. I sat up and guzzled it down. Caleb stood a couple feet away from the bed with a weird look on his face. I unashamedly checked him out in his boxer briefs. My guy was hot.

"I'll make some breakfast." He exited the room so fast I began to wonder if I'd done something embarrassing last night. He would tell me if I did, right? I couldn't see him missing an opportunity to tease me.

I was only a little dizzy when I stood up. Grabbing my duffel bag, I went into the bathroom to shower. A shower and brushing my teeth were definitely in order.

Thirty minutes later I walked into the kitchen where Caleb was already sitting at the table eating. He motioned for me to sit down in front of where he'd already served me. He still wasn't acting like himself and avoided my eyes.

"So anyways," I began. "What did we do after the club?"

He met my gaze looking suspiciously relieved. "You don't remember?"

"I remember up until we left the club and after that, nothing. Why? Did something happen?" Now I was beginning to think I'd done something crazy like streak through downtown naked.

"No, nothing happened," he assured me with a blank face. "We came back here, had a snack and you went to sleep."

"Oh, from what I remember, I had a good time. We'll have to do that again. Next time we could invite some friends."

Caleb finished eating and went to take a shower. I ate my food then cleaned up the mess in the kitchen. While waiting for him, I flipped through the channels. He appeared back to normal when he sat down on the cushion next to me and pulled me onto his lap. "I'm glad you had fun last night. I had fun watching you have fun."

"I didn't do anything stupid?"

"Nothing stupid," he reassured me.

I studied his face for a few more moments. Something had been up with him earlier. "I'm glad you had fun too."

"What time do you have to be at Cece's house?" he asked, rubbing circles on my back with his thumb.

"Not for two more hours." His touch was soothing and I burrowed my head into his neck.

"Do you want to go for a walk?"

I lift my head to look at him. "Sure."

Getting a pair of sneakers out of my bag in his room, I slipped them on. The weather was perfect outside. We leisurely strolled around the trendy downtown neighborhood for about an hour. He was sort of giving me a tour since all I'd seen of his neighborhood so far was the short walk between the parking garage and the apartment building. Caleb greeted a few people he knew, mostly girls. He told me he and his mom had lived here since the divorce.

When it was time to head over to Jared and Cece's house, we picked up my bag at the apartment. Caleb eyed my bag. "You could just leave it here."

"Well," I said drolly, "I'll need pajamas to change into tonight and clothes to wear tomorrow."

"You'll be wearing those pajamas here tonight and changing into those clothes here tomorrow morning," he insisted.

I was holding my duffel bag over one shoulder and I noticed he didn't offer to carry like he usually did. "Since when do you tell me what to do?"

"You're my girlfriend. My place is wherever you are and vice versa." He crossed his arms over his chest as if he weren't going to budge on the issue. "And I really don't want to have a sleepover at Jared's house. I don't think he'd appreciate me sharing a bed with you and Cece."

I laughed. "You're right, he wouldn't. Fine, we'll come back here, but I still need to take my bag because it has my outfit for tonight." Why not give in? It wasn't as if I wanted to be apart from him.

He narrowed his eyes at the bag. "Alright, I guess you'll need to take your bag."

"Jeez, thanks for permission, master," I joked sarcastically. Caleb was just too funny when he got possessive. I couldn't believe what he'd said about his place being wherever I was. It was funny how he could be sweet and bossy at the same time.

He turned around after opening the apartment door. "What are you smiling about?"

I wiped the smirk off my face. "Nothing."

"Uh-huh, sure. Let's go, princess." He motions for me to lead the way and locked the door behind us. He grabbed my bag out of my hand while I hit the elevator button to go down.

The whole crew was at the house. Cece came up to give me a

hug. "Where were you this morning? You missed ballet!"

I looked at her guiltily. "I had a bit of a hangover."

"What? You got drunk without me last night? How much did you drink? You never do that! Where was the party?" Cece didn't know how to limit her questions to one at a time.

"Yes, I got pretty drunk off about five drinks, but not at a party, at a club." I answered all of her questions in one go.

"At a club? With who? Didn't you say you weren't going to do that ever again after you-know-what happened? Are you okay?" Cece's questions were beginning to give me a headache.

"Don't worry, I was with Caleb."

"Oh, okay." She settled down and I guessed that was a good enough answer for her.

Jared walked into the garage and immediately spotted Caleb sitting on the couch up against the wall. Caleb smirked at him and Jared got a sour look on his face. "God, what's he doing here again?"

"*He* is my boyfriend and likes to watch us practice. You guys bring your little girlfriends all the time so why can't I bring my boyfriend?"

"Whatever, just tell him to stay out of my way." What a big baby he was.

We practiced for the next few hours and Caleb actually fell asleep. Either that or he was pretending to sleep to avoid talking to a girl one of the guys brought. At least I liked to think so.

After we were done practicing, a group of us went to the Ramirez family's restaurant. I loved their parents. They were always eager to feed people and I was one of their favorite people to feed. It worked out well all the way around. Afterwards, we went back to their house to change.

Cece rode with me and Caleb to the club we were dancing at tonight. Club owners paid dancers like us to show up and add some excitement to their atmosphere. Thank god for those dancing competition reality shows on television. They helped crews like us find gigs by adding to our popularity.

We did the routine we worked all afternoon on. Taye got the idea a couple weeks back for the routine while he was watching *Braveheart*. We all had one side of our face painted blue and were each wearing at least one piece of plaid clothing.

Cece and I had our hair plaited. We also put blue eyeshadow on our eyelid that was on the bare side of our face. She and I were both wearing red plaid skirts with black tank tops and black leggings underneath. Jared wore a red plaid hoodie and Taye wore red plaid cargo pants. All of the guys managed to find some clothing item to wear that was red plaid, whether it was on their head, body or feet. Any other clothing was black.

The music we'd chosen was an instrumental version of Eminem's "Bagpipes from Baghdad." Our routine consisted of a lot of aggressive popping and locking, plus some breaking. The crowd loved it. Making our performances a little theatrical made sure the club promoters remembered us and thought to book us again.

Dante met us at the club which I took as meaning he was really into Cece. I'd have a talk with the boy about treating my girl right, even if Jared already beat me to it. Cece was so sweet it made her a target for guys trying to take advantage of it. Caleb's best friend or not, Dante needed to know not to mess around when it came to her.

After our performance, Caleb embraced me tightly. "You did good, little warrior."

To give credit to where it was due, Ezra and Taye were the best breakers in the group while Jared was the best at popping. Cece and I had skills, but sometimes I worried we were more eye candy to our audience than anything else.

But other than skill, the most important part of dancing was confidence, so I told Caleb smugly, "I know."

"So it's like that, is it? Little b-girl has a big dancing ego?" he teased.

"Yep, it's the one thing I know I rock at."

He kissed me while gripping my butt. "Do you want to go back to my place?"

Before I could answer, Cece bounced up to us with Dante right behind. "Come on, guys, I want to go home and wash this paint off my face."

I laughed while wiping some blue paint off Caleb's cheek. "My mom is out of town, how about we go there?" Caleb offered.

"No way! Jared would kill me, plus I need to change at my

house."

"My bag is at her place anyways," I reminded Caleb.

He got an annoyed look on his face. "Fine, we'll go there first."

Cece ditched us to ride with Dante in his car, so it was just me and Caleb. Jared was about as interested in spending time with Caleb as Caleb was with him. When we got there, Jared and they guys didn't show up the entire time Cece and I were showering and getting ready again. Cece and I grabbed beers out of the fridge and took them to our boyfriends in the living room. I had no interest in drinking after the night before.

When Jared and the guys showed up, we were sitting on our boyfriends' laps. Cece quickly jumped off Dante. The girl could move fast. I'd sit on my man's lap if I want to. Jared wasn't the boss of me.

Following the guys into the house was a group of five girls. I didn't know them and from the way they were dressed and acting, I didn't want to know them. Cece and I were always irritated when the boys brought girls like this home from a club or battle.

They said *oh my god* every other sentence and screeched when they were drunk instead of talking in normal tones. They needed to learn to use their inside voices. To get attention from the guys they acted like complete idiots. Some of the guys would definitely get laid, which was why they brought the girls along.

"Oh my god, Caleb!" one of the idiots screeched.

"Damn," I heard Caleb mumble.

The idiot teetered over on her stilettos and plopped down next to my boyfriend. *Uh, hello, I'm sitting on his freaking lap! No matter how close you move next to him, I'm still closer!*

"Caleb! Where've you been? You never called me! I thought you liked me!" The idiot needed to shut her trap.

"Oh, um, hey, um. . . ." Caleb's discomfort was the only funny thing in this situation. He glanced at me and I stayed mute, merely raising my eyebrows at him.

"What's the matter, Caleb? Are you feeling alright?" The idiot actually had the nerve to place her hand on my boyfriend's forehead as if to check for a fever.

I'd had enough. Grabbing her wrist, I flung her arm away. "Nothing is wrong with him except while his girlfriend is sitting on his lap, some one night stand from his past shows up and he can't even remember her name."

"Oh my god! You did not just talk to me like that! I'll have you know that Caleb and I spent a beautiful night together! It was magical!" The idiot screeched and whined at the same time. *Talented.*

"Caleb, baby?" I said sweetly.

"Yes, princess?"

"What is this slut's, sorry, I mean girl's name?"

"Hell if I know," he answered, shrugging.

I bit back my laughter as the girl's face turned red. She swiftly stomped back to her OMG posse. First thing I heard her say to them was, "Oh my God!" Then it was like, "Blah, blah, blah, screech!"

At the end of her spiel, the volume in the room turned up. All of the OMG girls were trying to screech over each other in outrage. They were reassuring what's-her-name that she was the best, most beautiful, better than me and didn't need a guy like Caleb in her life. The song "Stupid Girls" by Pink began playing in my head. Unfortunately, not loudly enough to drown them out.

Caleb was shaking in silent laughter. I couldn't take it anymore. "That's it! Caleb and I are out of here!" I announced to the room.

"Don't leave me, Gianna! Take me with you!" Cece shouted dramatically.

While Jared was in the shower, Cece and I grabbed our things and snuck out with the guys. We ran out of the house, laughing as we saw one girl stumble into another in a drunken mess. It caused them all to start tumbling like dominos.

Jared was going to be so pissed when Cece didn't come home tonight, but he'd cover for her with their parents anyways. He was a good brother like that.

As Dante and Cece followed in his car, I finally let out my frustration towards Caleb. "Is that going to happen on a regular basis? How many girls have you slept with, Caleb?"

"Shit," he muttered. "I was just waiting for you to bitch me out over it."

Turning in my seat, I asked him, "Do you think I should be

okay with all these damn girls?"

"No, of course not."

"How would you feel if I'd slept with a ton of guys who all came sniffing around trying to get seconds?"

"I'd have very sore knuckles," he responded, staring at the road ahead. "I can't change my past, Gianna."

But would he even want to?

"Never mind," I told him, feeling ready to cry and not wanting to go there. Instead, I turned towards the window so I wouldn't embarrass myself if a few tears slipped out.

When he parked in his spot, he unbuckled my seatbelt and dragged me over to him. I hid my face in his chest, not wanting him to see how upset I was.

"I'm sorry, princess."

I nodded against his chest. Reaching out, I pushed open the door and climbed out from his side. Before he could see, I wiped under my eyes. He took my hand and we met Dante and Cece where they waited in front of the apartment building.

We mostly just chilled the rest of the night. When Cece used the restroom, I verbally pounced on Dante. I let him know Cece started the night as a virgin and she'd better end it that way. No deflowering on my watch. During our little chat, Caleb just looked up at the ceiling like he had nothing to do with the conversation, all but whistling to himself. Dante was a good sport. I thought Taye or Jared may have already given him the same talk.

The next morning, Dante took Cece home and I warned him to drop her off at the curb and speed away. *Beware Jared.* Caleb made me breakfast again and I cleaned up afterwards. It was homey, but I was still slightly upset about the night before.

After breakfast, Caleb asked, "How would you feel about doing number five today?"

Number five was a big deal. "Tattoo?"

"Only if you want to, it's sort of an important decision," Caleb said seriously.

I thought about it for a minute. "I'm ready."

Caleb smiled. "Then it's a good thing I brought the sketch, isn't it?"

We went to Donna's shop and several hours later, I had a two and a half inch tattoo on my hip of a boom box with wings. Caleb planned on licking it along with my belly button ring once they were both completely healed. I could safely assume that anything I got done at Donna's shop would end up being licked by Caleb.

CHAPTER TWENTY-NINE

"I think there's a great beauty to having problems. That's one of the ways we learn."
-Herbie Hancock

CALEB

I was so whipped.

How did it come to this?

I needed to reassert my manly authority in this relationship and quit letting Gianna get her way just because she was so damn hot. And Beautiful. And Funny. And Smart. Oh crap. I was in trouble.

I couldn't believe I was sitting in on an art club meeting after school. Wait, I could believe it because Gianna promised if I spent an hour at art club, checking it out, she'd spend an hour in my room tonight doing whatever I wanted.

Oh yeah.

Finally, it was over. When I left the art room, Gianna was outside leaning against the wall, smiling smugly.

"Why do you look so pleased?" I placed my hands on either side of her head against the wall, and swooped down for a kiss.

"Because," she said in between kisses.

"Because why?" I asked in between more kisses.

"Because I can tell by your face you enjoyed art club."

"It was alright," I said noncommittally. "What'd you do while I was in there? Sit out here, waiting for me? Yearning for me?"

"Psh, whatever! I went to the gym to watch cheerleading practice." She looked shy and embarrassed, avoiding my eyes.

"Thinking about rejoining?"

"Maybe," she admitted softly as her cheeks turned pink.

"You know I'll support whatever makes you happy, right?" I tipped her chin up to look into her blue eyes.

She sighed. "I miss it. Plus, it was a good dance workout Monday through Friday. I'm going to get out of shape if I don't rejoin or start going to the gym."

Holding her hand as we walked out to my car, I brought her hand up to my mouth and sucked on the tip of her index finger. "I can think of another good workout you could try."

Gianna gasped, yanking her hand away. “You are so bad.”

“You love it.” I ran the back of my fingers along her cheek. “And I love it when you blush for me.”

“It’s not every day that some guy starts sucking on my body parts,” she whispered as if we had an audience.

I laughed at her embarrassment. “I’d hope not. Don’t forget, you owe me an hour in my room tonight. There are many parts of you that have yet to be sucked on.”

Her cheeks went from pink to red. I imagined what other parts of her body I could make blush. Perhaps I’d find out tonight.

I teased my girlfriend the whole way home by hinting at all the things I was going to do to her tonight. I planned on doing everything short of actually having sex with her. I’d rather my nosy stepmother not be downstairs baking or knitting or whatever the hell she did, while I was having sex with Gianna for the first time. We’d go to *my* mom’s place for that. When my mom wasn’t there, obviously.

“My god, Caleb Morrison! You are such a pervert!” Gianna turned the radio up to drown out my naughty words, but the song on the radio was “Bedrock” by Young Money. I laughed as she fumbled to turn it back down.

“What’s the matter, Gianna? Does that song make you think of how I’m gonna make your bed rock tonight?” I grabbed high up on her thigh and squeezed. She squealed and pushed my hand away.

“I’ve made a deal with the devil. But it’ll be your bed rocking. Your room, remember?” Gianna didn’t seem too enthused. It hurt a man’s pride. Maybe she doubted my seduction skills. I’d just have to enlighten the poor girl.

“All this talk is making me hard-” I started saying.

Gianna interrupted so I couldn’t go on, “You are such a pervert! My virgin ears are burning!”

“That’s not all that’ll be burning by the time I’m through with you.”

“Pervert!” Gianna yelled, covering her ears. She was trying so hard not to laugh.

“Now that you mention it-” I began, but Gianna cut me off again.

“Crap!” Gianna sounded panicked and I swung my head to see

what caught her attention.

Pulling up in front of the house, I understood what she was referring to. Parked right in the driveway like it belonged was a big black truck. "What the hell is he doing here?"

Gianna had her face in her hands, muffling curses. "Take one guess."

"I'm going to kick his ass. *Again.*" I took my time getting out of the car and going around to Gianna's side.

"No, I'm not getting out. I don't want to deal with her."

When Gianna didn't budge, I reached down to unbuckle her seatbelt and pull her out. "You're making me think you're ashamed of me, princess."

Gianna looked at me with wide eyes. "I'm not ashamed of you! I just don't want to deal with my mother freaking out about you."

"In my opinion, I think Josh is doing us a favor. It's about time this came out in the open." I guided her forcefully towards the front door.

Before I could open it, Josh came waltzing out with a satisfied smile on his face. He looked momentarily surprised to see us, but his smile soon returned. I let go of Gianna to shove him to the ground.

Gianna stepped between us, placing her hands on my chest. "He's not worth it, Caleb. We have bigger problems to worry about."

I looked at her, then down at Josh, then back at her. "Let's get this over with." Before going into the house, though, I kicked Josh in his knee. As I slammed the front door shut, I saw him limping to his truck. I'd still beat that fucker later.

When I turned around, Gianna waited with a scowl on her face. "Are you done?"

"For now, unless he wants to come back for more." Shaking off the anger, I wrapped my arms around her. "It's gonna be alright. I'm sure your mother can be reasonable about this."

"Doubtful," Gianna muttered.

As if on cue, Julie entered stage left from the living room. Gianna tried to back out of my embrace but I held my arms tightly around her while steadily meeting Julie's shocked gaze.

"Please tell me what Josh said isn't true. Please tell me you two haven't been sneaking around behind our backs."

Gianna's spine straightened as she backed out of my arms. "Mom, quit being so dramatic. You make it sound so dirty and seedy."

"It's wrong! You two are stepsiblings! You aren't supposed to date!" Julie was about to lose it, if she hadn't already.

"We're related through marriage. It's not like we're blood-related. We didn't even know each other until recently," I pointed out.

Julie turned towards me, eyes flashing. "I don't want to hear your attempt to defend it, Caleb. I welcomed you into my home and this is how you repay me? By defiling my daughter?"

"Dammit, mom, quit making it sound like that. Caleb cares about me and I care about him. Plus, no *defiling* has taken place." Gianna then unthinkingly added, "Yet."

I groaned inwardly. That was not a smart thing to say right now.

Julie's face turned red with anger as she practically frothed at the mouth. "This is going to stop right now! I've already called Scott and he's on his way home. Gianna, go to your room. Caleb, wait in the living room for your father to come home. I'm going to go start dinner. This will all be settled shortly."

Gianna let out an exasperated sound and ran up the stairs. I did as my wicked stepmother ordered and sat on the couch. *This should be interesting*. Twenty minutes later, I could hear my dad pull into the garage. When he came in through the garage door, I heard Julie already bitching at him about me.

My dad entered the living room with Julie at his heels yapping like a dog. "Tell him to stay away from my daughter, Scott."

My dad looked tired and stressed. "Caleb, is this true?" He already knew it was true. He found out about it weeks ago, but maybe he didn't want Julie to know he'd been keeping it a secret for us.

Standing up so we were all on equal footing, I tried to explain. "Yes, but it's not the way Julie describes it. She makes me sound like some sort of sexual predator. I'm serious about Gianna. We haven't even had sex yet,"

Julie got in my face. "*Yet*? That'll never happen. Gianna is too good for you! Before you came along everything was perfect. It's probably your fault she quit cheerleading and broke up with that wonderful boy, Josh."

Now I was pissed. "My fault? It's your fault she quit cheerleading! Ask her yourself. And as for that prick Josh, why don't you invite him over for another talk and ask him about how he tried to force himself on her? Or about the time that he banged her head against a brick wall and knocked her out?"

"I don't believe a word you're saying," Julie stubbornly denied.

I looked to my dad. "You don't actually think I'm going to break up with Gianna just because Julie wants me to?"

I could tell my dad was confused by the whole situation. "No, I don't think you will."

"Make him!" Julie screamed, having definitely lost it.

"How do you suggest I do that, Julie?" my dad asked her. If she didn't watch it, his temper would rise too.

"I don't care how you do it! He's *your* loser son! You deal with him!" Julie stalked back to the kitchen.

My dad followed her and I let out a relieved sigh. It was good to have that crazy bitch out of my face. My dad and Julie were still fighting loudly in the kitchen when Gianna peeked her head into the living room. "Is it safe?"

I held out my arms. "No, but come here anyways." She rushed over and sat on my lap. Wrapping my arms around her, I tried reassuring her with a kiss.

Julie and my dad stormed back to the living room. Julie zeroed in on Gianna on my lap and went ballistic. "Gianna, get away from him!" Julie tried forcing Gianna off my lap, but Gianna was holding on tightly to my neck.

"Deal with it, mom! You can't make us break up!" Gianna yelled.

"No, but I can make him leave!" Julie hollered back.

My dad would only be pushed so far. "My son has a right to be here!"

Julie got in my dad's face now. "You don't seem to understand, Scott. I'll do whatever it takes to keep a delinquent like your son away from my daughter!"

"He's just a kid! You make him sound like the scum of the earth!" He wasn't backing down and it was clearly pissing Julie off.

"He's not good enough for her! I bet she doesn't even know half of the things he's gotten up to!"

Gianna interrupted their argument, "I don't care about his past, mom. I only care about his present and presently he's my boyfriend. You can't do anything about it."

Julie slowly looked from Gianna to me to my dad. She had a strange look in her eyes now and her face was going pale. "Take your son and leave, Scott."

My dad was taken aback. "What?" he asked faintly.

"I want your son out of my house and away from my daughter permanently. Take your degenerate son with you and leave." She moved away from him toward the doorway. "You can come home when you send him back to live with his mom."

"You fucking bitch," my dad whispered. Julie's face crumpled and she left the room.

Gianna jumped off my lap to follow her mom. A few seconds later, I heard Gianna and her mom fighting.

My dad still had a stunned look on his face. I didn't really know what to say to him, so all I said was, "I'm sorry, dad."

He cleared his throat. "Don't worry about it, Caleb. I wouldn't want to stay with a woman who looked down on my son, anyways. I think it's best if we leave right away. I still have the condo and it's in-between renters. We'll go there. Go pack enough for the next few days."

My dad looked defeated as he climbed the stairs. I'd never wanted to hit a woman before, but I was coming real close when it came to Julie.

I didn't really see any choice but to do as he asked. I ran up to my bedroom and grabbed my largest duffel bag. I was throwing things in there when Gianna slammed into my room. "What are you doing? Where are you going?" She was panicking and I wanted to comfort her but didn't know how. Things were so fucked up at the moment. More than anything, I was hurting for my dad. He loved that crazy bitch.

"Leaving. So is my dad. Since your mom kicked us out, we're

going to my dad's condo."

She had tears in her eyes. "Are you going to break up with me?"

Rushing over to her, I hugged her. "God no! It'll be okay, don't cry." I used my thumbs to wipe away her tears. "Please stop crying, Gianna. It's only twenty minutes from here."

Taking a deep breath, she forced herself to stop crying. "It's just that I've gotten so used to you always being here. Are you going to switch schools?"

"I don't see why I should. It's not that far. I can even pick you up every day." That finally got a smile out of her.

"My mom would love that," Gianna croaked sarcastically.

"She'll probably sit on the front porch with a shotgun." I laughed just picturing it. My Camaro would never survive.

"I'm trying not to freak out here," Gianna explained. "I need to talk to my dad. I'll be right back. Don't leave yet. I have to go get my phone because my dad needs to hear about how crazy my mom is acting."

Gianna went to her room to call her dad in Houston. Would he really back her up? Or would he agree with Julie that I wasn't good enough for their daughter? Julie said she'd do anything to keep us apart, but how much crazier could she get? She'd already kicked me and my dad out of the house in an effort to get rid of me.

Could Julie talk Gianna into breaking up with me? I didn't think so. Julie couldn't talk Gianna into something as small as staying in cheerleading, so I doubted she'd succeed in getting her to break up with me. The thought of not being with Gianna caused an ache to my chest. I didn't want to lose her.

Before I met Gianna, I'd thought I was living life to the fullest, wild and carefree. Now that I had her in my life I understood what it really meant to feel alive.

What could be done about Julie, though? Obviously something drastic would have to happen to get her to see reason. As I was zipping up my bag, an idea popped into my head.

Going into Gianna's room, I found her crying while on the phone. "Dad, you have to talk to her. She's gone psycho. You remember how crazy she can be."

Gianna barely glanced at me as I went to her closet and pulled out a suitcase. Opening it on her bed, I started throwing clothes and shoes in. I took the suitcase to her dresser and tossed in bras, panties and socks.

I heard Gianna tell her dad in a rush, "Um, dad, I have to go, call you later." She got up off her bed and watched me zip up the suitcase. "Caleb, what are you doing?"

"Get your toiletries and makeup out of the bathroom." When she just stood there, I said, "Hurry!"

She left the room, coming back a few minutes later with a large cosmetic bag stuffed full. I slipped it into front pocket of the suitcase, grabbed both our bags and said, "Let's go."

"Go where?" Gianna asked worriedly, following me down the stairs.

"Shh!" I warned her.

At the bottom of the stairs I didn't see anyone around, so I grabbed Gianna's hand and we quietly snuck out the front door. I threw the bags in the trunk and opened Gianna's door for her.

After a clean getaway, we were driving out of the neighborhood when Gianna's patience ran out. "Can you tell me where we're going, Caleb?"

I gave her the wicked smile I reserved for when I was doing something *really* bad. "We're going to do the last thing left on your list, number eight."

"Caleb, we can't do that right now! My mom will freak out!" Gianna shrieked.

I chuckled at the possibility of Julie getting any crazier. "Yeah she will."

Gianna had a dazed expression on her face. "I can't believe I'm going along with this. How far is the drive to Vegas?"

Book 2 of the *Beware of Bad Boy* series

Coming November 2013

Also by April Brookshire:

YOUNG LOVE MURDER

DEAD CHAOS

For info on upcoming books, playlists, my blog and newsletter,

Connect with me online at:

www.aprilbrookshire.net

Printed in Great Britain
by Amazon

81547735R00119